Dying Eyes

The First Brian McDone Mystery

Ryan Casey

Higher Bank Books
Preston, UNITED KINGDOM

Thanks to all my wonderful readers, my supportive family, Dad for the police technicalities, my editors and designers for making this thing as polished as possible, and Preston for the lovely cloudy setting

Prologue.

When she left the house earlier that night, she knew she was in some sort of danger.

What she didn't know was that she'd soon be lying dead in a filthy bedsit, her skin growing paler and paler, as the cold January night progressed.

#

She gripped the documents tightly. She couldn't risk dropping them or letting them fall, not after everything she'd been through to find them.

Her breath frosted as it left her mouth. Somewhere in the distance, a dog barked. Lights flashed and horns pipped, the goodwill of Christmas season replaced by the grumpiness of normal life. January. Parents would be back at work. Children would be bored of their new toys already.

But she had to do one thing. She couldn't leave it any longer.

They told her they'd be here. She just had to wait. Soon, it would all be over. She didn't want to involve them. She'd tried her best not to, but it had to be this way.

They caught her eye, walking through the car park. They startled her at first, their figure almost unrecognisable as they powered towards her, rubbing their hands in the cold.

She gripped the documents tightly. She had to do this.

#

She looked up towards them. Her vision was blurred, and her body shook. Damp goose pimples protruded from her skin as the dark figure moved above her, fuzzy and out of view.

Still, she gripped. She couldn't let go. She couldn't let that happen.

She tried to move her legs and hands, but they seemed magnetically attached to wherever it was she lay. *Why wouldn't they move?*

She could only keep holding. Keep holding...

If she held tight enough, someone would find her. She just had to keep gripping... keep gripping...

#

Moths danced around the dim light flickering in the corner. They wiped her hair out of her face and rubbed their damp hands against their dark black coat. Then they walked towards the door, taking a final glance around the room. Her eyes were still open with shock. She'd watched it happen. Even as they squeezed the final breath from her fragile, failing lungs, she had held on for dear life.

But not anymore.

They shut the door and disappeared outside, past the downtrodden buildings into the frost of night. The cries of locals roared through the claustrophobic little alleyways.

No one saw them leave. No one ever saw anything around here.

Chapter One.

The chiming of the church bells that morning was as welcome to Brian McDone as always—not one bit.

He slumped onto his side with a groan and looked at his clock: six a.m. Six-frigging-a.m. Surely the church figured by now that no one really cared about holy stuff at six a.m. Or maybe that was the plan? Maybe they knew no one really cared about the church anymore. One final form of revenge; a way to keep everyone aware of their presence.

He squeezed the bridge of his nose, his forehead aching. At the foot of his bed, he spotted an empty bottle of anti-depressants on its side. Some of the pills spilled out like a waterfall into a pool on the carpet. Beside them lay three empty bottles of beer, one resting against the other like tipsy dominoes.

The drunken detective. He had to play up the cliché. He couldn't let anybody know the truth.

Brian winced as he edged onto the side of his bed and rubbed his hands against his face. His white boxers stuck to his legs with the sweat of wearing them for the last few days. But it didn't matter. It was his time off. He'd worked Christmas and Boxing Day and barely seen anybody over the festive season, so what else did he have to keep busy except drinking and chilling out by himself over New Year?

The rattling of the phone against the table interrupted Brian, his head still in his hands. The one thing worse than church bells at six a.m. was his phone vibrating, especially on his day off. He reached for it, careful not to knock over the silver-plated photo frame on his bedside.

The ringing seared through his tender skull. He didn't bother looking who it was. Someone was calling him on his day off, which meant bad news regardless.

"Hello?" he said, his voice groggy. How many drinks did he have? *Snap out of it*—the drink wasn't causing the problems. He was just becoming too good at fooling himself that it was. He must be doing something right.

"What the hell you playing at?" the voice on the other end bellowed.

Shit. He hadn't...

He looked over at the miniature calendar on his bedside. *Oh, shit.* It wasn't Sunday...

"Price, I'm sorry, I—"

"First off, I'm *DI* Price to you," he said. Brian could almost feel spit splashing against his face from the other end of the crackling line. "And as for your apologies, I get it—you've got shit going on. I'm an understanding guy. Just sort yourself out and get in here as soon as you can, all right?"

Brian squeezed his eyelids together, his cheeks flushing. "Okay, okay. But seriously, Price— Detective Inspector. Seriously, I'm sorry."

DI Price snickered. "You can give me a proper apology when you get into work. You'd better get your lazy arse here quick, though—briefing's in five. There's something big gone down, and these rookies could do with some professional help. You up to it?"

"I'm on it," Brian said. The line cut out before he had the chance to say anything else.

He dropped the phone and looked around his living room. Or at least they called it a living room in the rental description. It had everything—built-in kitchen, bed, the whole lot. The only thing it didn't have was the most useful item you'd want—a loo. He had to walk into a little cupboard for that. At least when no one was around, he could just crack one out into the drainpipe underneath his window. Nobody had to know.

Brian stretched his arms out and lumbered past the empty bottles on the floor. He'd leave those there for now, just in case anybody from work came over and he needed an excuse for his lethargy. He couldn't have anybody asking questions. Vanessa visited a few weeks ago just to sort out a few technicalities, and she'd said what a tip the place was in. But what did that matter? He didn't have to make it nice for anyone. Not until the stuff with Davey was resolved anyway.

Davey. Probably best he kept him out of his head for the time being.

He stepped to the curtains and rested his arms on the metal window frame. Below him, cars headed to work, and buses left the station. The bloody bus station—Preston's one big grey chunk of pride. It was like a tumour on the city, but one to be proud of. People claimed they hated it, but the second an outsider poked fun at it, it was always, "Well, did you know it was the biggest one in the world before that one in Turkey got built?" Hypocrites, the lot of them.

Brian walked across the room to his desk, where his work clothes were draped over the back of a chair. He held them out, the creases snaking down the sides of the trousers. He'd sort that later. He'd thought the same thing yesterday too, but he really would sort it later.

Perhaps.

After slipping into his clothes, he looked at himself in the mirror. His chest became visible underneath his shirt as he rubbed his hands against his belly. He'd have to buy a new shirt eventually. Or go on a food cull. People dieted all the time. He could handle that.

What bothered him more was the growing patch of grey hairs just above his right ear.

He scratched the side of his head and leaned in towards the mirror. His cheeks flushed as the grey hairs stared back at him. Maybe it was better if he didn't look. Had they always been there, or had he just started to notice them since the split?

And his forearm. He pretended not to notice his forearm.

The phone buzzed against his leg again, just once this time. He pulled it out—Cassy.

"Where r u? Lazy git x"

He grinned for a second. She'd been good to him lately. She was the only one who had made any sort of effort since he'd come back to work. Screw the rest of them. Miserable gits.

He threw on his coat as he stumbled past his bed and opened the door onto the corridor, which constantly reeked of cigarettes and stale alcohol. Then again, one could expect little else from a hell-hole block of flats in the middle of town.

He locked the door of his tiny cabin and walked towards the stairs. All the other doors were shut. No one ever moved in around here unless they really had to. Brian could probably afford someplace else, but it was convenient enough for his needs; close to work and private. Neighbours—who needed them?

He skipped down the flight of steps and rushed out into the bitter air. *Something big gone down.* Price didn't use those words all that often. Nobody in Preston did.

#

As Brian walked past the early January discount shoppers gathered outside the St John's Centre, sitting under the glare of the bus station, he didn't think to check the headline of the Lancashire News on the display stands.

NEW YEAR TRAGEDY FOR PROSTITUTE GIRL.

Chapter Two.

The sound of phones ringing echoed through from the offices as Brian took the lift upstairs, coffee cup in hand. His stomach turned at the thought of seeing them all again, gloating about their lovely family Christmas. Stephen Molfer with his ridiculous face. DI Price and his disappointment.

As the lift door opened, everyone turned around to look at Detective Sergeant McDone. It was a sort of, "Isn't he going to be in trouble with the headmaster?" look that kids received when they'd done something naughty at school. He kept his head down and nodded at a couple of officers before edging over to his cluttered desk right by the door. He draped his coat over the chair.

"Feeling all right this morning, Brian?" Stephen Molfer asked.

Brian grunted. Stephen had only worked in Preston for two years and already considered himself top dog. Brian certainly hadn't missed Stephen's gaunt, mousy face while on leave. Weedy little bastard didn't stand a chance, not really. It was the same with most of them these days. It wasn't like the old times, not anymore. It used to be a laugh sometimes. Now, it was just a case of finishing whatever jobs came his way, going home, and drinking himself into forgetfulness, then doing the same again and again until he could retire into an eternal drunken stupor.

Or so he had them believe.

He flicked on his computer as the rest of the room returned to normal procedure. They'd been different with him lately, after everything that had happened with his family. He had to expect that though, really. They'd forget about it soon. Find something else to whisper about. Move on to the next piece of inane gossip.

The clattering of the door intruded again on the low hum of orderly conversation as DI Price stormed through, looking directly at McDone's desk. "Right, you lot—less faffing around. You all know the score. Well, most of you do, anyway." He looked at McDone for a few painful seconds, then at his watch. "To be fair to you, McDone, you've made it here quicker than I thought. DS Emerson's in the back. You two are going on a little mission nearby. Off your arse and into my office."

He turned his back without even letting Brian get a word in response and disappeared through the door. The rest of the office, open-jawed, looked at Brian again. He threw his coat over his shoulder, switched off his computer, and crept towards the wooden double doors at the other side of the computer-filled room.

Private meetings with DI Price were never something to savour.

#

Price's office stank of cheap aftershave, cheap leather, and cheap whisky. A chair at either side framed his desk. Price's own chair, large, black, and reclining, wrapped itself around him like a comfort blanket. The opposite chair was a grey hard plastic seat, fresh from the canteen. The lads called it the electric chair, because sitting on it was like being summoned to your death.

A number of framed certificates coated the walls of the office. Chief Constable Commendations, Divisional Commendations and Citations of Merit, all the credit given to Price despite the hard work and efforts of others. Numerous photographs also filled in the gaps absent of certificates—Price with the Chief Constable, Price with the mayor, Price with Mrs. Price.

What Price had failed to notice was that an unidentified, disgruntled officer with an artistic streak had somehow managed to doctor Price's name on each of the photograph, replacing the *E* with a *K*.

DS Cassy Emerson certainly hadn't failed to notice it, though. She was leaning against the bookcase in Price's office as Brian entered and flicked a nervous smile in his direction. She had to hide any sign of amusement, contact or sympathy, of course, in case Price decided to bollock her, too.

Price waddled over to Brian and pulled the coffee out of his hand. The hairs in his nostrils were growing bushier by the day. "Nice of you to bring me my morning coffee," he said before taking a swig. *Fucker.* Brian waited for Price's eyes, bothered by the heat, to sting and twitch, but he simply washed the drink around his cheeks and took another large gulp.

"Sorry for being late aga—"

"Ah, shut your face," Price said.

Brian looked at Cassy, who moved her gaze back towards the ground, her arms wrapped around her front. Recently promoted to Acting Detective Sergeant, she was more accustomed to taking shit than Brian. Had only been working in Preston for a few months, too, after transferring from Bolton. But that's just the way it was—the further you climbed up the ladder, the more people there were to shout at, the fewer to shout at you. Bullshit rolled downhill, and she didn't want to be at the bottom anymore.

Brian cleared his throat. At least his headache wasn't as intense now. There was no way in hell he could've put up with this grumpy bastard otherwise. Every cloud had a silver lining...

"What have you got?" Brian asked.

Price took another gulp of coffee. "I thought you'd never ask." Some of the coffee dribbled down his chin as his cheeks puffed out like a hamster's pouches. He picked up a newspaper and threw it over to Brian. "I'm guessing you haven't seen the news this morning."

No photograph. Just a bold, strong headline: NEW YEAR TRAGEDY FOR PROSTITUTE GIRL.

Brian looked back at Cassy, who was still quiet, arms folded. "So... there's a girl been murdered?"

"Your crash course briefing today is from the fucking *Lancashire News*," Price said. "One of the residents around the crime scene thought a morning call to the journalists would be more appropriate than a call to the police, and you know how the *Lancashire News* is acting with us lately. We've not even put a name on the girl yet. Some bloke just so happened to find this poor soul dead in her flat. Foster Road." He grabbed a sandwich from his desk and held it up to his mouth, even though the lettuce was going brown. "No prizes for guessing what he was up to down Foster Road, but anyway. You two know each other already, and you'll both be leading this investigation, so you'd better get down to Foster Road before the bloodies find something else to moan about."

Brian flicked the front page of the newspaper over. *The bloodies.* Price's name for the crime scene investigators. *"Always stating the bloody obvious, those lot,"* he'd say. *"Get paid for absolutely nothing."*

"How does the newspaper know she's a prostitute?" Cassy asked. It was the first time she'd spoken since Brian entered.

Price glared at her. "Emerson, have you ever *been* down Foster Road? Or were there no such things as prostitution hotspots in Bolton?"

Cassy opened her mouth to reply, but thought better of it and looked down at her shoes.

In the newspaper, the same old stories. A dog had learned to talk, or some crap like that. A rising charity company received funds for an awareness fair. Local businessman fiddled with taxes. Nothing out of the ordinary.

"Having a good read, Detective?"

Brian looked up at Price and shuffled the newspaper pages shut. "Sorry, Price—"

"It's *fucking* Detective Inspector, okay?"

"Detective Inspector, Detective Inspector. I'm guessing the CSI are already there to—?"

"Of course they bloody well are," Price exploded. His face was so red that a pinprick could have burst it.

Brian walked towards the door, smiling at Price as well as he could. He gestured for Cassy to walk ahead of him.

"Crime scene investigators," Price mumbled under his breath. "Crime scene investigators. Who the bloody hell are they kidding?"

Brian shut the door. He turned 'round to face the office, who stared at him, stunned at the lack of battle wounds. "Got yourself fired yet?" Stephen asked, his ventriloquist's dummy grin poking above his computer screen.

Brian laughed. "Actually, I've gone and got myself the dead prostitute case. What's it you're working on at the moment? Getting your pin dick up?"

Stephen sat red-faced as the rest of the office erupted with laughter, whooping and clapping their hands.

"Still got it, Granddad," DC Forbes shouted, his oval glasses shaking as he chuckled.

"As a matter of fact—" Stephen squirmed, refusing to back down—"I'm investigating a new street drug. Dramatically lowers inhibitions. Almost unidentifiable when blended with cannabis."

"Yeah, yeah." Brian walked away from Molfer, who continued to argue his case. "Come on, you." Brian smiled at Cassy. "Better get this scene checked out."

#

Foster Road wasn't too far from the offices. Then again, nothing was too far from anything in the city centre. It was hardly a sprawling place. Still, the residents found plenty of fresh things to moan about. Sometimes, the lack of cycle lanes. Other times, the distance between the bus station and the train station. *Lazy shits.*

Other cars already perched outside the flats as men in black leather coats with cameras flashed away. Yellow tape bridged the gap between the main road and the claustrophobic alleyway.

As Brian opened the car door, he noticed the handle had gone stiff. He turned to Cassy, who smirked.

"Quit messing about, Cas."

"What you gonna do? You shit yourself whenever you're around Price, and he's an old fart. What you gonna do to me?" She thumped him in the arm playfully.

"Whatever." Brian rubbed his arm. He liked Cassy. She was a tough, smart cop, new to the game over the last few years. "A new generation of officers," her previous employers at Bolton said. Price probably hated her for that reason, but then again, Price hated everybody. It probably didn't help that she was a woman. Hardly ticking many boxes on Price's "Perfect Police Officer" checklist.

The two of them got out of the car and immediately caught the eye of a nearby journalist. He rushed over with his camera like a fly towards dung, his gelled-back hair and thick-rimmed glasses hiding that punchable face underneath.

"Detective Sergeant, is there any news on the identity of the—"

Cassy pushed him away and he tripped backwards like a diving footballer. Brian kept his head down and walked towards the alleyway of flats.

More journalists flocked around their fallen com-rade like alarmed ants.

"Cheers for that," Brian said, when Cassy caught up.

"I did it for me, not for you." Cassy looked up and winked at Brian before they crossed the yellow tape and slipped through into the alleyway beside Foster Road.

The door to the house, painted in a flaking white, was wedged open, and the dim glow of a light crept out. The nearby buzz of voices echoed from the room like whispers in a museum. Brian turned to Cassy and handed her a blue, disposable forensic paper suit, which he knew would be sever-al sizes too large for her. "Ladies first," he said as they stood by the door.

Cassy pulled a false smile as the paper suit dan-gled over her neck before thumping his arm again and leading the way inside. "Tellytubbie 'Tectives!" she said.

#

The first thing Brian noticed on the girl was the purple bruises around her neck. Then the plastic ties around her ankles, cutting into her paling flesh.

The "bloodies" were already at the scene, sniff-ing out clues and evidence like well-trained dogs.

One of the men in a clear coat turned to face Brian and sighed. Jake Coolham, crime scene manager.

"What do we have?" Brian asked.

Jake slipped his glove off and grabbed a Soft Mint out of his pocket before tossing it down his throat, his flabby neck shaking as he gulped it down. Handling a dead girl, then tossing Soft Mints into his mouth. Brian tried to keep a straight face as Cassy cringed.

"Girl. Obviously." His cheeks wobbled as he spoke.

Nice sense of humour, too.

"Probably early twenties. By the nature of the wounds, I'd say she was probably held down, forced into submission, something like that."

Brian edged over to the side of the bed. The room was low on light and dingy, the air moist with sweat.

The girl was completely naked. Her eyes were open wider than seemed humanly possible, staring up in absolute terror at the ghost of her killer above. Around her ankles, sharp plastic ties squeezed into her flesh, piercing the skin. Bruises covered her pale, goose-pimpled body, and a blue one gripped around her neck. Fear lingered in her dead eyes—the realisation of her imminent fate glaring out between thick, stained eyeliner.

Brian put a plastic glove on and crouched down beside her. The goose pimples looked permanently engrained, crafted into her skin like a waxwork model. "Nothing at all on who she could be?"

Jake shrugged. "We're not sure yet. In fact, we're not sure about anything. No one's come forward about her after the vultures leaked the news. Probably just a whore, no family to give a shit, you know? Which makes it even more difficult for us. Thing is, she doesn't seem like your typical whore. No signs of malnutrition. No obvious signs of drug abuse. Looks a little grubby, but I bet she was a looker when she was scrubbed up."

Brian turned to Jake, took a deep breath, and moved to the other side of the room. A candle that had burned out long ago poured solid wax onto a fresh pack of unopened Durex on the bedside table.

"It's a shame for the girl," Jake said. "No one to spend Christmas or New Year with, now no one to look out for her. Real shame."

"Any prints? Hairs? Anything like that?" Brian looked around the room. An empty glass, red lipstick coating the surface, gathered dust beside the bed.

"The room's covered in 'em," Jake said. "As you'd expect from a filthy whorehouse like this, really."

Brian sighed. Hundreds of men and women would have been in here at some stage. Then again, with no identity for the girl, at least hundreds would narrow it down slightly from every damn person in Preston. "Get all the prints checked. We'll see what we can do with them."

Jake began to dust an empty glass. "I'll do my best, but you know what forensics is like for timing these days. Budget cuts—who needs 'em?"

Jake was right. Since the new government had been elected, every area of the police department was being squeezed to the point of incompetence.

"You get the idiots on the streets—the idiots in the press—blaming us for everything," Jake said, moving in to dust the bedside table. "If they want to complain, they should take it to bloody Downing Street!"

"What was she holding?" Cassy called as Brian rubbed his head and walked towards the door for some air. His headache was beginning to sear again.

"What d'you mean, 'holding'?" Brian turned to Cassy. She crouched down by the girl's side, looking at her fingers.

"Her nails." Cassy frowned intently at the girl's lifeless fingers. "They're dug right into her hand. It's as if she was holding on to something."

The girl continued to stare up towards the ceiling in fear. "I dunno," he said. "Holding on for dear life, probably. Who found the girl?"

"Well, 'anonymous report'. You know how they are around here. Place is practically the Amsterdam of the north. No one wants to admit any involvement or anything like that. But the bloke next door *was* lurking about a lot... Seemed very interested in everything, more so than anybody else. Just saying, that's all."

Brian crept out of the doorway and leaned his arms against either side of the door. The alleyway was narrow and unkempt, the smell of damp brickwork strong in the air. There was a series of four to five black doors, before a set of stairs that lead to another row of flats. He turned to the door next to the room they were in and nodded at Cassy. "We'll have a word with him after we've bagged and tagged everything for forensics."

The alleyway that broke off Foster Road was like all inner-city alleyways; damp, run-down, and not very pleasant. After gathering everything they needed for forensics, Brian stepped across the broken glass under his feet and walked towards the corroding door of the neighbour who had been lurking around the police and the press. Brian hoped for his own sake that the *Lancashire News* wouldn't pay him out for breaking the story. The last thing they needed was the incentivisation of crime.

Dry paint flaked from the door's surface as Brian knocked. Cassy twitched and sighed beside him.

"What you getting so het up about?" Brian asked.

"This bastard sold the poor girl out to that journo before contacting us. No time for lowlifes like that."

"Ah, you've got a lot to learn about the world, girl."

"Don't patronise me." Cassy frowned at him. "Just because you've got a morbid view of anything and everything doesn't mean you have to rub it off on everybody."

"I'm not patronising you. It's just called life experience. Come back to me when you've got more of it." He winked at her.

Cassy smiled back. "Life experience, right. How are your wife and kid again?"

Brian felt the weight of a bus hitting him. His smile completely crumbled to the ground. It was a good job the door in front of them opened, or he'd have had to dig himself a hole to fall down.

Brian cleared his throat and stepped ahead of Cassy. He didn't want her to see his cheeks flushing.

The man at the door had short hair and a big jaw that seemed to shoot itself out of his pea head. A mole protruded from underneath his eye. It was hard to tell whether he was smiling or pulling a funny face. He waited to be spoken to.

"Mr...?"

"Ad," the man spat. "What you doing? I've already had police around fucking asking me que—"

"Mr. Ad," Cassy said, slicing through the man's rant. "We just want to clear up a few things so we can work it out in our own heads, okay?"

Ad shuffled his feet and squeezed his hands together before tilting his head backwards. "Come in, then."

His flat was a carbon copy of the girl's, only more poorly decorated, which was hard considering the girl's room wasn't decorated at all. Empty picture frames were scattered around at random. Specks of tobacco and whatever else coated every surface. A dull hint of cannabis and sweat lurked in the air.

"Take a fucking seat." Ad fell back onto his bed.

Brian looked down at the seat, covered with something slimy. Cassy returned a disgusted gaze.

"It's okay." Brian smiled out of politeness. "We're only here for a few minutes."

Ad waved his hand in their direction as if to say, "Suit yourselves."

"First things first, Ad, we know you called the *Lancashire News*," Brian lied. "We've got evidence that links the location of the call to somewhere around here. There's no point lying about that anymore."

Ad held his mouth open then sighed. He'd fallen for Brian's bait. "Times are tough. We've gotta find a way to make a quick buck, y'know? But I was gonna ring the police, too. I swear I was gonna."

Singing like a bird already. Good start. "Okay, Ad. What happened last night, from the beginning?"

Ad leaned forward, polishing his voice as if he were telling a story to a classroom. "Well, it was about half-twelve, one-ish. I remember that, 'cause I was watching the fucking 'Football League Show'. Waited fucking ages for the Bolton highlights, and they went and showed them last again. Lost as well, so that pissed me off.

"Anyway, Barnsley are on—fucking Barnsley— and I hear this banging next door, and I think nothing of it, 'cause there's always fucking banging going on here... you get me?" His eyes glimmered for a moment before thinking better of the implications of his rhetorical question. A sort of naivety washed across his face. He must've known damn well the police were aware that Foster Road was one of the largest areas for prostitution, but clearly didn't want to say anything in case it involved him.

"And what was so startling that you decided to go 'round and take a look?" Cassy asked. She moved a tray of moulding cigarettes out of the way so she could lean against the small wooden coffee table, putting her sleeve down to stop her flesh touching any surface.

Ad stared at Brian as if Cassy wasn't even there. "There was a load of fucking around going on, I could hear that. Bloke talking a lot afterwards. Didn't hear what he said, but he was speaking loud, and then I heard a car go. Dunno what it was, but I went out in the morning and the door was open a bit, and I found her in there, as she is."

Brian rubbed his eyebrows. "The police said the door was closed when they arrived. That's technically tampering with evidence, Ad."

Ad waved his hand in their direction again, his face going red. "I don't know anything about fucking tampering with evidence. I just rang my old mate from the *Lancashire News*, and he came in the morning. Maybe he shut it, I dunno."

McDone glanced at Cassy. She knew what that look meant. They'd keep an eye on Ad; grill him with more questions, especially without a lead. He was the best they had right now.

"Have you seen the girl before, Ad?" McDone asked, leaning forward.

Ad shook his head, his eyes scanning the room. "There's lots of girls come here. Lots of 'em. Lose track, y'know? But I ain't seen her, which is weird. Must be a new girl. That's normal enough."

Brian kept his voice calm. "And if I were to speak to somebody and find out whether she is a 'new girl', then who would that be?"

Ad's eyes held contact with Brian's for a moment. He opened his mouth and shut it again. "I just keep myself to myself, y'know?"

"Of course you do, Ad. Of course. We might have a few more questions for you over the coming hours and days, though, you have to understand that. Until then, if you were to remember who this 'employer' is, then that would be a great help, okay?"

"No need."

The sound of the voice sank to the bottom of Brian's stomach like a rock. He turned around and saw DI Price leaning against the door, arms folded. Brian waited for him to speak. He cocked his head and gestured for Brian to leave the room with him. Brian followed him outside, nodding at Ad, who looked on with curiosity.

"Family of a girl gone missing just came in to the station." Price reached into his pocket and pulled out a photograph.

He noticed her smile first. Then her eyes. Those green eyes, beautiful and warm.

"Nicola Watson. Twenty-two years old. Didn't come home last night. That your girl?" Price asked.

Brian sighed. "That's her. I'd better be the one to, y'know—"

"You're good at that stuff, Brian," Price said. "See you back at the station."

Brian poked his head into Ad's room again. Cassy, still crouched against Ad's coffee table, frowned at him. "Come on, Detective," Brian said. "Ad—thanks for your cooperation. We'll be in touch."

Cassy followed Brian out of the door as Ad muttered to himself.

"We'll keep an eye on Ad, but right now we need to head back to the station," Brian said.

"And why would I head back to the station?"

Brian sighed. He hated this part. "The girl's called Nicola Watson. She's twenty-two. We're off to tell her parents."

As they passed the flat, he took a final glance at Nicola Watson's terrified, bloodshot eyes and walked towards the police car.

Chapter Three.

The long walk towards the public interview rooms felt like twice the distance when it was to deliver bad news. Telling parents their daughter had been murdered was the worst sort of news.

Brian stood outside the room where Mr. and Mrs. Watson sat. He could just about see them through the blinds. Mr. Watson was a big man, a grizzly bear with ginger hair and a distant, glassy gaze. Mrs. Watson, with bleached-blonde hair and a fake tan, held her husband's hand in the middle of the table. Neither of them spoke.

A hand fell onto Brian's shoulder. He turned 'round to see Cassy, her eyes sympathetic and understanding. "You sure you want to do this alone?"

Brian took a deep breath and nodded. He brushed the front of his shirt. "Someone's got to do it. You get back down to Foster with some DCs. I'll be with you in no time. Make sure the family liaison officer's fully briefed and at the ready."

"Brian, I—I didn't mean to insult you when I said about your wife."

"It's okay." Brian smiled to reassure her. He needed to toughen himself up. Three months off on the sick at the end of last year had turned him into a wuss. "The alcoholic detective with marital problems. I'm a walking, talking clichÉ!"

She laughed and stuck her middle finger up before disappearing past the other interview rooms and into the buzz of the main office.

She believed him. People were so used to seeing alcoholic detectives in fiction and on television that they took it as truth. He just had to keep playing up to that image—drinking when he needed to drink, smelling of booze when he needed to smell of booze. He just had to keep up the image and hope nobody asked to see his arms.

Brian took another deep breath and grabbed the cold metal handle of the wooden door. *Just go in there and get it over with.* He pulled the handle. The eyes of the desperate, searching mother and father stared up at him.

He didn't even have to say anything to them. He could tell by the way that they looked back at him, they already knew.

The interview room was completely silent for a few moments. Brian let the Watsons take their time to get their head around things. Not that a few minutes made much difference, but it'd be downright rude to start blabbering on and asking about their dead daughter immediately. He did note a few things, though. Firstly, they didn't seem like parents of a prostitute. Quite well-kept. Expensive clothing—nothing too scrotey. Unless Nicola had run away from home a while ago or something and made a bit of cash on the side. But that didn't make sense. They'd reported her missing right away. They'd come to the police station.

"Mr. and Mrs. Watson, I understand this is a really difficult time for you both, but I just need to ask you a couple of questions, what with the nature of—"

"Who did it?" Mr. Watson barked. "Have you got anyone?"

Brian leaned forward towards them as Mrs. Watson snivelled into her hands.

"It's... I understand your frustrations, but it's too early in the investigation to start pursuing any solid leads. That's where I was hoping you could help me. Tell me a little. Talk to me about Nicola."

It felt strange saying her name. *Nicola.* What had she done to deserve this?

Mr. Watson fell back into his chair. "She's... She was a lovely girl. Always thinking about others." Mrs. Watson spluttered and cried some more as her husband, his voice shaky, continued to speak. "I mean, like any girl in their early twenties, she did stuff behind our back, but we didn't think anything of it, y'know?"

"What sort of stuff?" Brian asked.

Mr. Watson's eyebrows twitched. "That look. Get that look out of your eyes. I didn't say that. Our daughter's no hooker. She had secrets, but she's no hooker, I swear to you—"

"Calm down, Trev," Mrs. Watson said. "Just... just calm down."

He sulked in his chair and wrapped his arms around his large belly.

"She drank, probably took a few drugs, but she was just growing up, right?" Mrs. Watson tried to put on a brave face. "All the kids do it—you know that better than anyone. But nothing... nothing like *that*. She was a good girl. She was going somewhere in her life."

"Until that little shit came along," Trevor muttered.

"Who are you referring to, Mr. Watson?" Brian asked.

"That boyfriend of hers. If she got into anything dodgy, it's his doing. Off the rails sort. Nicky thought she could 'rescue him' or some crap like that, but she was better than him. He just used her for her good nature."

"Trev, Danny was okay at times—"

"He was a scrote," Trevor roared. "A weedy little scrote. Not good enough for my Nicky. Not good enough." His arms shook as Shenice Watson, sniffing back the tears, rubbed her hand against them.

Brian took a note in his diary: *Danny. Boyfriend.* "Do you have an address for Danny...?"

"Stocks," Trevor Watson said. "Danny Stocks. Lives down by the old hospital on Walter Road. Number six, I think. Do you think he—"

"It's too early to start suspecting people. But hopefully he can shed a bit of light on why someone might have wanted to kill your daughter."

The pair flinched with Brian's words. *Too cold, Brian. Too fucking cold. Watch yourself.*

"Were there any arguments at home we should know about? Any indications that she might've been in trouble?"

Trevor Watson's eyes narrowed. "Are you implying something?"

Brian kept his cool. "I'm simply intrigued as to why you were so worried about your daughter's disappearance the morning after a night out, and more importantly, why you linked the death of a suspected prostitute with the death of your daughter."

Trevor and Shenice looked at each other, openmouthed. Shenice cleared her throat and wiped away a tear with a scrunched-up tissue. "She always came home," she said. "Didn't matter how late she'd been out, she always came home. And that road—those brothels and that seedy stuff—she always had to walk up by there. I guess I saw the age and I just... I just panicked. I always told her to walk with her friends, keep her wits about her, but she just saw the good in everyone, y'know? She never saw this coming. Poor girl. Poor, poor girl..."

Brian flicked through the pages of his diary, giving Trevor and Shenice a moment to calm themselves. "Is there anybody else that might be able to give us a few details about your daughter? Any friends or work?"

Shenice's eyes struggled to focus. "Um, I don't...
I don't know about her friends now. Since... since
she met Danny. But, I don't know."

"There is her workplace though," Trevor interrupted. "That charity. BetterLives."

"What about BetterLives?"

"She was helping out there. Doing a load of ad-
min work, helping out with the accounts. She
seemed to love doing it, even though it was voluntary. She always was into her politics and stuff."

Brian closed the diary and slipped his hand into
his pocket. He shot a sympathetic smile at Mr. and
Mrs. Watson. "Thanks for your time, both of you.
Here's my card—if you remember anything, or if
you just want to speak, give me a call, any time. I... I
realise how hard it must be to lose a child. So
please, don't forget me. My colleague will take you
to see... To identify the body. Thanks again for
your cooperation."

Trevor walked up to Brian. He looked much tall-
er than the impression he gave when seated. "Have
you ever lost a kid, Officer?"

Brian's gaze twitched towards the ground. His
neck burned, and he tugged at the top button of his
collar. "No, I—"

"Then you don't understand. You can't possibly
understand."

The pair left as Brian slumped into his chair, slicking his hair back with the sweat that had formed.

#

The chatter of the briefing room immediately died down the second Price, grinning, walked in. He held his Starbucks coffee cup so tightly that it looked like it might just crumble in his hands. He sat down next to DC Peters, who was quite visibly hungover, and plonked his large pad onto the table. The force snapped Peters out of his trance; he rubbed his eyes and took deep, steadying breaths.

"Hello, all. So it's not ideal to be calling another briefing so soon after this morning, but at least you're all here this time." He glared at Brian then opened his pad. "We've made huge progress, though. Bloody huge. Peters, what've you got for us?"

DC Peters, whose face was growing paler by the minute, shuffled the papers in front of him.

"Come on, Peters," Price said. "You're gonna be keying this info into H.O.L.M.E.S. this afternoon, so you'd better be clued up."

"Okay, okay." Peters fumbled his glasses from his collar. "Well, so far I... The girl. The girl's call—"

"Peters, have you been drinking again? Fucking hell. Keep your hands still. For God's sakes." He shook his head and edged away from Peters, who squeezed his hands together to try to stop them shaking. "Do you want to go to the bathroom?"

Peters pushed his chair back and clenched his stomach, already jogging towards the door. "Please, Detective Inspector." His cheeks expanded as if blowing an imaginary trumpet as he ran through the corridor, before a chorus of "Oh's!" and "Are you okay's?" erupted. Poor Peters evidently hadn't quite made it to the bathroom.

Price shook his head. "Brian, what have you got? And please, don't go being sick on me. It's not a good look."

Brian cleared his throat. "The girl we found this morning is Nicola Watson. She's twenty-two years old. I've spoken to her parents, and they've just identified the body. They don't seem to think she has any links to prostitution."

DC Pennison tutted behind his huge glasses. "That's what they all say." He took his glasses off and wiped his eye. He always looked frog-eyed without his glasses, like a little mole blinded by the light.

"I think it would be advisable to keep a team down at Foster Road to do some further investigations in the surrounding area. I'm not entirely sure they're the most honest sets of neighbours."

Price nodded. "And what's this about the boyfriend?"

Brian turned his paper over as another acting DC took handwritten notes. The H.O.L.M.E.S. system was playing up lately, and they didn't have the financial support from the government to fix it, so they had to make do with the intermittent system they had. "Daniel Stocks. Aged twenty-three." Brian paused as he leafed through the documents he'd just about managed to print prior to the briefing. "Few previous offences—possession of drugs, vandalism—but nothing major. Nicola's parents didn't seem too keen on him though."

Price grumbled something under his breath. "One of you two check him out."

"I'd like to let DS Emerson do the honours, sir."

Price stuck his bottom lip out, slightly puzzled by Brian's reluctance to lead. "Thought you usually liked to stick your dick right into the action, Detective?"

Brian smiled. *The Lone Ranger*—another detective clichÉ he'd managed to convince them of over the years. "I think the new Detective Sergeant is more than capable of investigating this lead while I pursue some others."

Price nodded slowly. "Very well. Well, you all know your duties. DC Pennison, when Pukey Peters has stopped spewing, you get back down to Foster Road and get pursuing those leads. And when I say 'pursuing leads', I mean pursuing leads and not stopping off at McDonald's, regardless of how good their limited edition Taste of America burgers are. The rest of you, off you go. See you soon."

The officers scooted up from their chairs and disappeared out of the room. Price stormed off, looking frustrated at how quickly he'd drunk his coffee. Brian and Cassy remained.

"To what do I owe the pleasure?" Cassy smiled teasingly at Brian.

He reached into his black 2011 diary, even though it was 2012 now, and tore out a little page on which he'd scribbled the boyfriend's address. "We have this address on record for Danny's most recent location. Check it out, and have a chat to him." Brian walked towards the door and threw on his big black jacket.

"And where d'you think you're going, anyway?" Cassy asked.

Brian smirked. "Charity work."

Chapter Four.

The office blocks where BetterLives was based were one of the newer buildings down by the docks, overlooking the marina. *Marina.* Who the hell were they kidding? Sure, it looked half-pretty in the day, but McDone knew what it was like at night. A cesspit. You'd be lucky not to get mugged walking from KFC to McDonald's. Then again, who'd walk from KFC to McDonald's? You'd be surprised by the youth of Preston.

He pulled up in one of the newly paved car spaces overlooking the depths of the docks and took a final look at the papers in front of him. "BetterLives: New Fundraising Fair to Bring Smile Back to Preston." The smiling, grinning face of their leader, Robert Luther. Apparently, he helped get people working again, aiding the disadvantaged. People seemed to like him. Brian had seen a million versions of him in the past—smiling for the cameras, probably slipping whisky into his Coke before bed every evening. The fact was Nicola Watson had worked here, which meant she knew people. Potential leads. Maybe even suspects. Someone had to know Nicola Watson, what she did, where she stayed, what food she ate, and all that.

He left the car and walked towards the entrance of the office blocks, one of those big, circular, all-glass things with blue tinted windows, which a bunch of companies hired out. BetterLives was on the fifth floor, which gave Brian a good chance to get a little bit of exercise in his legs.

Brian entered the building. The man from the photograph was already standing there, waiting to greet him in the airy reception area. It was like a reception area you'd find on a cruise ship, spacious and open, the opposite of the claustrophobia of Foster Road earlier that day. The man, dressed in a suit, his tie poking from underneath his collar, walked towards Brian. Sign of a man who still had everything done for him. He smiled, but not too cheerily. He knew why Brian was here.

He extended his hand. "Robert Luther. Pleasure to meet you, Officer...?"

"Detective Sergeant Brian McDone," he said. Robert had a standard grip handshake, not too tight or too slack. Clearly practiced a lot.

"Would you like to follow me to my office? It's only on the fifth floor, but I can call for a lift, if you want?" Robert's brown eyes investigated Brian's waistline. He didn't say anything, but he didn't have to. An awkward moment of silence passed.

"I... Yeah, sure, whatever." He followed Robert into the lift, and they ascended to the fifth floor. He could get his exercise some other time.

#

"Obviously, I'm greatly shocked by the news," Robert said. He sat in a brown leather chair behind a mahogany desk. Deer horns, and a framed series of group photos and newspaper cuttings of his achievements, decorated the wall. Clearly a man with self-confidence issues. When in doubt, one could imagine he'd stare at the wall and give his ego a good stroke. Brian sat opposite him in the rather more conventional office chair. He looked beyond Robert's head and out onto the view of the roundabout near the water of the docklands.

"It isn't the first time it's happened to someone in our department," Robert said, before reaching for a bottle of water and pouring some down his throat. "Oh, do you—water?"

"No, it's fine. It's happened before? What do you mean?"

"All this talking. Like sandpaper on a man's throat. But anyway, yes—it happened a while back. Old lad called Jim. Used to help out with some of the filing. Cancer got him in the end. But of course, nothing like... like this, anyway."

"How well did you know the victim?"

Robert scratched at his lip before shuffling some papers about on his desk, tapping when he reached a particular one. "Nicola. Lovely girl. Always had a smile on her face. Hadn't worked here long, but she always seemed pleasant whenever I saw her. Always gave a damn about event organisation and things like that. It's... it's weird. This speech I was about to do this afternoon, announcing a new scheme we're putting in place. She organized that sort of thing. Contacting the venues, sorting out times. It's... Ah, it's just surreal, really. It's knocked us all for six."

Brian scribbled a doodle of some sort of extra-terrestrial being in his diary, but it seemed to create an atmosphere of authority about the meeting.

"What exactly goes on at BetterLives? That's something I've never quite got my head around."

Robert's expression slipped into public figure mode. "BetterLives is a different kind of charity. We open up new volunteering opportunities to get people working. We share our donations with close affiliate charities, such as Air Ambulance and hospitals. We don't discriminate; our only goal is to give people a—"

"Better life. Right."

Luther nodded. "I want to put Preston on the map. I want to make a difference here and prove that this sort of model can work elsewhere. I've never believed in anything like I have this."

Brian pretended to note something else down. Why would anyone want to put this crap-hole on the map? "Well, I wish you the best of luck with that, Mr. Luther. How long ago did Nicola join BetterLives?"

Robert skimmed through the paper again. "Ah, it'll be... Yes. September just gone. Three months ago. Feels like longer; then again, it doesn't feel like a minute ago."

"Do you always have such glowing opinions of your staff, Mr. Luther?"

"I try my best. It helps if we have a positive working environment. Same with any workplace,

right? I mean, there's always going to be the hot-
heads. There's always going to be... the slackers,
and personality clashes. But I like to think we
have—had—a nice balance at BetterLives. Obviously, without Nicola, it's going to be very hard to
handle for a long time. I don't know. Do you have
any suspects?"

"It's still pretty early. We have a few leads. We're
just trying to get the best sense we possibly can of
the sort of life Nicola lived, so if you can help enlighten me on anything, then that'd be a great
help."

Robert sank back into his chair again. "Well, like
I say, she seemed a lovely girl. Always smiley and
bubbly, so I'd imagine she has a lot of friends. Early
twenties, too? It's great, isn't it? All the young'uns
so motivated to do good for their city. Really sets
an example."

"You're hardly ancient, Mr. Luther."

Robert laughed. "So I keep telling myself.
Doesn't stop the grey hairs from ignoring me."

Brian waited for Luther to continue.

"But, um, yes, like I was saying. I didn't really
know the girl outside of work. I'm really busy at-
tending charity events, public speaking—all the fun
stuff my colleagues force me into. But yeah—if it
would help to chat to her co-volunteers from the

organisation committee, I can bring them right up here, or you can go downst..."

The door creaked open, and a short man with glasses poked his head through. He looked back at Luther, who raised his hand and gestured for the man to enter.

"Detective McDone, this is Michael Walters, my friend and adviser of—what, sixteen years?"

Michael Walters and Brian shook hands. Limp handshake. Slightly damp. Walters wore a grey jumper under his blazer. His curly, balding hair would have benefited from a shave.

"The pair of us practically invented BetterLives from the ground up," Luther said. "And the charity before this, and the charity before that. This chap keeps me right in order and stops me making the daft decisions."

"Don't flatter yourself, Robert. I was here first. I just needed a ventriloquist's dummy to do the hard work!" Michael laughed and smiled nervously at Robert, who tutted and shook his head. Not as confident as his boss. Not as self-assured. Probably still an egomaniac.

"Detective McDone here has just been chatting to me about Nicola Watson. I was just about to take him down to meet some of our team myself, but if you could do the honours, Mike, then I'd be grateful."

Michael nodded cautiously. "Don't see why not. But most of them aren't back from their Christmas holidays yet."

Luther turned back to Brian. "Yeah, being voluntary, there's not a lot we can do about the holidays."

"That's okay. Just let me have a quick chat with whoever is here. We just want an idea of the sort of girl Nicola was more than anything." Brian pulled a card out of his pocket. "If you remember something, or if a little fact or detail comes to mind, just give me a call, okay? Number's on there."

Luther gripped it between his fingers. "I'll be sure to. Good luck with the investigation. I'll mention the girl in my speech later."

"Thank you, Mr. Luther." Brian followed Michael out of the cosy wooden office and towards the lift.

#

Michael Walters walked down the corridor, shaking his hips, every step over exaggerated. Probably fancied his boss. Probably the main reason he stuck around. *Yes, Mr. Luther. Of course, Mr. Luther.*

"Nicola's team is just down there." He pointed to a little section in the corner of the office where old computers were stacked up beside ancient monitors. The room was empty aside from a young man with slicked back hair.

Michael smiled at Brian. "I've cleared the room out for you so you can chat to Nicola's colleagues in private."

"Thanks." *He definitely said "colleagues", didn't he?* And yet, there was only one man in the room. Walters nodded and began to scoot off.

"Did you know Nicola Watson?" Brian asked.

Walters stopped and spun 'round. "Me? Oh, I don't know anybody around here. I'm just the figures man. Recognised the girl, though. Terrible shame. I'll get someone to see you out when you've finished. Anything else, Detective?"

"That'll do for now. Get in touch if you find any info out."

"I'm planning on getting a full questioning of the staff sorted once we're all back. Of course, I'll be in touch." He smiled and walked back towards the lift.

Brian turned to the office room, the one man in his baggy clothes staring back at him.

#

The man was called Joshua Clements. He'd worked at BetterLives for just as long as Nicola, so they'd sorted many of the events out together.

"She was always a laugh," he said, twiddling his tie. The steam that should have risen from his half-full teacup was non-existent as the tea lay still like a cold, stagnant pond.

"What do you know about her personal life?"

Joshua puffed his cheeks out. "Only that she had a boyfriend."

Brian looked down at his notes. *Danny.* "And this boyfriend. Did Nicola ever talk to you about him?"

Joshua smiled and shook his head.

"What's so funny?"

"Nothing. Oh, nothing's funny," he said, sniffing. "Her boyfriend? I dunno. I saw him storm in here one day kicking up all this commotion. She seemed upset and weird whenever she saw him or mentioned him. Always dead cynical, like. I dunno, I might just be looking into things too much. I dunno."

Brian put pen to paper and expanded his doodle. Should he risk it? *Screw it.* "This is all very good, Joshua. But I sense that you had feelings for Nicola that might go beyond your work?"

Joshua looked like a rabbit caught in the head-lights. He reached into his pocket. "You've got that wrong, and you're running down the wrong track."

"Well, you certainly seem a bit defensive. All I'm saying."

Joshua planted a photograph onto the table. It was a picture of him and another man with a streaked quiff, both dressed in suits. They were signing a piece of paper in what looked like a regis-try office.

He held out a silver ring. "Been in a civil part-nership for a year. Very happy in it. I love him, he loves me. Like I said, you're running down the wrong track." He smiled again.

"I have to ask these questions," Brian said. "Just procedure, y'know?" In his gut, he felt punched. He was getting nowhere.

"I know. I understand you're just doing your job. But it's tough, y'know? She... Nicola. She was just so... so normal. I don't understand why anyone would want to do this to her. She was just an ordi-nary girl, you know?"

Brian pulled another details card out of his pocket as his phone buzzed. "Like I say, if you have anything else to tell us, or any of your colleagues have anything to say, give us a ring, all right? Sorry about your loss. And sorry, I have to take this." He handed the card to Joshua and pulled the phone to his ear.

"What is it?" he asked.

"Brian, you need to get down to Danny's as soon as possible," Cassy said.

"What—what's going on?"

Cassy sounded out of breath. "He's gone. Hasn't been seen since yesterday afternoon."

Adrenaline rushed through Brian's body. "I—I'll be right there," he said, before running out of the room and down the stairs.

At least he'd finally got his five flights of exercise for the year.

Chapter Five.

It seemed like forever ago that driving with the siren on had last excited Brian.

He used to love it, whirring through the traffic, filled with youthful excitement and adrenaline. Now, it was just routine. The sound grew irritating over the years. In the films, sirens were a sign of an impending chase—a high-tempo shoot-out with a group of crooks. In Preston, sirens were usually due to a Chihuahua terrorising some neighbours, or something along those lines.

He shot through the parting traffic as the old hospital emerged in the distance. It used to be sprawling inside, full of life. Now, it was an empty shell, ghostly and abandoned. A thick film of dark-green moss coated the red brick, which was wearing away, on the side of the clock tower. He'd dealt with a few druggies and delinquents in there, but nothing too serious.

Brian pulled up outside the grey brick house on the opposite side of the road to the hospital. Cassy stood in the garden with an elderly woman. Looked too old to be Danny's mother. Maybe a grandparent or a neighbour.

He walked over to Cassy and the other woman. The woman folded her arms over her grey cardigan. A massive mole sprouted out of her left cheek, and her scraggy, unkempt grey hair clung to the sides of her face like an animal with separation anxiety. Cassy held her hands out, trying to calm the woman down.

"Not my lad," she was saying in protest. "My lad wouldn't do a thing. Nope, not my Danny."

"Mrs. Stocks, we're not trying to accu—"

"It's *Ms.* Stocks, alright? *Ms.* Learn to get it right before you start bossing me around, lady. All the same, the lot of you. All the same..."

"Can I help you, Madame?" Brian looked at Ms. Stocks with concern. Cassy shook her head, battling to resist saying anything inappropriate.

Ms. Stocks eyed Brian closely. "Just this woman of yours. Us women, we shouldn't be in the police.

We don't have a clue about things like that. In my day, it was just the fellas. Back to those days, I say!"

Cassy rolled her eyes. The way she tensed her jaw, Brian knew she was dying to say something.

"Look, it's all right," Brian said. "I'm here now. Cassy—you grab a coffee. Got one in the car for you. Okay?"

Cassy, her mouth dangling open, stared at Brian. Then she shrugged and walked over to her police car. "Whatever."

Ms. Stocks tutted. "So rude, that girl. So, so rude."

Brian sighed. This woman was going to be hard work, but he'd dealt with worse in the past. "Sorry about my colleague. First off, I just want to assure you that we're not here to do anything to your son—"

"Grandson. He's my grandson, our Danny. Mum died a few years back. Got the breast cancer. Never was strong enough." She slipped a long cigarette between her chapped lips and took a drag, then let out a tickly, chesty cough. Stale, smoky breath clouded around Brian's face. The way she coughed, she'd probably want to keep an eye out for "the cancer" herself.

"Your grandson. Now, we don't want any trouble, Ms. Stocks. All we want to know is where he could've got to. We're worried about him, okay? That's all. We just want to ask him a few questions about his girlfriend. You with me, Ms. Stocks?"

"His ex," Ms. Stocks said, sharply. "Never was good enough for our Danny, that girl. Didn't give two shits about him. He thought the world of her, y'know? Thought the world of her. Fool. Silly fool."

Brian leaned against the garden wall. He felt something sticky in his hand and turned to see he'd rested his palm on a thick, slimy slug.

"Oh those bloody slugs," Ms. Stocks said, pulling the cigarette out of her mouth and ramming it into the slug's back. It shrivelled and dropped to the floor, drying up almost instantly.

"You say they split up?" Brian asked, cringing as Ms. Stocks continued to smoke on the slime-coated cigarette.

"I didn't say that, did I? His ex, I said. 'Cause she's gone now. Long gone."

Brian wasn't convinced. She seemed to know more than she was letting on. Her eyes, the way they twitched. Her evident animosity towards Nicola Watson.

"You weren't fond of Nicola, then?"

Ms. Stocks coughed. "Hope you aren't trying to say nothin' about me or my family, 'cause I swear we ain't done nothin', I tell you!"

"Ms. Stocks, I can assure you I'm not trying to do anything of the sort. I just want to know a little more about Nicola Watson. Try to build the best sort of character picture that I can. You can see how much that could help us, okay?"

Ms. Stocks took another spluttering drag on her cigarette. "My Danny, he was obsessed with her—crazy about her. At first, she was all right. But then she'd end up cancelling coming 'round for tea, 'cause she had stuff better to do. Broke our Danny's heart, she did. Then she'd stop coming at all, and Danny would end up having to pay to go see her. Was as if she thought she was too good for us, y'know?"

All this was good information, but Brian wasn't getting anywhere concerning Danny's whereabouts.

"Ms. Stocks, I don't mean to pry, but do you have any idea where your grandson might be? Any friends or relatives, or just somewhere he might go to when he wants to be alone?"

Ms. Stocks squeezed her eyes shut in deep thought. "He was always here or with that girl. Other than that, I've no idea. I'd tell you or go find him myself if I did, y'know?"

Brian sighed. He put a hand on Ms. Stocks' shoulder. "Thank you very much for everything,

Ms. Stocks. I realise it must be a very stressful time for both you and your grandson."

She glanced away. "He was crazy about her, y'know? Crazy about her, silly fool."

Brian looked back at the police car. Cassy stared through the window, fidgeting with agitation like a dog locked inside on a hot day. Brian tilted his head at her and she rushed out, sucking on a straw wedged into a carton of coffee.

Ms. Stocks' eyes widened when she saw Cassy approaching. "What's she doing back here again?"

"Ms. Stocks," Brian said. "With your permission, of course, DS Emerson and I would love to take a quick look around your grandson's room. It's nothing serious, just a quick check to see where he might have got to. Is that okay?"

Ms. Stocks looked out at the street, uncertainty in her expression. "Do you 'ave one of them things? A warrant, or whatever they call them on the telly?"

Shit. They could usually take advantage of old women, especially with a few friendly manners. "Ms. Stocks, it's only a quick look, I—"

"No," she snapped. "You can come back here with a warrant. I don't have to let you in, not if this girl you're with is saying things about my boy. No, no."

Brian gave up speaking. He turned to Cassy, who fumbled in her pocket, and shook his head. There was nothing they could do until they got a warrant. *Good job, Cassy, good job.*

"Ms. Stocks," Cassy intervened. "Would you like us to file your grandson as a missing person?"

Ms. Stocks looked to Brian, then Cassy, and chewed at her lip. "Yep. Yep. He's just done a runner. Gone missing, that's all. Missing person. Good lad, our Danny. Missing person."

"DS Emerson, we'll just have to—" Brian started.

"And would you like to make that an official missing person report?"

Ms. Stocks nodded. "Yes. Yes, I would. My boy needs finding. He needs bringing back. You need to do your jobs."

Cassy took some more notes in her daybook and smiled reassuringly at Ms. Stocks. "If you'd just sign here, please, we can make that official." She handed the pen and book to Ms. Stocks, who wedged her half-smoked cigarette between her fingers whilst she scanned and signed beneath the entry.

What was Cassy doing? They didn't need a missing person's investigation open. The budget was stretched as it was. They needed to treat this as one case.

"Thank you," Cassy said as Ms. Stocks passed back the daybook. She offered it to Brian, who glared at her, puzzled. "Ms. Stocks, now we've got your written consent and report of Daniel Stocks' disappearance, we are entitled to take a look around your grandson's room for any clues as to his location. Or in the event that he may just be hiding underneath his bed."

Brian's stomach tingled as he realised what Cassy had done.

"What?" Ms. Stocks said, her lips shaking. "But I... but I thought... What?"

Cassy smiled. "You filed the report, Ms. Stocks. That was your decision, not ours."

Ms. Stocks twitched her head and muttered some inaudible words before holding her arm in the direction of her house. "Oh, whatever. First door on the left up the stairs."

As they followed Ms. Stocks inside, Brian nodded in thanks, and Cassy's lips formed a wide, sarcastic smile.

\#

The hallway was narrow and claustrophobic, the lighting dim. The once-white wallpaper curled at the edges as brown mould peppered across it. The washed-out ceiling looked like a coffee drinker's teeth, yellow and grimy. Stale cigarette smoke clouded the staircase.

Ms. Stocks stumbled up the stairs with Brian and Cassy in tow. She held her back and winced with every step.

"You don't have to come with us if you don't want to, Ms. Stocks," Brian said.

"No, I do," she said sharply. "My house, I'll do what I want. I think I can climb my own stairs."

Cassy tutted as the pair of them waited for Ms. Stocks to take another step.

And another.

And another.

When they finally reached Danny Stocks' room, Ms. Stocks stood beside the door, her arms folded like a nightclub bouncer's. "I'll be out here if you need 'owt," she said, staring at Brian and refusing to acknowledge Cassy.

"Thank you, Ms. Stocks. We appreciate your co-operation."

She shrugged and mumbled something under her breath as Brian and Cassy walked into the room.

A double bed sat at the opposite side of Danny's large, spacious bedroom, thick bedding spilling out of cracked buttons at the bottom of the sheets. Several posters hung on the walls: Preston North

End Football Club, women, rock stars. A big glass display cabinet sat at the foot of the bed. It housed medals, video games, a digital camera, and scraps of weed and rolling papers.

Brian opened up the glass cupboard and reached for the digital camera. It looked quite new, perhaps a recent Christmas present.

Cassy dabbed some of the weed onto her fingers. "Old mare out there could do with a joint or two. Sorry, I shouldn't insult your new lady-friend right under your nose, should I? What the hell was that all about? 'DS Emerson, kindly go sit in the car like a nice little lap dog.'"

Brian, ignoring Cassy's sarcasm, held down the power button of the camera. "Anything on the computer?"

Cassy clicked the mouse and scrolled around. "It's a new one by the looks of things. Not a scrap on it. No photos, no music—nothing."

"It's not new."

"Hear what I just said? The box is here, right next to it. The thing's still got fucking tape on the screen. It's brand new."

"Or, he's a very organised guy, and he deleted what little stuff he had on the computer in a rush but forgot to take his camera along with him." He passed the camera to Cassy. She looked at it and clicked through the photographs, her mouth widening.

"2nd January... and that's—hold on, is that...?"

"Yes, it is," Brian said.

Cassy flipped the camera back around and pointed to the tall guy in glasses, who was sucking on a joint. "Who d'you think this is?" she asked.

"Ms. Stocks," Brian called. "That's what I'm about to find out from my lovely new lady-friend."

Ms. Stocks pottered into the room. "Did you call, Officer?" She ignored the weed and the mound of smelly underwear beside her grandson's bed.

Brian smiled at her and rolled the digital camera around in his hand. "This is a very nice bit of kit. Big fan of photography myself. Is it new?"

Ms. Stocks squinted at the camera as if it were an alien object. "Oh, that thing. Yes, my Danny has been saving up for so long for one of those things. He's a good lad, my Danny. Likes his photographs."

"Sure." Brian held the camera up to Ms. Stocks so she could see. "This photograph was taken just a few hours before Nicola Watson was murdered. Can you tell me who the third person in this photograph is, please?"

Ms. Stocks blinked rapidly. "That's... But that's her brother, isn't it?"

"Her...her brother? *Nicola's* brother?"

Ms. Stocks nodded. "Yes, yes, her brother. Nice lad. Got on well with our Danny in school, he did. Yeah, lovely boy. Lovely, lovely boy."

"They never told us anything about their son," Brian said to Cassy. "Do you remember Nicola's brother's name?"

"I... I don't, I'm afraid. Lovely boy, though, I can assure you."

"I'm sure he is. Ms. Stocks, would you mind if I kept hold of this camera?"

Ms. Stocks frowned. "Why? Why would you want to do that?"

Brian pulled his diary out and placed it in her hands. "It's the missing person thing. This might help identify his location, and the sooner we do that, the sooner we can get your Danny back to you, okay?"

Ms. Stocks hesitated for a moment before shrugging and jotting her signature in the diary. "But I want that back," she said. "He's saved up so long for one of those things. Please, Officer. I'd hate him to be upset if it got lost."

Brian patted Ms. Stocks' shoulder. "I can assure you I'll take very good care of it, Ms. Stocks. Thank you very much."

Brian and Cassy left the house, and Ms. Stocks, who lit up another cigarette and leaned against her slug-infested garden wall, waved them off. Brian told her to be in touch if Danny returned home to her at any point, but she didn't seem like the most cooperative of ladies.

"Well, aren't you going to thank me?" Cassy asked, as they sat in Brian's car.

"Thank you?" Brian pretended he didn't know what she was talking about, but to her credit, she'd done well, fooling the old woman into the missing persons loophole. "For what?"

"You know damn well what for. Where would we be right now without me?"

"You did all right. But if anything, you've only gone and got us more questions than answers."

"Like, why didn't the Watsons mention they had a son?"

"Well, it depends how you look at things. Either they didn't really see the need to, or—"

"—or they're covering for him."

Brian lifted the camera out of his pocket again and had a final look at the picture as Cassy stepped out towards her police car.

Nicola, Danny Stocks, and Nicola's brother. Together, smoking weed, at eleven p.m. on 2nd January. Last night.

The night of Nicola Watson's murder.

Chapter Six.

A school stood just around the corner from the Watsons' house on a quiet, tree-lined street, one of the nicer parts of Preston. Brian had lived in the area when he was a toddler. The construction of a new water works forced his family to move out. Three years after the construction, the water works closed and had been abandoned ever since.

Brian and Cassy slammed the doors of their cars and walked towards the Watson household. Brian took another glance at Danny's camera. This lead had to go somewhere. It just had to.

"I'll do the talking," Brian said as Cassy knocked on the frosted glass door of the traditional, semi-detached house. A bunch of cards were wedged in the low letterbox at the foot of the door. Red ones, blue ones... It was either somebody's birthday, or the hand-delivered sympathy cards were already beginning to fly in.

Trevor Watson pulled the door open. His red-eyed face was vacant and distant. He gestured Brian and Cassy inside without saying anything and dragged his feet towards the kitchen.

Trevor placed the small pile of sympathy cards from the letterbox onto the kitchen worktop. Opening those couldn't be easy. What was he expected to say? "Thank you for sending me the sympathy card..." It wasn't like a birthday, or Christmas. Cards would be the last things you wanted when you'd just lost something, especially your daughter. Card after card, reminder after reminder...

Trevor walked over to the fridge and grabbed a colourful drawing from behind a magnet. He grinned and walked over to Brian and Cassy, dangling the green and blue crayon-covered sheet in front of them with shaking hands. "She drew this, back when she was in primary school. Always... always was an arty girl, my Nicola." His voice was shaky, the tears in his eyes growing heavier.

Brian attempted a smile. "Your daughter sounds like a lovely girl, Mr. Watson."

Trevor scrunched the drawing up into a little ball and pressed it in his palms as tightly as he could, then stormed over to the kitchen bin and tossed it inside. His face was completely red, and he panted like an animal.

Then, breaking free from his fixated trance in a split second, he perched on the side of his kitchen table and stared into space. "How can I help you, officers?"

Brian cleared his throat. "It's actually your son we want to have a word with."

Trevor looked between the two officers. "Scott? And why would you want to have a word with him?"

Cassy stepped forward. "We believe your son might have been one of the last people to see Nicola Watson with her boyfriend, Danny Stocks."

Brian bit his lip. Why did she always have to interrupt and be so forward like that? A bit more subtlety wouldn't go amiss.

Trevor wiped his fingertip against the dusty table. He looked back up at Cassy. "Well, I appreciate your honesty, Officer. But from what you're saying, Danny did it?"

Brian's stomach sank. Typical. This is why he'd told her he'd do the talking. He fired a stare at her and intervened. "No, we aren't saying that at all."

"We have reason to believe that Danny Stocks might have been the last person to see Nicola Watson, and we have evidence that he was with your son, Scott, sometime before her death."

Trevor rubbed his hands against his cheeks. "Danny. Danny. If I see him... if I see him, I swear, I'll kill him. I'll kill him." His soft voice made the words even more sinister.

"That's why we'd like your son's help," Cassy said. "Danny's gone missing."

"It's him isn't it? It's him. I knew it. I knew it."

"Mr. Watson," Brian said. "My colleague is not saying that, only..." He realised Cassy and Trevor were staring somewhere behind him. He turned around slowly and saw him, standing like a model in the spotlight.

"Scott Watson?" Cassy asked.

The skinny, acne-ridden boy cowered and scratched the spot on the bridge of his nose underneath his glasses. "Y-yes?"

Cassy walked towards Scott. Brian and Trevor stayed put.

"We'd like to have a word with you about your friend Danny. What say we sit down for a cuppa?"

#

Trevor paced around outside the kitchen door. Talking to Scott where he was most comfortable—

his home—was a ridiculous idea, really. He'd rather have done it in private. They could've brought him in as a witness and recorded what he had to say. But here they were, sat around his kitchen table.

Scott twiddled his fingers as Cassy pushed the camera towards him. The reflection of him, his sister, and Danny glowed in his thin-framed glasses.

"What were you doing out with Danny and your sister that night?" Brian asked.

Scott shook his head, mumbling inaudible words. He was hiding something, there was no doubt about it. The way he shook; the way he looked so uncomfortable and out of place in his own kitchen. Brian would have no trouble breaking him if he had to.

"Scott, you're not getting yourself anywhere by staying silent. Now by all means, keep your mouth shut. You're certainly making our job a lot easier."

Scott looked up at Brian with bloodshot eyes. He opened his mouth to speak and gulped back an interrupting air bubble. "I know it looks bad. But I promise, we didn't do anything wrong."

Brian laughed. "Usually kids who do things wrong say they haven't. Since when were you and your sister's boyfriend such good friends, anyway?"

Brian nodded at Cassy, and she changed the picture to the one of just Scott and Danny together, smoking joints. Nicola was nowhere in sight.

Scott dropped his forehead into his hands. "I just didn't want to say. I didn't want to say because I knew it'd get me into trouble, and I... I just couldn't."

Cassy leaned in towards Scott, who couldn't hold his gaze with either of the officers. "Couldn't what?"

He took a nervous breath and glanced over at the door, where Trevor was staring into the kitchen, red-faced. "The weed," Scott whispered. "I was getting it off Danny. It made me feel cool, I dunno. But we weren't really friends. He just smoked with me a few times. I didn't want to say. I didn't want it to get me in trouble."

Brian slumped back into his seat. *Weed.* That was all the kid was scared about. "Believe me, kid—a bit of green is the last thing on our list of priorities right now."

Scott snivelled. "I just... I just want my sister. She wouldn't do anything wrong."

"I know, kid," Brian said. "I know it's tough. But you can help us. I know it's hard—all this bullshit with people you thought were your friends, losing family... Yeah. But right now, you are the only person who can tell us where Danny Stocks might be. I *know* he helped you out. I know he gave you weed, but between you and me, maybe we can ignore that, all right? We just need to know where you went to smoke. Where is that place on the pictures?"

Speechless and shaking, Scott looked up at the pair of them.

"Scott," Trevor shouted. "You tell these officers where that scrote is, right now."

"I don't know," Scott said, his gaze wandering. "I... There could be a few places. I don't know."

"You're telling me you were so stoned that you didn't even know where you were? How very convenient. Speaking of which, where were you when your sister went missing, anyway?"

Scott looked at his dad anxiously then slumped his shoulders like a school-kid being told off by a teacher. "I... I was at work. That's why I couldn't... The spliff, I couldn't..."

"You irresponsible shit," Trevor shouted, shaking his head.

Brian leaned back in his chair and shook his head at Cassy. Little bastard went out for a smoke before work, of course he did. Careless git. "Where do you work?"

Scott fiddled with his hands. "I drive. I was doing nights and... I drive."

"Oh, now the plot thickens! So, you were not only doing drugs that night, but you were driving under the influence. Mr. Watson, I was beginning to think you were an intelligent lad, too. So admission of substance abuse *and* driving under the influence. Maybe we should head down to the station where it's a little more... cosy. What do you think?" Brian had no real intentions of wasting petrol, but he just wanted to strike a bit of fright into him, break him down even more. From the way Scott Watson glared nervously at Brian, then the window and back again, he figured he was doing a good enough job of freaking him out.

"I—I'm sorry, I really am," Scott said. "Just, please. My sister. I know I was stupid but... but my sister. Please."

Brian let out a sigh. "The way I see it, you have two options: the easy option and the difficult option. The easy option—you tell us where you and your good friend Danny smoke those drugs, and perhaps we could send you on a nice, low-profile drug rehabilitation programme for a couple of weeks, keeping it quiet, y'know? Or the difficult option. Well, it makes it very easy for us, but for you... I can only offer my sympathies."

Scott's arms began to shake even more. His breathing intensified as he stared at the table with tired, reddening eyes.

"Scott," Trevor called. "You tell them. You tell them right now, or I'll fucking shake it out of you."

Scott scratched at the table with his long fingernails. Then, like a burst balloon, he gasped and collapsed onto the table. "The old hospital," he said, snivelling. He looked back up at the officers. "That's where we usually go. Just—please, don't tell him I told you. Please."

Brian nodded and reached his hand towards Scott. "Thanks a lot for your help. We'll be in touch about that drug rehab thing." He patted Scott on the shoulder and departed through the kitchen door.

Trevor Watson gritted his teeth and stared at his son sitting at the kitchen table.

"We'll need Scott in for an official statement later on. If you can contact my colleagues, they'll be able to sort that out for you. And, um... go easy on him, Mr. Watson," Brian whispered. "He's been through a lot."

Trevor looked right into Brian's eyes. "He's my son. I'll deal with my own son, okay?"

Brian half-smiled at Trevor as he and Cassy let themselves out.

They could hear Trevor Watson's shouts from outside.

#

Brian and Cassy returned to the station shortly after. They needed to pick up two Detective Constables to accompany them to the old hospital and drop off one of their cars. The department was low on cars, so they often had to double up nowadays. The budget was tight; they just had to make do with what they had.

"I don't think we have to worry about Scott Watson so much," Brian said as he and Cassy waited for the DCs. "But Danny—we need to get down to that old hospital. We don't need any of this messing around or waiting for people."

Cassy rolled her eyes and shook her head. "You're such a grumpy so-and-so. We could do with the cover. I swear, you're gonna get your cock burned one of these days." She jabbed Brian in the stomach playfully.

"Yeah, well, we all get our cocks burned from time to time."

Cassy's face turned serious, and she tilted her gaze towards the ground.

"If you don't stop dicking around, I'll cut your cock off, let alone burn it, DS McDone."

Brian's stomach sank as he turned 'round to see DI Price's bloodshot eyes staring at him. "Detective Inspector, I'm sorry about..."

"'Course you aren't. Now you'd better tell me where the fuck you're at with this case. It's five p.m., and I still feel like you're doing a bloody dot to dot without a pencil."

"We're off to find the runaway boyfriend now," Cassy said. "Danny Stocks. We were told to come back for some support? From two DCs?"

Price mulled the words. He looked at his watch. "You finish in an hour."

Brian and Cassy looked at each other, unsure of Price's intentions.

"Do you... want us to leave it 'til tomorrow then, or...?"

"I want you to get your thumbs out of your arses and get the fuck down there right now," he barked.

"What about the DCs?"

"They're on their bloody way down there already. Just get on with it!"

"Right, right, Detective Inspector, we'll be right on it."

Price, shaking his head, disappeared down the corridor.

"Told you you were gonna get your cock burned," Cassy said.

Chapter Seven.

The car pulled up outside the derelict old hospital just down the road from lovely old Ms. Stocks' house. Brian passed this place often. Its decaying brick and ghostly presence stared down at him like something out of a haunted-house flick. At night, stoners and scrotes filled it. Now, they knew that Danny Stocks and Scott Watson were amongst those people.

Brian brought the car to a sudden halt, and Cassy jerked forward, her food almost flying across the dashboard. "Smooth parking, Brian. Very smooth."

"I'd like to see you do better."

"Yeah, yeah," she said, closing the lid of the half-finished box of Won-Ton noodles.

"Nervous?" Brian asked, smiling for reassurance.

She looked up at him with a sort of "What the hell are you on about?" face that gave Brian his answer.

"It's okay," Brian said. "You'll grow to love Preston's finest abandoned old buildings soon enough. They aren't as creepy as they look on TV, I swear."

Cassy rolled her eyes as she ejected her seatbelt. "Oh, it's not the abandoned buildings I've got a problem with. I saw to plenty of those in Bolton. It's just... I dunno. This case. It's bigger than anything I've been involved in before. Raises the stakes a bit.

Brian shrugged. "We'll be fine. I know my way around this place."

"I get that, but... Brian—your phone. You've got Location Services switched on, haven't you?"

"Wouldn't have a bloody clue." He handed his phone to Cassy. She seemed to be a whizz with all this technical stuff, like most of the young ones were.

She tapped around on his phone. "It brings your location up. Just in case anything happens and we need someone to come for us, y'know? I always prefer to be cautious."

"Don't go soft on me now, DS Emerson. The cavemen didn't have bloody Location Services, did they? We'll be fine. Come on."

The sound of Brian's radio crackled as the pair stepped outside the car and into the fresh January air. "DS McDone, we're at the west side of the hospital. What's the P.O.A?" DC Peters said.

"Finished spewing your guts out yet, Peters?"

"Har-har, very funny. Now come on. I want to get home as much as the next man, so let's get this done with."

"DS Emerson and I will go in there and have a look around. We have info that suggests the ex-boyfriend could be inside. If he is, we'll bring him in for questioning. Doing a runner the day after his girlfriend goes missing isn't the smartest thing to do."

"Okay, okay. Do you need us, or...?" Peters sounded eager not to get involved.

"Stay outside. We'll give you a shout if we need any backup. The sooner you rest that poor little head of yours, the better."

DC Peters muttered something inaudible then switched his radio off.

Brian looked at Cassy. "You ready?"

"Why the hell not, eh?"

#

The door echoed through the vast expanse of the derelict hospital as Brian pushed it open. A thick layer of dust coated the filthy reception area. Old chairs lay on their sides, the long-lost voices and drones of receptionists and life-support machines still audible if you listened closely enough. Wall-mounted telephones dangled from their cradles. Crumpled papers and cracked vodka bottles lined the floor. It was like the opening scene of 28 *Days Later*, where Cillian Murphy wakes up with his cock out and the whole world's gone to shit.

"Where do we start in a place like this?" Cassy asked.

Beside the abandoned opening desk, a long corridor led towards the old maternity wards. The door to the corridor was slightly ajar, and barely any light peeked through the boarded-up windows.

"Used to be one of the best maternity hospitals, this place," Brian said as fragments of broken glass crumbled beneath his shoes. "My mum gave birth to me in here. Strange, isn't it? This shithole was the first building I ever lived in." He brushed his hand against the dusty old documents on the desk. Something clattered down the corridor. A flock of crows flapped about, squawking at the disturbance. It was their territory now.

"What happened to this place?"

Brian moved closer towards the corridor door. "The same thing that happens to everything good in this city—it went to shit. Hospital just got closed by the government one day, along with a few others in the north, because, y'know, we're less important than those rich toffs down south. Nobody bought the place. Nobody knocked it down. It's just kind of... here." He crouched down; somebody had been here recently.

Very recently.

"Cassy, come over here."

"What is it?"

Brian dabbed his finger in the blood on the floor and wiped it off on his dark trousers. More blood trailed through the slightly open door. "Certainly looks fresh to me. Either we've got a dying animal on our case, which would explain the crows, or we've got... well, something else." He pulled himself up and winced as he pushed the door completely open, shining his torch down into the boarded-up darkness.

"Wait, shouldn't we call for...?"

"Let's just have a quick look around, okay? See what we can find."

"If you say so, I guess."
"Good girl. You're learning."
"Piss off."

#

The farther they walked down the corridor, the messier it got. Things creaked, and sudden movements glimmered in the light of their torches. Damp, sticky glass cracked under their feet. It was an industrial jungle, filled with mysterious old cures and undiscovered secrets. A man-made Amazon gone to waste.

As they progressed farther into the mouth of the beast, Cassy began to cough. Brian glared at her. "Keep it down," he whispered.

"Weed."

Brian's eyebrows twitched. "You've done *what*?"

Cassy held her hand to her face and covered her mouth to prevent further coughing. "No, *weed*. I can't handle weed. There's someone been smoking in here."

Brian twitched his nostrils like a sniffer dog, and the ghastly dull smell hit him. How hadn't he smelt it before? Was a decline in the sense of smell another thing the curse of middle age stripped away?

"We'll go a bit further in, and see..."

"Brian," Cassy whispered. She stared somewhere beyond him and switched off her torch.

"What's up?"

"Look. Up there."

Brian squinted ahead and kept his torch low. At first, he didn't see anything. Then a miniscule light, flickering just in the distance, became visible.

He turned back to Cassy. "How shall we go about this?"

"I thought *you* were the fucking expert?"

Brian gulped and lowered his torch even more. The person had to have seen them. It *had* to be Danny.

"We'll go in quiet," Brian said. "Keep your light off. Anything happens, we turn them on straight away and blind the bastard. Okay?"

Cassy turned back to the door they'd come through. "You sure we shouldn't call for backup now?"

Brian mulled the thought in his head. *Call for backup or get it done with?* "We're here now. Let's get it done with."

Brian took lead and started walking. He waited for the sound of Cassy's footsteps behind him. No chance he was venturing too far into this dark abyss alone.

The light grew even closer as broken glass cracked beneath Brian's feet. Had he seen them? Was he even there?

Then, the light went out.

Brian stopped walking, and Cassy edged into his back. What now? Did he turn the torch on, or what? Danny could be anywhere, waiting to ambush them...

Fuck it. He pulled up his torch and aimed it in the direction of the light.

That's when he saw him lying there.

Thick vomit trickled out of his mouth. A bottle of pills rested between his limp fingers.

"Call a fucking ambulance," Brian said as he rushed over to Danny's lifeless body and eased his neck upright.

A solitary spliff lay on the floor as the lit end gradually burned out.

Chapter Eight.

Brian couldn't get the image of Danny Stocks out of his head that night. Bottle of pills in his hand. Lone spliff burning out beside his fingertips.

He couldn't sleep. He knew what he had to do if he wanted to sleep, but he didn't want to do it. Nobody in their right mind would want to do it. But it wasn't about want. It wasn't a choice.

He should've felt triumphant about their discovery of Danny, but a part of him couldn't help but sympathise.

Danny was to spend the night—maybe longer—in hospital, on suicide watch. Any form of interviewing was postponed until the doctor considered him "fit for questioning". Just what they needed.

If only they'd got to the hospital quicker. If only they hadn't taken a detour back to the station on the way back from the Watson household, they could've had him. Now, they just had to hope.

Brian took a sip of whisky and cringed. He hated the stuff, but he had to keep up the image at work. Keep it on his breath. *The recovering alcoholic.*

His phone vibrated. Who would be calling him at eleven p.m.? He grabbed it from his cluttered bedside table and lifted it to his ear the second he saw the name on the screen: Vanessa. *Shit.* He was drunk, too. Was he drunk? *Shit.*

"'Ness, I, erm... Hi." *Smooth, Brian. Real smooth.*

"Sorry to call you so late," she said. "I just... Well, I heard about it on the news. The boy you found. Is that it? Is it over?"

He hadn't spoken to his wife since Christmas, and now she was ringing up and asking about the case. That meant the media were all over the events. The powers above keeping the press sweet after a recently strained relationship.

"Hard to say. We won't know more until we have a chat with the boy. But it doesn't look great for him, in my opinion, anyway. Running off and trying to kill himself. Either depressed that his girl-friend's gone, or something more complicated."

Vanessa sighed. He pictured her twiddling with her long, silvery blonde hair as she always did when she was on the phone. "How you doing?" she asked.

"Good." Brian gripped the bottle of whisky in his other hand. "And you? How's Davey?"

"We're good. He's good. He got a new toy car today. Can't wait to show you."

"I bet. I bet he loves it."

A moment's silence passed before Vanessa started speaking again. "Listen, I was wondering if you wanted to meet up for a coffee tomorrow?"

"I... A coffee? Course, course, that'd be... Will Davey be...?"

"Just me and you," Vanessa cut in. "I wanted to talk about, um, the divorce. Get things moving further with that. If that's okay?"

"Oh... yeah." Brian's enthusiasm deflated. He cleared his throat to mask the disappointment in his voice. "I mean, yeah. I'm busy lately. Probably better if Davey and I hang out when I'm a bit more focused... or something like that." He gritted his teeth after saying the words. They sounded as if an alien was speaking through him.

"That sounds very mature of you, Brian. You have a lot of making up to do. If you're busy, then maybe now isn't the best time."

He knew what she was implying by the way she said "busy". *Judgmental cow.* But who was he to argue, lying here with empty bottles around the room, whisky in his hand? Still, only he judged himself. What he did in his spare time was nobody else's business. No doctor's. No therapist's. Nobody's.

"What time would be best for you tomorrow?" Vanessa asked.

"One-ish, perhaps? Lunch?"

Vanessa kept quiet for a few seconds. "All right," she finally said. "One it is. Be there, Brian, seriously. Goodnight."

"Good—"

The phone cut out. He pressed it against his cheek for a few moments, then popped it back on his bedside table, next to the turned down photo. He started to turn the photo up, have a look at them again, just to remember. Just to remember how it was.

He stopped himself. He screwed the bottle cap on the whisky before walking to the bathroom cubicle. He pulled the flimsy light cord and saw his bushy stubble staring back at him, ready for a shave.

He picked up the razor blade. The sense of dread welled in his stomach. *You know you have to do it. You know you'll feel better if you do it. You know you'll be out of control if you don't do it...*

He closed his eyes and squeezed the handle of the razor. He didn't have to do it. He was seeing Vanessa tomorrow—he would feel better then. She would make him feel better.

"I wanted to talk about the divorce..."

He pressed the razorblade against his forearm and clenched his jaw. *Almost over, almost over...*

The tang of whisky seared the back of his throat as the metal cut into his flesh, but soon he would be okay again and he'd be able to sleep, and everything would be back to normal.

The drunken detective. He wished it were as simple as the clichÉ.

#

Brian's breath frosted like steam from an engine as he walked down to the police station the following day. He smelt of sour whisky. His clothes stuck to his skin, but he hadn't found the time to take a shower. He'd done the usual—dabbed a bit of whisky under his armpits and on his neck, just to give off the strong boozy smell. He'd cleaned the wound on his arm and wrapped a bandage around it, but soon after that, he'd fallen to sleep. Maybe back in the day, he would've made an effort to impress his colleagues. But as age progressed, it was becoming less and less important.

As he walked inside the station, Amanda, the desk officer, did a double take and nudged the work experience intern by her side. Both of them had a little giggle and avoided eye contact with Brian. *Perfect.* He must have done a good job of looking the drunken mess. Then again, Amanda always seemed to find something to laugh about, like a high schooler who never quite matured.

Cassy scanned Brian from head to toe as he walked through the chatter of the main office. "You okay?"

"Fine," he said. "Just fine. Is the boy here?"

Cassy nodded reluctantly and pointed towards the interview room doors. "Came out of hospital this morning. Asked him if he wanted to pop down for a little chat, and he seemed okay with that. His grandma—your new girlfriend—she's been on the phone, but you know what she's like with me. So I couldn't say much to her, y'know?"

Brian pulled off his coat and threw it onto his desk. DS Stephen Molfer jumped as the coat knocked over his pot of stationary, sending a bunch of freshly sharpened pencils to the floor. He glared at Brian with narrowed eyes.

"At least it'll get you off your arse," Brian said, and some of the other officers laughed as Molfer got down on his hands and knees.

Brian turned back to Cassy with a smile on his face. Cassy, however, was not smiling.

"What aren't you telling me?" Brian asked.

Cassy sighed. "The press. They're all over this." She grabbed the copy of the *Lancashire News* from the desk and held it up. *BOYFRIEND SUICIDE ATTEMPT AS MURDER TWISTS.*

Brian punched the paper out of his face and started walking towards the briefing room. "Murder 'twists?' What does that even *mean?*"

Cassy scrambled to pick up some notes and ran to catch up. "I dunno. But the press seems well-informed."

Brian looked around the room at the officers at their desks. "Not surprised. Just the way things go. I bet half of these young rats are earning an extra few quid a day from the press. The problem with rats is, someday they get caught."

"Do you think I'm a young rat?" Cassy asked, raising her eyebrows like an innocent puppy.

"For that, darling, you'd have to be young."

She punched Brian in the arm before leading the way to the briefing room. Brian winced with pain. Nobody noticed, and he was completely content with that.

#

DI Price already sat in the middle chair, arms folded and cheeks more inflamed than ever. White hairs sprouted out of his nostrils like weeds in a garden, unstoppable and never-ending. He looked at his watch as Brian and Cassy entered. "On time for once. Maybe you'll actually make some progress today, right?"

Brian bit his lip. "That's certainly my intention."

"None of that cockiness with me," Price said. "Take a seat."

Brian sat down at the corner of the table, Cassy beside him. DC Peters was clean-shaven and fresher looking than yesterday. He was perched in front of a laptop, keying in notes from a black notepad.

"H.O.L.M.E.S. up and running again?"

"For now. Got a few complaints through to the ACS. He says we're using it wrong. I'd like to see him come down here and bloody use it right."

"Don't you get lippy, Peters, or I'll make you spew again," Price said. A few of the officers around the table snorted and sniggered. "McDone, the lad's in the interview rooms. The boyfriend.

Looking a bit fidgety for my liking. Stares into space like a fucking junkie. Not sure I like him."

"DS Emerson and I will have a chat with him. He tried to kill himself last night. If that's not a sign of guilt, then I'd like to know what it is. We have a clear motive for his attempted suicide. Now we just need to work out whether he might have a motive for something much darker."

Price offered a slight nod in agreement. "We'll have to interview under caution. He's free to leave at any time. You'd best hurry up. Thanks to the press, I'd expect the girl's parents'll be paying us a visit today."

"What are you trying to say?" Brian asked.

Price stood up and began rubbing out some old notes on the whiteboard with his dusty sleeve. "What I'm trying to say is that you'd better find out as much about this kid as you can, before the parents come in here and bloody kill him, or before he decides he's had enough and takes off. Well, what are you waiting for?"

Brian and Cassy scrambled to their feet on cue as the rest of the officers, tired-eyed, remained slouched in their chairs.

"Carter, any word from forensics on Nicola's body?"

DC Carter, a bulky man with a face like a bull-dog, shook his head. "No word. Forensics staff is down to the minimum. Can only do one thing at a time."

"And the CCTV?" Brian asked. "Pennison?"

DC Pennison shrugged and held out his hands. "Council CCTV doesn't cover the crime scene. A complete blind spot, which is *very* handy for a seedy area like Foster Road."

Typical. Forensics was taking its time, and CCTV was a dead end. Two leads down the pan, all thanks to inadequate council budgeting. "Right. We'll go speak to Daniel. The rest of you, make sure the system is up to date, and check in on Scott and the Watsons. We need to make sure that lad doesn't think he's got away with things too easy, in case he does anything silly again. Get on the phone—I want an official statement from the boy, okay? A few of you get back down to Foster Road and expand the house calls. We need every single house in that surrounding area accounted for. Price will split you into groups. Understood?"

Pennison and Carter nodded as Peters contin-ued to key into the laptop. Brian and Cassy walked to the door.

"Oh, McDone?" Price said.

Brian turned back to face him. "Yes?"

"Get a shower. You fucking *stink*."

Chapter Nine.

Danny Stocks wasn't alone.

One of the duty solicitors, Jonny Marsden, moved up to the desk and held out a hand to Cassy and Brian. He was short and plump, with a ring of hair above his ears and a pair of wonky glasses gripping his shiny head. Danny, his hair matted and greasy, stared into the distance. Brian pulled a chair out for Cassy then one for himself before opening up his diary and getting comfortable. He clicked the record button on the tape recorder as Danny scratched at his arms.

"DS McDone and DS Emerson interviewing Mr. Daniel Stocks as an exceptional witness in the Nicola Watson case."

Danny blinked.

"Also present is duty solicitor Jonny Marsden, who is representing Mr. Stocks." Brian nodded and smiled in Marsden's direction, who returned a nod out of politeness. *Fucking sap.*

"Mr. Stocks, firstly, I should make you aware of your rights. You—"

"He's very aware of his rights," Jonny snapped. "He knows very well he doesn't have to be here so soon after his incident. And he knows very well that he can leave whenever he wants."

Brian attempted a smile. These duty solicitors always had to stick their noses in where they weren't wanted, regardless of whether it was in the case's best interests or not. All they cared about was their paycheck. "Thank you, Mr. Marsden. Mr. Stocks, can I call you Daniel?"

He looked at Brian. "Danny." His voice sounded weak.

"Danny. As you're aware, you're being treated as a witness in the Nicola Watson case, hence the need for recording. We have reason to believe you were the last person to see her alive. First of all, and I hope you'll excuse me if I'm blunt, but I don't particularly care. Why the big show yesterday?"

Danny opened his mouth, but Marsden leaned forward and interrupted. "Mr. Stocks would appreciate a bit of sympathy on his behalf. He is still in a fragile state of mind after recent events, and your aggressive line of questioning, especially targeted at a witness, is only going to upset matters." Marsden's raspy, forced-posh voice indicated he was probably from Blackburn, really. Stupid bastard.

Danny, looking between Brian and Cassy, sat back into his seat and closed his mouth.

"Why did you do a runner yesterday, Danny?" Brian asked.

Danny reached for a pen on the table and twirled it with his finger. His grey eyes were vacant, his body rigid underneath his green Converse t-shirt. Dandruff dangled from his thin, greasy hair.

Marsden leaned forward again. "Detective, I would appreciate it if you—"

"It's all right, I can speak for myself." Danny glared at the duty solicitor then turned his attention back to Brian and Cassy. "I needed to get away from all this shit."

Brian took down some notes. "Your grandma didn't see you yesterday morning when you went missing. It all just seems a little too convenient for me. How did you know about any of 'this shit' if you had nothing to do with your girlfriend's death?"

Danny shook his head at Jonny. "I thought this was...? I don't see why that matters."

"It matters if you want to clear your name, because the way I see it, you're not in the best position, son—"

"All right, Scott told me. He called me as soon as he found out she was dead. And the night before, me and Nicola, we... Well, I saw her. Scott just thought I should know, so I ran. My... my girlfriend was dead. Someone told me my girlfriend was dead, so I needed some space. Satisfied?"

Brian shuffled in his chair. Scott Watson hadn't told them anything about contacting Danny Stocks. "Right. You realise how this looks right now though, don't you? You realise you're our main lead. You realise you, the main lead, did a runner when the news came out and tried to kill yourself." He reached into his pocket and slammed the camera down in front of Danny. "You realise that you, the main lead, were one of the very last people to see Nicola Watson before she was killed. So talk."

Danny smiled when he saw the camera. "I knew this is what it'd come to. I knew you'd start throwing accusations at me. Just knew it."

"Care to elaborate, Danny?"

"The camera. I knew I'd have left something that could 'smear' me or put me in the shit one way or another. That's why I deleted the stuff off my hard drive. I was in the middle of putting the pictures on the computer."

Brian took another note. "So what you're trying to say is you deleted the pictures from your hard drive, but not the camera? Sounds to me like you went to a lot of trouble to cover these photos up, Mr. Stocks."

Danny laughed, and Jonny opened his mouth before being interrupted.

"Not enough trouble, though, eh, seeing as we're sat here now?"

"Mr. Stocks has a point," Marsden said, his bald head a plum-red shade now. "If he were so desperate to cover up for something, then why would he leave a camera lying around with potentially incriminating evidence?"

"Maybe he was in too much of a hurry to get away," Cassy suggested.

Danny closed his eyes and held his hands to his face. "And I really looked like I was trying to get away when you saw me, did I?" Tears collected in his eyes. "I didn't want to *live* anymore. I deleted the pictures because I couldn't bear to look at them. I just wanted to be back there with a spliff and to see my days out." Danny's eyes twinkled in Brian's direction. Marsden stared at his hands.

"Mr. Sto—No, Danny," Brian continued. "I appreciate what you're saying, but you've got to see it from our angle and how this looks. You're not in a good position. Where were you after eleven p.m. on 2nd January?"

Danny shook his head. "I... I was hanging out with Scott and Nicky. Smoked some new blend. And then I..." He froze. "Scott left for work. I chatted with Nicky. Not for long. Then I left."

"New blend?"

"Cannabis. There, I said it—I smoke. Don't pretend you didn't already know."

Brian noted down a reminder to mention this 'new blend' to Stephen Molfer. Perhaps it could help him with his little case. Not even on the drug lead and still bailing Molfer out. "What did you talk to Nicola about? Did you leave alone?"

Danny began to fidget in his chair. "Just—just stuff, y'know? Just general stuff. But we had a bit of a disagreement and... and then I left. I don't know where she went after that."

Brian took note as Jonny wiped his steamy glasses. "So what you're telling us is that you and Nicola had a row, and then you left. After that, no one saw her. The following day, you try to kill yourself." Brian threw his pen onto the desk. "You'd better have a good alibi, Danny."

"I do."

Brian smiled sarcastically. "Well, your grandma didn't see you again that night, so you'd better enlighten us."

Danny's cheeks blushed, the first bit of colour Brian had seen in them all interview. "Turn the memory card 'round."

Cassy frowned. "Memory card?"

"The memory card, in the camera. Flip it over, then stick it back in."

Marsden arched his neck over the table towards the camera to see whatever it was. McDone fiddled with the silver camera until the memory card port popped open. Bloody technology. There was a reason he hated it; it hated *him*. He pulled out the tiny memory card and flipped it onto its side, slotting it back into the camera with a satisfying click.

He switched it on again. New photographs. *Bloody hell—double sided memory cards.* Technology just got better and better.

"Those are the pictures I deleted from my computer, all right?" Danny said. "I didn't want her to find them. Then I found out about her."

Brian flicked through the photographs. Some portrayed another girl, blonde and naked, her nipples erect. Others showed Danny holding the camera above him and the girl, legs intertwined, sweat dripping from their bodies.

But the time-stamp proved most interesting about the pictures. All between eleven and twelve. And then they stopped, at twelve.

"This doesn't disprove anything, Danny," Brian said. "You can only account for your little sexual encounter until twelve o'clock, you cheating little toerag. If we call this girl now, she could tell us that you stayed with her all night, could she?"

Danny smirked. "You told me Nicola was killed some time after eleven. You asked me where I was after eleven. That's where I was."

"So you have a little argument with your girl-friend and then you go and cheat on her to prove a point. Do you make a habit of sleeping around, Danny? Are women all just meat to you?"

The door handle rattled. Jonny tried to rest his hand on Danny's tense shoulder, but Danny knocked it away.

"McDone," the voice at the door said. It was Price. Brian zoned back into the room now. Screaming and shouting in the corridor. "If I get my fucking hands on that murderer, I'll fucking kill him, I'll fucking kill him!"

Price lingered by the door. "The girl's parents are here. You'd better bloody tell them what you've found and get them out of my police station before I let them loose on the boy myself."

Jonny whispered something to Danny. Danny's voice was rising, getting more het up and uncomfortable. Cassy stepped up and walked towards the door.

"Something wrong, Danny?" Brian asked.

Danny's eyes were red. His hands shook as if a volcano inside his flesh was waiting to erupt.

Jonny Marsden stood up and eased Danny to his feet. "I think that's enough for one day, don't you, Detective?"

"Danny, if there's something you have to tell us, tell us. Otherwise you're getting thrown to the wolves whether you like it or—"

"I wasn't cheating."

"Right, come on." Jonny tried to link his arm through Danny's and squeeze him out of the other door.

"McDone." Cassy and Price stood by the door, hesitating and mumbling to one another as the shouts of Nicola's mother grew closer to the interview room, definitely beyond the front desk.

"What do you mean, you weren't cheating?" Brian asked.

The duty solicitor pulled the door open and poked his head out to check the coast was clear. Danny followed with his shoulders slouched.

"Danny, tell me what—"

"I wasn't cheating, because she was seeing someone else." He disappeared through the door and out into the safety of the corridor.

Chapter Ten.

Dealing with the newly bereaved never seemed to get any easier.

Shenice Watson threw herself at DI Price as Brian and Cassy walked out of the interview room.

"If he's in there, I'll fucking kill him myself," she shouted. "I'll fucking kill him myself!"

Brian glanced at the door where the duty solicitor and Danny had made their escape. *She was seeing someone else.* Who was she seeing? He needed to know.

He walked over towards Shenice Watson, held back by her husband and a police officer. His face was blank and expressionless as his wife's reddening, manic eyes shot evil glances at everyone in her path. She was like an escaped zoo animal, desperate not to be dragged back to the cage. Apparently, anger was the second stage of grief.

"Mrs. Watson," Brian started. "We need you to just listen—"

"I've done enough listening." She launched herself free of Price's arms and towards Brian. Her husband, half-heartedly holding his wife back, just stared into space.

Brian continued to edge closer to her. "Mrs. Watson, please, we just need to talk to you about a few things." He raised his hand to rest it on her shoulder. She hit it away, continued to scrap at it, but her protestations grew weaker and her eyes welled up with tears. "Please, Mrs. Watson..."

Brian reached for her, and she tumbled into his arms. At first, she tried to break for the door of the interview room, but Brian pulled her head to his chest. "It's okay, it's okay," he said. Trevor Watson stared at Brian, allowing him to comfort her as she whimpered and snivelled into his uniform.

"It's just... my girl, my baby girl..."

Cassy and Price squinted at them, hunched forward in case Shenice made another runner towards the interview room. Other than Shenice's nonsensical whispers, complete silence radiated through the corridor.

"Shenice, it's time we had a sit down again and speak about things, I think?" Brian said. "You go in that room there. Cassy will bring a coffee through for you. And we'll talk. Talk about where we're at, and what we know. That's okay, isn't it?"

Shenice yanked herself from Brian's arms. For a moment, Brian thought she would make a lunge for the interview room door again, but she stumbled back towards her husband, who still hadn't said a word.

"How's that sound? Mr. Watson?"

"Was it him?" he asked. His sharp, cold stare seemed to gaze into Brian's soul.

"It's too early to—"

"We're treating him as a witness," Cassy interrupted. "But we're keeping an eye on him."

Trevor Watson snatched his wife's hand. She reluctantly interlocked fingers with him. "Find him. Find him, and get back to us when you've found him. No more fucking around. Just... just find him."

Holding hands, he and his wife lurched down the corridor, escorted by a short police officer Brian didn't recognise.

"What about that coffee?"

"Just find him," Trevor said, dragging his wife along. "We'll sit down and have a coffee when you find him."

They disappeared through the door.

Brian lowered his head into his hands as Cassy let out a huge sigh.

"Bit of good news and bad news to cut through the misery," Price interrupted. "Bad news is Danny Stocks has an alibi. The blonde piece is named Heather Graham. Confirms that she had a one-night stand with Danny. Good news is one of the lowlifes from 'round the Foster Road area is coming in. Keeping it anonymous. He's due in at one o'clock."

"Get Daniel Stocks back in that interview room as soon as possible," Brian said, and barged past Price.

Price frowned. "I beg your pardon? Did you not just hear what I said? He has an alibi. And more importantly, someone's coming forward with information. Could be exactly what we're looking for."

Brian looked Price directly in the eye. "Daniel Stocks just told me that he and Nicola Watson weren't even together at the time of her death, because she was seeing someone else. If that doesn't scream motive for murder to you, then I don't know what does. Get him back in this room, and lock that half-witted solicitor in a cell for ten minutes if you have to."

Price was initially speechless. "There's technicalities to that. But I'll get him back in here later. You can't just go following your little hunches every time you get one. It's never got you anywhere in the past. Anyway, speak to this bloke we've got coming in. See what he has. If he has nothing, I'll get Stocks back for a chat. I suppose the girl could be covering for him."

Brian bit his tongue. "Time's he due in, again?" He tried not to sound too intrigued.

"About five minutes. One o'clock."

A weight dropped to the bottom of Brian's stomach. One o'clock. *Shit. Shit, shit, shit.*

"You all right, Brian?" Cassy asked.

Brian yanked his phone from his pocket. A text from Vanessa: "Where r u? x" She'd definitely said one o'clock. He had no excuse.

"I... Cassy, you see to the bloke we have coming in." Brian tossed his phone back into his pocket and broke into a jog down the corridor.

Cassy's eyes widened, and Price looked on the verge of exploding. "What d'you mean—?"

"I'll be ten minutes," Brian called. "It's really important. Start speaking to the guy. I'll be back soon, I swear."

He trotted down the office stairs and out into the cold, then headed towards the city centre. He was already out of breath.

At least now he had an excuse to get some proper frigging exercise.

Chapter Eleven.

Vanessa was already leaving Costa when Brian finally stumbled into the town square, out of breath and drenched in sweat. She wore her big wool coat, the one he bought her, and was looking over her shoulder and checking her phone.

"Ness," Brian called, as loud as he could. It came out as a whimper. His heart would probably throw itself out of his chest if he ran any farther. Exercise—who needed it, anyway?

Vanessa did a double take as she saw the sweaty, chubby man pounding down the street towards her. Hooded youths whispered to each other and sniggered. Other people gave him funny looks. Vanessa's cheeks blushed as she glanced down at her feet.

When he reached her, Brian stooped over to catch his breath. He wiped his fingers through his damp hair. "Ness, so sorry I'm late."

Vanessa shuffled around in her handbag, trying not to make eye contact with Brian. "It's okay; I just wanted to... to give you some forms, anyway."

Brian's stomach sank, especially as he'd done all this running. "Can we at least go and sit down? Have a drink?"

Vanessa continued to rustle through her leather bag, her cheeks growing pinker as she peeked up at passers-by. Brian stood beside her in a sweaty white shirt, unbuttoned at the collar, leaning back as if he'd just run a marathon.

"How's Davey? Where is he?"

"At school. He's fine."

Brian scratched the back of his neck. "And you, are you...?"

"I'm fine." She pulled out a brown envelope from her bag and handed it to Brian. He grabbed it with damp palms and stuffed it under his arm.

"I'd better go, anyway," she said. "Obviously now's not a good time." She turned away and signalled an oncoming bus.

"Oh, come on, Ness. Don't be like this. I had work. It completely slipped my mind. Just this case, it's really getting deep, and—"

"And that's why now's not a good time," Vanessa said, staring into Brian's eyes. It was the first time they'd been connected properly for a long while. But he didn't feel that warmth he used to, back when things were good.

"Read through the forms. Get your case sorted. And then get in touch. You look a mess, Brian. I don't want Davey seeing you like this, especially after last time." She diverted her stare to the ground.

Irritation weaseled its way up his trachea. She'd always turn to what happened back in September—the reason he'd taken a few months off sick. Always.

"Come on, Vanessa, for God's sakes. It was an accident. It's just with everything going on... Davey doesn't have to worry about anything, and you know that."

"Your five-year-old son constantly asks me why his daddy doesn't come home anymore," Vanessa snapped. "You have no idea of how much shit I—we—have to put up with."

"Ness, I'm sorry." A lump grew in his throat. "It won't happen again."

"No, it won't, Brian. You need to keep on visiting the doctors, like we agreed. You need to finish your case, and you need to get yourself straight. I'm so sorry if I sound insensitive, Brian, but I can't risk our son going through all that again. I want him to see his daddy like he used to be, not like he saw you in September."

"Ness, I—"

"I'm sorry, Brian," she said, and stepped onto the bus.

Brian stood in the rain and watched as the bus disappeared. He felt completely lost as avid shoppers rushed past and chavs cycled by on their BMXs outside Footlocker and McDonald's.

He walked up the hill towards the library, heading back to the police station. Stuck outside in the rain again, with nobody for company. What an idiot. All he had to do was remember to meet her at lunchtime. That one little thing—that was all he had to remember—and he'd blown it. His phone vibrated in his pocket. He ignored the first three vibrations, then pulled it up to his ear without bothering to check who was calling.

"Hello?"

"The bloke she was seeing was pretty financially well off," the male voice said. Brian's eyes widened, and the spring in his step returned.

"What... Danny? You do realise the sort of shit you're opening up for yourself by making this phone call, don't you? You'd better have a good reason for this."

"Okay, okay. I couldn't speak before with that suit dragging me out of the room."

"I'm sure you couldn't. Got off nice and lightly there, didn't you?"

"I know what it looks like, but I'm trying to help you here."

"How did you get my number?"

"Your card. I picked one up on the way out of the station. Seriously, listen to what I have to say."

Brian sighed and began to rush back to the station. "Right. Who was she seeing? You'd better bloody talk to me, okay?"

"I don't know. But I found out about him that night. Yes, I know how that looks, but I didn't fucking kill Nic, all right? I slept with a girl as a rebound. I didn't kill Nicola. So I'm assuming she went back to his place that night."

The words rang through Brian's skull. He wasn't sure what to think. "Very convenient, Danny. Very convenient. This other guy—tell me what you know about him. How long had she been seeing him? Anything, just anything."

Danny paused before speaking again. "I don't know, and I wish I could tell you, but I noticed she was being a bit weird. Saying she was spending more time on this charity job. I didn't think anything of it, but now I think back, yeah. She was probably seeing someone else all that time."

Brian waddled across the road and stepped under the shelter in front of the Guild Hall. Buses ploughed through the rain, splashing puddles onto the pavements. "So you think—"

"All I know is that she was probably seeing someone else for a while, and he was probably well off."

"What makes you think he had money?"

"He gave her a bracelet. Silver one. I dunno much about jewellery, but it was all right. But she only wore it once. Never told me where it came from. Shrugged it off, and then I didn't see it again. Just... the more you think about things... Yeah." The other end of the line buzzed. "That's all I know, I swear."

The line went dead.

Brian made his way back to the station. The rain washed away the sweat on his body. Something wasn't quite right. He didn't want to believe Danny. His gut told him he was more involved than he'd been letting on to. But the bracelet. And the "seeing someone else". He'd have to have another think about things. He'd have to bring Danny in and have a proper chat with him.

Price and Cassy were already waiting for him at the top of the stairs when he reached the station.

"Nice of you to join us again, fatty." Price folded his arms. "You've got a bit of explaining to do."

"Detective Inspector, I—"

"It's all right, McDone," he said. "Your partner here's done half the work for your lazy ass. Cassy, brief this fucking dodo, would you?" He turned away and bombed back down the corridor towards the main offices. Cassy was shaking.

"What's going on?" Brian asked.

"A charity car." Cassy's shifty eyes met Brian's.

"What do you mean, 'a charity car'?"

"The man who we brought in at one o'clock. I spoke to him. He saw a bloke leaving Foster Road around one a.m. in a black charity car. That's just minutes after Nicola Watson's death." She pulled a magazine from underneath her arm.

"I don't get what you're getting at," Brian said, before seeing the car on the front of the magazine.

"Thank me later." Cassy walked past Brian and into the main office.

Brian stared at the picture of Robert Luther stepping out of a BetterLives branded black car on the front of Preston Life magazine.

Chapter Twelve.

"And that, ladies and gentlemen, is why Preston will rise again!"

The small crowd gathered in Avenham Park cheered. Flashes from the local media's cameras lit up the grey sky. Robert Luther took a bow after talking up his volunteers and all the good they had done for the city, as well as the increased stature of the city as a result of many of BetterLives' schemes. People were working again. A sense of community was returning to Preston. BetterLives were the heroes, Robert Luther their poster boy. He sat down as the mayor grinned and spoke of plans for national expansion and growth.

The police car came to a halt at the top of the hill. Brian and Cassy stepped out of the car without saying a word then walked in the direction of the crowd down the hill.

"And charities like these make it possible. They make us realise that in hard times, we can achieve. We really can have 'better lives'!"

Some kids near the front scoffed and rolled their eyes as the mayor delivered that last line. Brian knew enough about the mayor to know that he was the last person to give a shit about "better lives" or opportunities for people. It just wasn't in his résumé. He must've been rubbing his hands that somebody else was doing all the good work for him. *What a dick.*

A few people glanced over at Brian and Cassy as they shuffled their way through the crowd towards the makeshift podium, but the crowd clearly didn't think anything of it. They just turned back and clapped their hands every time the mayor said the right words.

"Growth!"

Applause.

"Happiness!"

Applause.

A security guard held his arm out as Brian made a break for the podium. "Gonna need to see some form of ID, officers."

Cassy reached into her pocket and negotiated with the security guard as Brian stared up at the podium. The mayor's eye caught Brian's; he stuttered and tried to continue talking. The crowd grew restless.

"So... so as I was saying, I..." The mayor stepped towards the edge of the podium and crouched down. "Detective, is there a problem?"

The bald security guard stepped aside as Cassy grabbed back her warrant.

Here we go...

Brian took a deep breath and climbed onto the podium. He walked towards Robert Luther, who looked around the stage and frowned at all the commotion.

"Robert Luther," Brian said, standing above him. The crowd's chattering came to a sudden silence, but the journalists' cameras did not.

Luther stared from Cassy to Brian. "Detectives? Is there... what's wrong?"

Brian smiled and waved at the security guard. "I think we should take a trip down to the station, just to go over a few things, shouldn't we? Oh, and I suggest you follow us without kicking up a fuss.

Wouldn't want to draw any more attention to you now, would we?"

Luther, struggling to speak, blinked rapidly. After a few moments of hesitation, he walked down the steps with the officers, his head lowered. The crowd wasn't holding back from whispering now. Old women in posh coats and bulgy eyes leaned in to one another to gossip. The cameras kept their focus on Robert Luther as he followed the police officers up the hill towards the police car. The mayor looked on, open-mouthed.

#

The press was already beginning to gather outside the police station as the police car arrived.

"Mr. Luther, what is this about?" one of the journalists asked, bustling his way to the front of the crowd and knocking a notepad to the floor.

Another journalist scrapped with his colleagues and prodded a digital voice recorder towards Robert Luther's mouth. "Is this about the Nicola Watson case?"

Luther didn't say a word.

Brian and Cassy escorted Luther to the interview rooms and shut the door, then turned the blinds down as passing officers peeked in. Cassy stood by the door, watching and waiting. Brian was well aware that what they were doing was not *tech-*

nically by the book, so they'd have to keep their wits about them and act fast.

Brian sat opposite Robert Luther and scrutinized his body language. Subdued. Submissive. Silent.

"Mr. Luther, I hope you'll excuse our little intervention back there..."

"Do you realise what you've just done to me?"

Brian turned to an empty page of his diary and pretended to spot something of significance before looking back at Luther. "I don't believe so, Robert. Elaborate, please."

"That stunt you pulled. You could've destroyed me. All the work we've done. I don't care what you think I've done or why you think I'm here, but you can't just go doing things like that. At least call me, or cooperate with me. I told you I was willing to aid the investigation, so—"

Brian slammed the magazine cutting of the BetterLives car onto the table. "Cooperate with me about this picture, Robert."

"Without legal assistance? Why should I? I have absolutely no reason to be here or to answer any of your questions in these barbaric and downright insulting circumstances."

Brian stared deeply into Robert's blue eyes. Technically, he had no right to be doing this. He had to hurry. He had to get as much out of him as he could whilst Robert was backed into a corner. It was the best way to get anyone, by surprise. Robert Luther had to know something. It was his car, so he had to be involved.

Luther sighed as he scanned the picture. "Well... it's me getting out of a BetterLives car. What more do you want me to say? Do you want me to comment on the substance of the magazine paper? The type of camera the shot was taken with?"

"You can start by telling me how often you drive this car, Mr. Luther."

Robert shook his head. "Why should I? I... Well, every now and then, when we're spreading the good word. But why does it... Is this to do with the case?"

"Which case, Mr. Luther?" Brian asked.

"The... Nicola Watson. Our employee. Has something happened?"

"McDone, you'd better hurry." Cassy, standing by the door, grew more agitated. He ignored her and glared at Robert Luther.

"Your car was seen down by Foster Road on the night of Nicola Watson's murder. Did you head out for a little drive that evening, Robert? Stretch your legs?"

Robert's mouth dangled open. He snapped it shut and licked his lips.

"McDone, seriously—Price does not look happy."

"Shut it, Cassy. Just for one second, shut it." He took a deep breath and turned to Luther. "So did you?"

Robert leaned back and folded his arms. "Detective Sergeant, you've got this all wrong. If you'd done your research, you'd learn that we have five BetterLives branded cars, and I wasn't in any of them that night."

Brian paused. His heart thumped faster as Price's footsteps grew closer. "Five cars? Who drives them?"

"Well, whoever's on the rota that evening. Look, if I can help put you in the direction of someone in our department, or if you're suspecting someone, or... Ah. I see what this is about now. You think it's me? You think I have some... You think I'm involved in this in some way?"

Brian gritted his teeth. "How can I see that rota?"

The door swung open. Cassy lowered her head as Price barged through. His face was redder than Brian had ever seen it, as if he was on the verge of bursting. He walked over to Luther and shook his hand before whispering something in his ear. Then he turned back to Brian.

"A little chat. My office. Now."

Luther straightened his tie as Brian reluctantly followed Price towards his office. He—and the rest of the department, judging by the way they avoided eye contact with him—could tell it wasn't good news.

#

When Price was angry, he wasn't afraid to let people know about it. When he was furious, he'd give people the silent treatment. The tension would build in the air to a point where the guilty party just *had* to say something.

And then the grilling would commence.

Price poured himself a glass of Diet Coke and swished it around his mouth before looking up at Brian.

"Detective Inspector, I—"

"What the fuck do you think you're playing at, Brian?"

Brian stared at the floor, hands behind his back. "I thought you wanted me to investigate the Robert Luther lead?"

Price almost choked on his Diet Coke and reached for a tissue in which to spit. "I said to investigate the fucking *lead*, not go storming into a

charity speech like something off BBC-fucking-
Four. Not to mention gatecrashing a public event
like that without an official arrest warrant. And you
wonder why the police department gets such a
bloody bad rep these days?"

Foolishness settled in his gut. Maybe he had
been a bit hasty.

"Detective Inspector, with the facts we knew at
the time, with regards to the vehicle and—"

"You didn't know jack bloody shit, son!" He almost knocked over his half-empty can. "You saw a
bloody picture of Robert Luther getting out of a
bloody black car in a magazine, and you assume it's
the murder vehicle?"

McDone cleared his throat again. "You said it
was a BetterLives car."

Price slapped a blown-up photograph of a black
car, barely visible in the dim glow of the street
lamp, onto the table.

"That's the only shot we have of a black car on
CCTV, just minutes before Nicola Watson's supposed death. What's that look like to you?"

McDone studied the picture. "The black Better-
Lives car, from the magazine—"

"Wrong—there's no fucking BetterLives logo in
sight, McDone." He shoved the magazine cutting of
the BetterLives car next to the CCTV photo. "The

logo is on the *left*-hand side of this magazine photo. See any logo on this car? Didn't think so. The
smack-head from Foster got it wrong, didn't he?"

McDone slumped back in his chair. All his en-
ergy drained out of his body, Price feasting on it
like a hungry lion.

"You'd better bloody sulk. First you go gallivant-
ing off on a personal call when we're about to chat
to an eyewitness, then you go dragging DS Emerson down and breaking the rules at a bloody major
media event. Do you have any idea what the press
are gonna say about us? They're gonna absolutely
destroy us. Nice job, McDone. Nice job."

He'd just tried to do the right thing. He'd just
tried to get this thing done with, for his family.

"I can only say I'm sorry for my misjudgment,
Detective Inspector, and can assure you it won't
happen again. What would you like me to do next?"
He squeezed his eyes shut and waited for the
words. He'd been kicked off cases before. He knew
what the buildup felt like. Price eyeing him up,
contemplating his fate.

"Go home. Get your feet up. Have a fucking
bath. You're on a thin line, Brian. A very, *very* thin
line. Don't make me get the Chief Superintendent
involved. Then get yourself back in work tomorrow
and back down to Foster Road. And properly inves-

tigating. I mean *properly*. None of this hunch bull-shit, and all of it by the book, you understand? There must be about fifty zillion pimps and prozzie rings down there that you've neglected to investigate so far."

McDone let out a small sigh of relief at remaining on the case. He thought he smelt something. Probably himself. Two beads of sweat dribbled down the side of his chubby neck. His damp shirt clung to his chest.

"Thanks for the second chance, Detective Inspector. I won't let you down again."

"No, you won't," Price said smugly. "Final straw, McDone. No more messing up. Keep your private life well away from this place. I don't want a repeat of last time. I like you, contrary to what you might think. Don't fuck that up."

McDone nodded. A smile crept across his face as he left the office. Price actually *liked* people?

Outside of the room, Robert Luther put on his coat and chatted with Michael Walters, the short, balding assistant Brian met when he'd visited BetterLives. Walters did a double take at McDone then walked towards him.

Here we go. He didn't need to deal with another dickhead today.

"DS McDone." Walters held out his hand as he balanced his jacket over his arm. "Michael Walters. We met the other day—"

"Yeah, I remember." McDone grabbed Walters' hand and shook it. It flopped like a limp, lifeless fish.

"I expect a full and frank apology from the police in tomorrow's papers for their smear campaign towards Robert Luther and BetterLives. We want to help with the investigation. Don't abuse that trust."

"Just doing my job." McDone held his smile and waited for Walters to speak again.

Walters pulled his hand away and turned back towards his boss. He sauntered back down the corridor. "Good luck with the investigation, Officer. We've got a media storm to tame."

Walters patted Luther on his back and led him out into the roars of the press. At least the press had something to talk about for the day.

"Shall we grab a drink?"

Cassy stood behind him. She buttoned up her red checkered jacket and slipped her bag over her shoulder.

McDone smiled. "A date with a lovely lady like yourself? Who am I to refuse?"

Chapter Thirteen.

The beer's stale, dull taste kissed Brian's lips. God, he hated beer.

"I've not been in here for ages," Cassy said, edging forward on her barstool.

"I've not been in a pub for ages," Brian said, taking a swig of beer. The pub was pretty empty for late afternoon. The chubby, baldheaded bartender was already wiping down the surfaces, as if he wasn't expecting much business. A couple of scraggy looking locals whispered to one another in the corner of the room, half-pints in hand. "If you want to see the recession, go to the pub," DC Kelly had told him. He wasn't sure what he meant at the time, but now he thought he understood.

Cassy frowned. "You aren't trying to tell me you're not a drinker anymore, are you, Brian?"

Brian looked down at his shaking hand. *Play it cool.* "I'm just a drinker of finer spirits these days. The kind I can enjoy in better company." He poked a thumb into his chest theatrically.

Cassy fixed her gaze on Brian. He moved in his seat, trying not to make eye contact with her. Was she still looking? Why did people do that?

"What's going on with you, man?"

It felt strange, hearing those words. It had been a long time since anyone had tried to do anything other than brush his problems under the carpet. Did she know? Did she suspect something? He scratched at his arm automatically.

"Just this case. We've been rushing 'round for what—two days? Already it's doing my nut in. Feel like we've got absolutely nowhere." He took a larger gulp of his pint and focused on the door. His cheeks tingled.

"No, I'm not talking about the job." Cassy smiled as she dangled her pint below her mouth. "At home. What's going on?"

Brian shrugged. "Nothing. Nothing's going on."

"Brian. You were off sick from September to December. You turn up smelling of booze every single day. What's going on?"

Brian almost took another sip of his pint, but sighed and placed the glass down. At least the booze smell trick was working. "Just Vanessa. My wife. Well, ex. I'm trying to, y'know, do the right thing for her and my boy."

"And what do you think is the right thing for her and your boy?"

His hands weren't shaking anymore, just lightly tingling. Brian folded his arms and looked away again. He was like an oyster, closing off from the world. It wasn't often he got asked about these things. "I just want to get the divorce sorted and to prove to her that I'm fit to see my boy again. I just miss him."

Cassy took a small sip of her drink and diverted her gaze towards the bar. "Y'know I have a son?"

"I didn't know that, no."

Cassy cleared her throat. She avoided eye contact with Brian. "I was silly, really. Got pregnant when I was seventeen. Gave him up for adoption. Really wanted to keep him, but my dad wanted me to go to university and all that, and the kid's dad wasn't around to support us. It's weird. It's been well over ten years now. Sometimes I think I see him. I dunno."

Brian tried to catch Cassy's wandering gaze. Her eyes started to well up. At least the conversation had moved from him to her.

"Just work on building bridges with your wife, Brian. It'll take time, but don't give up. You have a son, after all, and I know you don't like talking about what happened, but if you ever want to talk..."

Brian closed his eyes. "I'm not fit to be a dad. My head, it's... It belongs in the police. I've done some bad things, and I don't expect her or him to forgive me. But what happened, I've gotta live with that."

Cassy bit her lip and averted her eyes. He knew she was preparing to ask him the question.

"What *did* happen, Brian?"

Brian smiled and stood up, stuffing his coat under his tender arm. "Maybe another time, okay? I should... We should get an early night. We'll have forensics calling for us to see the body any day now, and we've got to properly investigate the surrounding area of the crime scene. Don't want to go missing any vital pieces of—"

"Brian." Cassy shot to her feet. "If you ever want any company, you can always, y'know, sleep on the sofa. It's not great—in fact, it's pretty shit—but yeah. Just a thought." Her cheeks were turning pink.

"Thanks, Cassy. I appreciate that, but I'll be okay. Now come on—there's a cab outside with your name on it."

Brian's breath frosted as he waved Cassy off. The taxi disappeared down the road in an unhealthy cough of engine fumes. He blew warm air against his fingers and walked into the 24-hour shop a few doors down.

"Mr. McDone," the Asian man behind the counter said. "The usual?" He reached for a bottle of Bell's whisky.

"Make it two," Brian said, and slid a Gillette razor blade over the counter.

#

The routine was growing all the more familiar: throbbing head, scent of booze, aching arm. The vultures from the press already gathered around the door of the police station made it worse, all wrapped up in wool coats and scarves, not a bit of skin on show. Some held cameras and some held microphones with their thick mittens. *Soft bastards.*

"Officer, do you have anything to say on the Nicola Watson case?" one of them asked, pointing a microphone towards Brian's face. He knocked it aside and kept walking.

"Officer, is it true that the police made a massive error of judgement with regards to BetterLives?"

The questions buzzed and buzzed in Brian's already tender ears. He held his frown, acting as if he hadn't noticed the press, and hopped up the steps at the entrance, where they followed him like flies on shit.

"DS McDone, is it true that you were responsible for using wrongful methods to arrest not one, but two, suspects? What do you have to say about the decline in policing standards in Preston? Is it because of the cuts?"

That particular journalist's whiney voice stuck with him. Short. Wearing glasses and a green coat. Somewhat different from the others. Unshaven, student type. He rolled his eyes downwards as McDone looked at him. He thought he recognised him from somewhere.

Then it clicked. David Wallson, the guy who'd written the first piece on Nicola Watson. The guy who'd broken the news of a dead girl before the police had the chance to. "Wrongful methods". How would he know? Who was providing him with his information? Brian gritted his teeth together and resisted lashing out.

"DS McDone, is it about time you stepped down for good? Got back to fighting for that wife and kid of yours?"

Brian stopped. His heart started thumping. He approached David Wallson and stared right into his eyes. "Would you like to repeat that question?"

David Wallson turned to his notepad and cleared his throat, his cheeks flushing. "It's just... I heard a report that you're distracted at work. I heard that..."

Brian clenched his fist. But no—he couldn't allow himself to react. He couldn't get the department into any more trouble. He took a breath to calm himself. "I don't comment on speculation or personal matters. As long as you are all aware that we are trying our very, very best to apprehend the culprit of this awful crime, and we are getting closer. Thank you, that'll be all."

He stepped through the door, the weight of having spoken to the media lifting from his shoulders. Since his time off, relations with the press had been strained. Price always liked to be the face of the investigations and kindly asked Brian not to get involved after rumours surrounding his lengthy absence emerged. He always used to deliver press conferences, but now he was just another face in the crowd. A fat face, at that.

In all honesty, he preferred it that way. Media types were the lowest of the low.

As Brian stumbled into the office, Cassy already stood by his desk. "Survive the vultures?"

"Just about." Brian tossed his lunch bag onto his desk and cleared his beer-throat of phlegm.

"Don't tell me you have a hangover after just the one pint," Cassy said, her eyebrows raised. He sensed the sarcasm in her voice. Sensed what she was implying.

"Getting less tolerant nowadays. Didn't sleep great."

"Such a lightweight these days," DC Pennison shouted, a smirk on his face.

"Yeah, I thought I saw you getting dizzy off half a pint of Coke the other day, didn't I, Pennison?" Brian said.

Pennison laughed and shook his head. It might have been banter, but banter only really happened with friends, and Brian certainly didn't class many of the good-for-nothings working at this place as friends.

The door opened, and Price walked in with a spring in his step. He clapped his hands together. "Right, morning. DS McDone and Emerson, good news for you. The mad doctor is waiting for you. Finally found a free moment in his hectic schedule to investigate the body of, y'know, only the highest profile murder case in this city for years."

Brian stepped to his feet, gesturing Cassy to follow him. "We'll be right down there, Inspector. Constable Carter, any further information from Foster Road?"

Carter shrugged his heavy shoulders, looking as lifeless as ever. "Nothing in particular. We've spoken to a bunch of known pimps, but we can't get anything helpful out of them. And every place 'round there is either empty for escorts or has an alibi. There are two places locked up that we haven't had the chance to go to yet."

"Right. We'll get down there later. I guess the priority is not to run before we can walk. We need to be steady about this so we don't overlook anything."

Price scoffed. "Wise words. If only you'd taken that approach towards your little show on the park yesterday. Do you have any idea how much trouble that's got us in?"

Brian sighed. "I apologise. DS Emerson, let's go to forensics. Everyone else, get digging around Nicola's social media profiles. Any friends, family, or anyone she spent a lot of time with. It's all we have to go on right now. Then we'll head back down to

Foster Road and try to contact those two no-shows."

Everyone remained still.

"Well, you heard the man," Price said.

The officers jumped from their seats and turned towards their computer screens. A chorus of clicking keyboards erupted.

Price handed Cassy and Brian a clear protective jacket each, then winked at Brian before walking away.

"Did you see that?" Cassy slipped her protective jacket over her shoulders.

Brian tried not to face her. "No, I..."

"You did see that. Price *winked* at you. What went on in his office yesterday, huh? I thought you looked a little... red-faced, but I didn't want to say anything."

He ignored Cassy and attempted to button up his protective jacket. Some of the officers giggled at him as his flabby belly poked between the plastic buttons. He saw Cassy cover her mouth too, trying her best not to laugh.

"This your first?" Brian asked her.

Cassy nodded. "Learn something new every day, eh?"

"Prepare to see the human body in a whole new way," Brian said as the pair took a left and headed towards the forensics department.

#

It never got any easier, seeing a dead body on the slab.

It was something Brian tried to believe you could grow a tolerance to over time, but that was just a lie to make it easier for the newbies. That feeling inside that one day, everyone was going to be nothing but a lump of meat filled with broken mechanics lying on a table. Terrifying.

"DS McDone. DS Emerson."

"Jeeves," Brian replied, holding out a hand and pulling it away before he got the chance to shake it. "Just a joke Jeeves and I have. Not wanting to touch his... Yeah, you get it."

Jeeves, the forensic specialist, was a short man with greying hair and a big nose. He wore glasses and a constant frown, like a schoolteacher. His posh voice was as fake as they came. Brian was convinced Jeeves couldn't possibly be his real name. He'd clearly watched too many crappy detective TV shows and tried to model himself on the creepy pathologists.

He pulled back the cover from Nicola's body, like a magician revealing his latest contraption. It was weird, how different a body looked when it was on that slab, compared to how it looked at a crime scene. At the scene, there was a sense of detachment, like a re-enactment of a historical event in a waxwork museum or a still from a movie. But right here, nobody could deny the reality of it. This was death, and it was coming for everyone.

Cassy flinched as she looked at Nicola's eyes. Thick, purple, bloodshot streams ran from her greying pupils.

"As you know," Jeeves began in his little presentation voice. "Nicola Watson. Aged twenty-two. Cause of death: strangulation." He pointed towards the thick red and purple marks coiled around her neck.

"Any word on the precise time of death?"

Jeeves sighed. "As was predicted, between 12 a.m. and 1 a.m. on 3rd January."

Brian circled the body. Nicola's feet were close together, the finely cut toenails just about creeping over the sides of the slab.

"Any semen traces?"

Jeeves licked his lips. "Nothing out of the ordinary. Nothing to suggest any forced intercourse. There are a few samples that we'll have checked out. But the way it looks to me, either it wasn't sexually motivated, or he cleaned her up very, very well, which is rare but not impossible."

Brian scratched his forehead. "Anything we don't already know?"

"Ah," Jeeves said with a little smile. He enjoyed doing this, probably a bit too much. He always started with the normal things, then followed with an "ah" moment. It was like an absurd cat and mouse game of who could solve the mystery first. "Look at her hand."

Brian and Cassy crouched down to look at Nicola's fingers. "Looks like she formed a fist," Brian said. "Probably the terror. Like when people grit their teeth. A subconscious reaction, right? She knew she was gonna die. Had time to think about it."

"Ah," Jeeves said again. *Fuck.* Another bloody "ah" moment, which meant Brian was wrong. "That's what *I* thought. But open the fingers up a little... Actually, I will do that." He squeezed the fingertips from the hand, their grip as solid as rock. "See it?" Jeeves tapped the fingernails with the end of a pointer.

"What is it?" Cassy asked.

"This, my friends, is paper."

Brian squinted and finally saw little specks of white under her fingernails. "Why would she...?"

"Because she didn't want somebody to see something," Cassy interrupted.

Jeeves shrugged, a suggestive, "That's for you to find out" look on his face. "Perhaps. But whatever it was, she was holding it very tightly."

Brian's arm throbbed with pain, and he felt a slight lightness in his head. He really had drunk a little too much last night. Maybe all this fake alcoholism would turn him into a legitimate alcoholic at some stage. What a twisted turn of events that would be. "So all we have is a black car, which may or may not have been a BetterLives car, an ex-boyfriend who she breaks up with for someone else, and a bit of paper between her fingertips. Jeeves, I'm sorry, but I've no idea what to make of it."

Jeeves tilted his head again. "Ah," he said. "*Ah*" *number three.* "Look closer at the paper. What do you see?"

Brian squinted at the little pieces of paper. What the hell was Jeeves getting at? "It's, erm, just a bit black, and—"

"It was wet," Cassy interrupted.

Brian frowned. "Wet? But what does that mean?"

Jeeves edged around the slab towards Brian and Cassy. "I took a closer look at her underwear." A creepy, elongated smiled worked its way across Jeeves' face. *Weird bastard.* He certainly didn't strike Brian as the sort of man to be trusted with a load of underwear. "Look at this picture. See that?"

Brian narrowed his eyes. It was a close-up of several circular molecules that looked like tiny islands, as green as fresh peas from a pod. He'd seen a picture like it somewhere before, but he couldn't quite make it out. "Some sort of molecules?"

"Unless I'm very much mistaken, which I doubt, these are cyanobacteria."

Brian had no idea what Jeeves was talking about.

Jeeves turned back to the picture and tapped it with his middle finger. "Cyanobacteria, you might know better as blue-green algae. These molecules are very easy to wipe from the skin but stick to clothes like flies to faeces."

Cassy scratched her head and looked away from Nicola's cold, pale body on the slab. "What does blue-green algae have to do with anything?"

Jeeves smiled. "Unless Miss Watson decided to go for a fully clothed paddle on a cold January evening, I'd say someone tried to drown her."

Brian shook his head. "But... if they tried to drown her, then why didn't they just finish her off there? Leave her wherever they drowned her?"

Jeeves smiled again. "I think the question is, why did your culprit take her to a well-known prostitution hotspot to dry her body off before they killed her?"

Chapter Fourteen.

Brian and Cassy sat in the police car. Cassy slurped the last remnants of a thick McDonald's milkshake, the straw scraping the bottom of the carton. Fifteen minutes had passed since their trip to forensics. Neither of them had spoken much since seeing Nicola Watson's body again, draped across that slab.

"What d'you make of it?" Cassy dangled the straw between her teeth and blew bubbles of milkshake out of the other end.

Brian flicked his heater up towards his windscreen, waiting for the frozen condensation to recede, and rubbed his purple hands together. His breath clouded.

"I mean, she's been found in a prostitution den. Price wants us to pursue that lead. Do you think maybe she's been picked up? Got herself embroiled in something nasty? I dunno."

Brian wiped his sleeve against the car window, making a hole in the condensation so he could see where he was going.

"But then, the paper in her hands. And then the water. Something doesn't fit."

"We go back to Foster Road, and we ask around. Chances are she's got involved with some bad people, and she's not the good girl her parents and her work colleagues make her out to be."

Cassy frowned as Brian revved up the engine which spluttered out exhaust fumes. "You don't really just think that. What's getting to you?"

Brian tried to kick start the engine again.

"Come on, man." She tossed her empty carton to one side. "You don't have to be dicky with me. I'm your mate, for God's sake."

Brian finally got the engine going. "I don't know. That's the thing. I just... I usually get my head 'round shit like this. But I just don't know. My gut tells me that Danny Stocks knows more than he's letting on to. And then there's BetterLives, who seem all happy to help when we aren't accusing one of theirs. And then there's her family... I don't think they're being totally honest with us. Something's just not adding up."

He put his foot on the accelerator, and they headed towards Foster Road. "I have a feeling they aren't being completely honest down at Foster, too. And whatever did happen, we can't take anything away from the fact that she was killed there. That's where it happened."

"What if it didn't?"

Brian let the thought play out in his head. The water. The paper.

"We find out." He took a left turn onto Foster Road as a group of hooded kids cycled past, flicking two fingers at them when they thought they were out of sight.

#

They got out of the car and walked down Absom Road, which ran parallel to Foster Road. It wasn't quite as much of a shithole, but it still reeked of sewage and sweet, sweat-tarnished perfume. It was a poor excuse of a road, and no decent sized cars could fit down there. But as long as hookers could take their clients somewhere out of sight, it served its seedy purpose.

Brian and Cassy walked up to the first redbrick building on the right. Brian stopped at the door.

"I'll start at this one. You work your way down. We'll try to speak to everyone. It doesn't matter if they've already been spoken to—we speak again."

Brian knocked on the first door as Cassy knocked on the doors on the opposite side.

A little thin-haired man, his balding head peeling like a mistreated potato, came to the door of the first house. He was holding a cat, and his white vest was browning at the armpits.

"I don't see nothing," he said. "Now't bad to see 'round 'ere, officer. The young'uns, they 'ave their stuff to do, but we were all kids, ain't we?"

Brian held up the picture of Nicola. The man squinted at it.

"Have you ever seen this girl around here before?"

"Well, I see a lot of girls coming in an' out of this place. But she don't look like the type." He frowned and drew out his last words. He was like a scruffy version of Wallace from *Wallace & Gromit*.

Brian sighed. "Thanks, sir. If anything does come to you, you'll give me a call, won't you?" He handed his card to him.

The man waved Brian off. Another dead end. Cassy was at the bottom of Absom Road, engaged in conversation. They would never get anywhere like this. People didn't talk. Probably all had some silence pact or something. That's if they knew anything at all.

Something caught Brian's eye in the distance. A person stepped out of their front door. He was wearing a blue jacket, a cap covering his eyes. Brian walked towards him, even though the man was beyond Cassy.

The man turned around and looked at Brian. Brian raised a hand, but the man pretended he hadn't seen him. He shuffled down the alleyway and took bow-legged strides away from the officers.

"Sir, can you wait up a second?" Brian called. The clouds of breath above the man increased in number as he continued walking. Cassy turned to Brian to see what he was doing and then spotted the man ahead of her.

"Sir, this is the police, can you..."

The man ran.

"Shit. Cassy, get the car and bring it 'round here right now. I'll get him."

Cassy frolicked around, caught in the moment. She took a quick look at Brian's bouncing waist. "But you—"

"Just go!" Brian said as he sprinted past her and towards the man, who climbed the stairs at the side of the buildings and kept on running.

Brian had always intended to start exercising as a New Year's resolution, but not exactly in this manner. He launched himself up the stairs and past the doors of houses, some derelict, some as good as new. The frosting breath of the man in the distance grew larger as he turned a corner.

The man wasn't slowing down for anybody. He darted down the metal grating and froze at the end before disappearing right around the corner. *Shit.* Out of sight. Brian would have to be careful. All sorts of bad things happened to police officers when the suspects weren't in vision.

Brian slowed down before the turn and poked his head around, half-expecting something to smack him in his face.

The man stood at the very end of the walkway, elevated fifteen or so feet above the ground. His cap had fallen off. Brian could see his face now, panicked and wide-eyed. He faced Brian and took a pained glance at the ground below him. *Shit.* Not a jumper...

"Sir, step away from the edge of the walkway, slowly." Brian had seen people jump from this height before. He wasn't high enough. As a rule of thumb, suicide jumpers needed to jump from at least three times their actual height to kill themselves, and even then, only fifty percent died. This was just shy. Once, a few years back, a woman had jumped from this height. Instead of killing herself, her thighbones crunched into her pelvis, which pierced through her flesh and mashed her colon. She lost her legs, and the damage to her digestive system meant that she defecated into a bag to this day.

The man's eyes were huge and animalistic. He was panting now. "Just—just leave me, okay? Just let me go, and... Just leave me the fuck alone." Something small dropped from his hand, tumbling from the elevated platform and to the ground below.

"Sir," Brian said. Cassy's car approached from the other side of the road, behind the man. "Sir, we just want to ask you a few questions about Nicola Watson. The girl who was killed. You know how it looks—if you jump, you'll never get away with it, whether you like it or—"

"I don't care how it looks," the man shouted. His entire body shook. He moved one foot backwards and dangled it over the edge teasingly.

Flashbacks of the staircase.

Brian took a step towards him as Cassy crept out of the car. The man's eyes widened as Brian treaded closer.

"This doesn't have to end in tears, mate," Brian said. "We just want to talk. A few questions, that's all. So get away from that edge, and we can talk."

Cassy moved stealthily up the road below them. She grabbed the item that the man had dropped. Brian had to keep the man talking. Just a few more seconds...

"Just a stupid mistake... a stupid mistake." The man dragged his foot back onto the metal grating and moved shakily towards Brian.

"Come on," Brian said. "We can talk about that mistake. Come on, that's it. Another step. Another step."

The man looked up at Brian and shook his head. "You've no idea. No idea." He laughed before stepping backwards and closing his eyes.

If Cassy had arrived at the top of the ladder a moment later, she'd have fallen to the ground to whatever fate awaited her pelvis and colon below. Instead, she caught the man's back and pushed him forward. Flailing his arms, he went flying face-first into the grated flooring.

Cassy charged towards the man and sat on his back and dangled the small item he'd dropped over

his face. Brian rushed over to help pin him down.
The man cried out with pain.

"Sir, we're taking you into custody for the possession of a suspected illegal substance," Cassy
said.

Brian let out a snigger of disbelief when he
faced Cassy. They had no right to arrest him for
fleeing a scene. But drugs... Cassy was good. Really
good. "You... You'd better be more careful in the
future."

"Thanks for the concern. Now let's get this bastard down to the station."

The man didn't put up any sort of fight. He just
smiled as they pushed him down the stairs and towards the car.

"Price," Brian radioed in. "I think we're on to
something."

Chapter Fifteen.

The man didn't say a word on the journey to the station. He just kept looking down at his hands and scratching at them. A constant smug smile clung to his face. Something was distinctly unlikeable about him. Maybe it was just the '70s-style moustache.

Maybe it was what they had in common. The willingness to jump.

They pulled him down the corridor and towards the interview rooms. Heads turned. Whispers started. But the man just smiled through it. Defeat in his eyes—the chase over. No jumping off buildings today.

They had to question him about the drugs. The possession of drugs was their excuse for bringing him in here. Then, they could take the interview in a more extra-curricular direction.

Brian placed him in a chair and sat opposite, flicking the recorder on. "I don't know whether you're familiar with this procedure, but you have a right to inform someone of your arrest, a right to legal advice, and a right to look at the police codes."

The man smirked. He wiped his mouth with the sleeves of his blue jacket.

Brian plonked the small bag of weed against the table. "Well?"

"What's the point in arguing any of it?" the man grunted. "You've made your minds up about me. You can throw me to the wolves. They always do."

Price appeared at the door and tapped his watch. He didn't have long to talk to him. Not this time. The man was entitled to a duty solicitor, so he'd get one. That's just how it worked.

Cassy slipped the printed sheets that Price had given her over to Brian. The man sat back and folded his arms.

"Adrian Priles," Brian said. "Forty-six years of age. Cinema attendant down at the docks. Suspiciously away from your flat the two previous times we paid visits. But strangely... that's all we have on you, and *that* we pulled from your driving license and ID card scans. Tell me, Adrian, if you're so squeaky clean, how long have you been lurking around brothels with drugs?"

"It's not what it looked like, okay?"

"Well, I'll tell you what it looks like, Adrian. We turned up. We were just about to ask some nice, friendly questions. You do a runner. You pull yourself to the top of a staircase, and you get yourself all ready to jump. And this is just days after a murdered girl is found on the street parallel. So apologies if, in your opinion, it's 'not what it looked like', but it is exactly what it looked like. Start talking."

"You think I was something to do with *that*?" Adrian slammed his palms against the table. "I just wanted a toke. It's not what it looks like."

"New blend, by any chance?"

Adrian shrugged. His nostrils twitched. "Perhaps."

"I have a colleague looking into this supposed new blend. I'm sure he'd love to hear what you have to say."

Adrian shook his head. "Unless?"

"Well, you could talk to us about what you were doing at the brothel in the first place if you really did just want a 'toke'. How about that?"

Adrian twiddled with his finger before reaching into his pocket. "Don't bullshit me. I know I'm not here because of the drugs. I know how you people work. Let me show you something." He pulled a ring out of his pocket and slipped it on his finger. "This is my wedding ring. I have a wife at home. She's expecting a second kid. I tell her I go out with Dave and Andy a few nights a week. Dumb bitch still thinks Dave and Andy exist."

"Unfaithful git." Cassy shook her head.

"So while your wife's however-many-months pregnant, you're going out there getting your kicks from someone else? Is that what you're trying to tell us? Is that your defence?"

Adrian smiled, revealing his coffee-stained yellow teeth. He toyed with his ring some more. "Like I said, it's not what it looks like."

"Where were you on the night of Nicola Watson's murder?" Brian asked. "Were you 'out with Dave and Andy' then?"

Adrian's left eyelid twitched. He inhaled sharply. "I'd like to see that solicitor now, please."

Shit. He knew his rights. He knew he had every right to sit around and wait for his solicitor. They had him. They had to press him. "He's on his way. If you'd just—"

"Adrian," Cassy cut in. "You could save yourself a lot of trouble if there's something you want to tell us. If there's something you're hiding and you're not telling us, we need to know."

"And why should I tell you when I'm entitled to legal advice?"

Cassy rubbed the side of her neck. "You don't have to. But if you want to save your ass, you might as well start saving it now."

Adrian opened his mouth then closed it again. He straightened his back and laid his hands out on the table. "I'm a pimp," he said. "I'm a pimp, okay? My wife doesn't know. I don't sleep with the girls. I wouldn't look at another woman. I just... I just couldn't let my wife and family find out. That's what I thought this was about. That's why I ran."

Brian's eyes widened. He leaned over to Cassy and whispered, "How didn't we know about him?"

Adrian stared back at them and rubbed his tongue against his teeth. No previous charges against him and he wasn't on the "Red List"—a comprehensive list of known pimps both in and around the North West area. On his papers, no indication of what he was doing.

"Bit convenient, isn't it? This whole family sob story?"

"Like I said, I know how it looked, but I guess I just got scared. I dunno. I've not lived here for long. It's just the money... since the cuts. We had to earn somehow. My children and my wife... I had no choice. I needed to keep it on the low, y'know?"

"Where did you live beforehand?"

"Edinburgh. Only been here a few months."

Edinburgh. That's why there was no trace of any potential previous wrongdoings—he'd be in the Scottish system. Brian took a note to remember to contact the Scottish Police. He reached into his pocket for the pictures of Nicola Watson and spread them out in front of Adrian. One of her as a child, on a swing. Another from a school party, smiling with her beautiful big eyes. And another, purple veins protruding inside her dying eyes. Her neck, painted with bruises like a piece of Expressionist art.

Adrian groaned and looked away as Brian pushed the images in front of him. "You're like one of these charities. Showing us all the sob stories in Africa to try and get some sort of emotion..."

"Did you ever see Nicola Watson around Foster Road?"

Adrian shook his head. "She's not one of my girls. I'd know her if she was. And I haven't seen her before."

"Which makes things all incredibly convenient once again, doesn't it, Mr. Priles?"

Adrian plucked at his trousers. "Can I see that solicitor now?"

"Tell me about your clients," Brian interrupted. "Any strike you as the murdering type?"

"No," Adrian said, loudly. "I work with better, respectable men. Men that treat women well; men that just want a break, you know?" He looked at Cassy as he spoke.

"No, I don't," she said in a monotone. "But carry on, anyway."

"Well, yeah... My clients, they aren't the sort of men that would want their families to know. So I try to keep things discreet. Keep things respectable. They're... I guess they're a bit like me, really." He shuffled in his seat, his gaze twitching around the room.

The heat of the room was beginning to get to him. Price still hovered around the door, red-faced, a ticking time bomb.

Brian placed the picture of the black car in front of Adrian. Adrian shifted his gaze away from it and stroked his hairy forearms.

"Right now, this is all we have. A black car that left the scene of the crime around the same time as Nicola Watson's death. If you've seen this car before, you can help us. Otherwise, I don't know what to make of you. You've still not told us where *you* were when the crime occurred."

A bead of sweat dripped from Adrian's moustache. "Can I see that solicitor now?"

Brian tossed the photograph of the car in his face. "They're on their way. Adrian, have you seen this fucking car or not?"

Price shook hands with somebody outside. *Shit.* Time was almost up. He had to get it from him. He was so close. Price walked towards the door.

"Adrian, have you—"

"Yes," Adrian exploded, his eyes bulging out of his skull. "Yes, I... It's my client's. It's my client's. Just, my wife. Please—my wife. Don't tell her about this. I'm begging you."

Price leaned in through the door. "McDone, an urgent word, please." His face was purple, his voice more subdued than usual.

"One sec," Brian said, waving a finger in Price's direction and turning back to Adrian. "A name, Mr. Priles?"

Adrian was whimpering. He rubbed his hands up and down his arms and looked around the room at everything that wasn't Brian's eyes. "We don't go by real names. It's anonymous. It protects them."

"McDone," Price repeated.

Brian pretended he hadn't heard Price's voice and moved closer to Adrian. He could feel his defences falling. They were so close.

"A description? What was he like? How often did you—"

"McDone, get the hell out of that chair and get over here right now," Price said. "This man is entitled to legal advice. That's an order."

Adrian's jaw snapped shut again.

Brian lowered his head into his hands and sighed. Adrenaline raced through his skull. He turned to Cassy, subdued, and raised his eyebrows sarcastically. "You'd think they didn't want us to fucking solve this thing, wouldn't you?"

Brian threw his chair to the other side of the room. Adrian folded his arms and sat upright for the first time. Price's face was the colour of a dark grape now, and his lips quivered.

"You stay in here with him for now," Brian said to Cassy. "I'll be back in a sec. Say hello to his solicitor for me." He followed Price out of the door.

He'd been so close—so close to getting more out of Adrian. "Why did you have to do that, Price? I don't get it. We were so close, and—"

Price squared up to Brian. "If you'll shut your noisy trap up for two seconds, I'll tell you. Now follow me, and zip it."

Brian nodded reluctantly and walked with Price towards the computers in the main office. Colleagues stared at him. Whispered about him. Price stopped at the third computer and pointed his finger at the screen. DC Peters sat beside it. He fumbled around the keyboard and hit the space bar as Brian slumped forward against the desk.

"I just don't get what could be more important than—"

"Just watch," DC Peters said.

The date was marked in the bottom right corner of a video. 27/12/12. 1:34 a.m. A week before the murder. Brian sighed. Probably just another loose lead.

"Wait, I thought you said there was no CCTV coverage for this..."

He spotted a figure in the bottom of the screen with his hands in his pockets, scuffling around. A recognisable blue cap on his head. *Adrian.*

He picked himself up from the desk and shook his head at Price. "No, we know he's just a pimp now. I got that from him. So if you'll let me—"

When he turned his eyes back to the screen, he saw the black car, arriving in the distance. Adrian looked up at it.

"That's... that's the—"

"The car," DC Peters finished. "But what's more interesting is who gets out of it."

Brian's knees weakened when the man shut the door and walked towards Adrian. He looked over his shoulder and scratched the side of his head before shaking Adrian's hand and giving him something. Then he looked over his shoulder again and walked towards the door on the left.

Brian was still. A fuzziness floated around his stomach. Price chewed at his chapped lip.

"Where did you...?"

"It just so happens that Foster Road isn't the CCTV blind spot we thought it was after all. Have a look at this." Price placed an A4 print in Brian's hands. Brian's eyes widened.

"BetterLives shares an office building with the CCTV control for West Preston. It's a private firm called CityWatch—basically, the council outsourcing so they can sit on their arses and get paid for doing nothing. And this photographic evidence also shows our friend from the Foster Road footage entering the CityWatch offices the morning after Nicola Watson's murder."

Brian stared back at the screen as DC Peters rewound the footage. The handshake. The look over the shoulder. The walk towards the door.

"I think it's about time you paid another little visit to BetterLives, don't you?"

Chapter Sixteen.

Brian pulled up outside BetterLives. The office building overlooked the murky water of the docklands. Clouds had formed over Preston; clouds always formed over bloody Preston. It was like *living* in a cloud sometimes, but it gave the community something new to moan about, to take their frustrations out on.

Brian looked over at the empty seat beside him. Cassy's finished McDonald's milkshake carton rested on its side, a speck of strawberry dribble staining the fabric below. He smiled and turned to face BetterLives offices. He had to play it cooler this

time, Price had told him. "No more major fuck
ups." The last thing they wanted was the media
getting on their backs again. The *Lancashire News*
had just about got over the fact that they'd arrested
Robert Luther last time. They couldn't give them
another excuse to start sniffing around.

Preston didn't need it.

He zipped up his jacket and stepped out into the
rain. He walked towards the fancy office blocks,
back into the unknown.

A smiling woman sat behind the desk in reception area, a white shirt buttoned up to her neck and
blonde hair dangling onto her shoulders. Brian
tried to force a grin back at her, but remembered
the sight of his coffee-stained teeth in the mirror
every morning. Age—what a bastard.

"Are you here to speak to BetterLives again, Officer?"

Brian nodded.

"It's not serious, is it?"

Brian saw the woman's false smile beginning to
droop. She was employed to smile nicely. Make
people feel good about themselves. Legal prostitution, with stricter limits. She didn't need the police
causing any potential job jeopardy for herself or
her colleagues. This affected everybody.

Brian smiled at her. "Just a few questions about our discussion the other day. It shouldn't take long." He walked over to the elevator; the car was at floor 28. *Damn.* "Is Mr. Luther free now?"

The woman moved around the desk and rustled a few papers. "Well, he could be, but... I'll give him a call. That'd be better, wouldn't it? If I just let him—"

"Thanks," Brian said, before walking to the stairs. "I'll find my way up."

#

By the time he reached the fifth floor, his knees ached. It'd be good for him. Vanessa always told him to start exercising. *"It'll keep the flab away,"* she'd said. And the therapist—*"Exercise will burn the depression away."*

If only he'd listened to them earlier.

Robert Luther's door was already open. The fifth floor had a different feel to typical offices. There was a warmth in the traditional wood and cream of the walls. Classic paintings hung from them, and archaic oak doors stood tall.

Luther slouched against his desk, legs crossed, as Brian approached. His assistant, Michael Walters, was vulturing around him. Brian entered without knocking.

"Officer," Robert Luther said. "How can I help?"

"New evidence has come up." Brian rubbed his muddy shoes against the cream carpet. "I want to get straight to the point, so if you'll allow me..."

Luther, edging towards Brian, held up a newspaper. It was a picture of Luther getting out of the black car, and the blurry picture of the car that the CCTV had shown. The headline read, "Preston Charity at Centre of Scandal".

His lip quivered. "I don't know what you think you're doing, Officer, but we don't deserve it. We're trying to do the right thing. I've told you, time and time again, we'll disclose everything. I'll let you speak to every single one of my staff ten times over; I'll let you search my home inside-out; I'll let you check every last log. You just can't keep creeping up on us like this. It's not right."

Brian weighed up what Luther was saying. The adrenaline was still building inside him from the video clip he'd seen on DC Peters' computer screen. "I respect that, Mr. Luther, I really do. BetterLives—great cause and all that. Big hope of a dying city. I get that. And I get you've lost a member of staff; it hurts, all that, yeah, I know. But the part about 'disclosing everything'? I've got to take you up on that, I'm afraid."

Luther's eyes twitched. Walters, fumbling through papers and continuing his day's work, frowned in the background.

Brian waited for his moment. He wanted to milk this for all it was worth.

"What do you mean? Has... What's going on?"

Brian stared beyond Luther and right at Walters, a triumphant smile on his face. Walters looked up and slowed down leafing through his papers.

"Officer, what's happened?" Luther asked, glancing between Michael Walters and Brian.

Brian reached into his pocket and stepped over to Luther's wooden desk. He dropped the photographic still from the video onto the table.

"New footage from one week before the death of Nicola Watson, at the place of death."

He placed the other photograph from the second clip of footage on the table. "And *more* new footage from the same place, a couple of weeks prior, similar time of night."

The room was silent. Luther picked up one of the photographs, his hand shaking.

Brian rested his hands against the desk. Wet soil dripped from his shoes. "So, take a look at those pictures and tell me, is that not you, Mr. Walters?"

Walters stood rigidly. He dropped the documents in his hands onto the desk. His mouth struggled for words. "I... I..."

"Well?"

Luther shook his head. "This has to be a mistake. It has... Michael?"

Walters' glance back at his boss said it all. He could hide things from some people, or try to, but there was no hiding it from the man he had been best friends with for years. He turned back to Brian, in slow motion. "I—"

"You can save your talk for down at the station. We're arresting you on suspicion of the murder of Nicola Watson. You do not have to say anything, but it may harm your defence if you do not mention when questioned something that you later rely on in court. Anything you say may be given in evidence."

Brian slipped the handcuffs around Michael Walters' wrists. Two more police officers appeared at the door.

"I'll be in touch, Mr. Luther," Brian said. "If you want to keep this on the low, you might want to make a few excuses. It might be a while before you see your man again."

Luther stared on as Brian took Michael Walters through the door. Michael Walters didn't look back at Luther, nor did he say another word. He just walked, mouth closed and head high, as Brian and the other officers led him towards the police car.

Chapter Seventeen.

Michael Walters' eyes hazed over as he watched recorded clip after recorded clip, the starring role in every one of them. The routine was the same. The times were the same.

Arrive, shake the pimp's hand, disappear inside, repeat. All the same, except for the night of the murder. All the CCTV evidence, removed by this man.

"We found it strange from the off." Brian circled Walters. "Y'see, at first, we thought that we'd found ourselves a little CCTV blind spot. But we did a little digging and it turns out the local council—

God bless them—have outsourced CCTV in certain parts of the city. It just so happens that the company they outsourced to shares a building with... Come on, let's have a drum roll here... BetterLives!"

Walters clenched his fists. DI Lawrence had scanned his fingers for a potential match inside the crime scene. He'd refused legal advice, adamant that he could fight his own battles. They almost had him.

Brian stepped around Walters as Price watched, clicking his pen. He liked it when Price believed in him and let him do his thing. It was very redeeming, to say the least.

"So when my good friend and colleague found this information out, he took a trip to the archives with a nice search warrant, only to find that the CCTV from the night of Nicola Watson's murder was missing."

Michael Walters slowly shook his head. He clasped his hands together in front of his face.

"But it gets better. When my friend asked to see the CCTV covering the main door leading to CityWatch offices, he only found a shot of you walking in there the morning after the murder, then leaving with a DVD moments later. Coincidence?"

"I don't believe it," Michael said quietly. "I don't believe it."

"Why did you remove that DVD, Michael? Why that one and no others? If you've got a filthy habit of seeing prostitutes, why remove a DVD from the night of the murder and not the other weeks? A bit sloppy, no?"

"I didn't remove that DVD," Michael said.

"Oh really? So, what—you just paid a casual morning visit to CityWatch offices? Catch up for a gossip with some of the guys? What was it?"

Walters took a deep breath and sipped his water. He cleared his throat. "I wasn't removing a DVD from that night. I work part-time with City-Watch and there was a problem, so I had to go down there."

Brian smirked. He'd have to remember to contact CityWatch for any records of Michael Walters. "Right. A problem. Convenient. So if we searched your home, which we are in the process of getting a warrant for, and if our officers searched the Bet-terLives offices, which they will be doing very soon, they wouldn't find that missing CCTV DVD, would they?"

Walters looked Brian directly in the eyes. "No."

"You see, this is how it looks. I think you lurked around Nicola Watson at work. Hell, maybe you had a relationship with her. Or maybe she had a relationship with someone else at your workplace. I think she was waiting to go home that night, and I think for whatever reason, you couldn't get your kicks from a whore, so you took her for a ride, and you raped her, and you killed her."

"I'm not in a relationship with Nicola Watson," Michael said. "I barely remember her. There's a lot of people at—"

"And then I think you washed her, scrubbed her down, removed all traces of yourself, and dumped her in that brothel when you'd finished with her, where you knew some lowlife could take the blame in your place. Then you removed the DVDs, forgetting you'd visited in the past, and hoped for the best."

Michael glanced at Price, who sat tall and silent but ever so present. Brian leaned back in the chair opposite Walters. His circling performance had run its course. Walters was speechless.

"Are you sure you don't want to pursue any legal advice now, Mr. Walters?"

Michael Walters removed his glasses and rubbed his eye. A sigh respired from his chest, and he collapsed onto the table. "I visited prostitutes lots of times. Maybe ten, maybe twenty, over the last few months." The way the words suddenly cut through his self-imposed silence was as if he was possessed, a demon speaking from within. "I was in a bad place. I—I know it's bad, but I... Okay. I tried to remove a DVD recording of me visiting Foster Road from some weeks ago, because I heard news of journalists buzzing around. I panicked, and I guess I got the wrong DVD. I didn't visit any prostitutes that night. It's a coincidence."

"You're forgetting something, Michael. We have eyewitnesses who claim they saw a black car matching the one in the CCTV footage. We have stills from further down the road of a similar vehicle arriving at the same time as it always does on a Monday. Good theory, but it's taken you a while to come up with that one, so excuse our skepticism."

Michael, still in a trance, was shaking. "I couldn't risk it coming out. The hooker storyline. So I tried to get rid of it. I thought it'd worked—I thought I'd done it—but clearly not now. I just wanted to do the best for BetterLives. I thought that was the right thing to do for the city."

"I'm sure you did, Mr. Walters. I'm sure you had the interests of the city in mind through every second of strangling her."

"I didn't see any prostitutes that night. It was New Year, for God's sakes. I had better things to do at New Year weekend."

"Like?"

"I was at a BetterLives get-together. Some fund-raiser thing. Just a few members of staff. Mainly big public figures. Maybe a few smaller people, too."

Brian sighed. "And can anybody confirm your attendance at that party?"

"Sure." Walters licked his lips. "About five or ten people."

Walters listed seven names, and Brian jotted them down. "Get on the phone to them," Brian said to DC Peters, who shot out of the room obediently. "You say you were at a party until what time?"

"Probably around twelve, one-ish. Late enough."

Brian slapped the photograph of Walters getting out of a car and walking towards a petrol station onto the table. "Then explain to me why you're getting petrol at eleven-thirty." His very own "ah" moment. Jeeves would be proud.

Walters stared at the picture, his eyes growing ever more restless. "I suppose I left earlier than I thought," he said. "Ah, that's right. I went to fill up and then I went back."

"McDone," DC Peters shouted. "A Mr. Stanton has confirmed that Walters was at the BetterLives function that night."

Brian scratched his head. He wasn't letting Walters go just yet. "Did he say when he left?"

"Around one, he says. But he's not sure."

Price shifted in his chair and looked at his watch, his face growing ever more purple. "Get us a meeting with the alibis arranged. I want to know more about Walters and his actual whereabouts that night."

Peters walked back out of the room. Walters sat upright, his controlled manner restored. "Why did you go for petrol?" Brian asked.

Walters' eyebrow twitched. "Because I needed to fill my car up."

"Okay, that's enough," Price said. It was the first time he'd spoken throughout the entire interview. "We're done here."

Walters threw his rucksack over his shoulder. "If there's anything else I can help you with, officers, I'd be delighted to, but I really need to get back to work right now."

Brian stared on, speechless, as he watched Price allow Walters out of the room. *What the fuck was he doing?*

"He's got no concrete alibi, Price."

Price slapped his hands together. "I know you want it to be him, and I did, too, but people saw him at that party. And I just now got the prints back from the flat on Foster Road. There's no trace of Michael Walters, Brian. Sounds concrete enough to me."

"DI Price, DS McDone." DC Peters held a paper in his hand. "I've contacted CityWatch. They do have Michael Walters on record for doing various technical assistance jobs."

Price shrugged his shoulders at Brian.

"Don't you think it'd have been better if we'd at least kept him in here for a while? He could go back and do anything now. Hide evidence. Anything."

"We could've kept him in here, but that'd be a bad idea for..." Price wiped his mouth. "He's got an alibi, McDone. His prints didn't come up at the flat. Let it go."

Brian's hands tingled, tension mounting in his chest. "I cannot believe this. Go on—a bad idea for who? You might as well say it, Price."

DI Price was frowning at Brian. "It's a bad idea for us. To fuck up again. And it's a bad idea for your reputation, if you want to keep any more of it."

Brian laughed. "Don't bullshit me. I know exactly what you meant to say. You're worried about BetterLives. Worried about the great fucking hope of Preston being tarnished. Worried about what the press would say about us if we damaged them. Whose payroll are you on, anyway?"

Brian regretted the last words almost instantly, but it didn't matter anymore. He knew what was coming. He might as well cross the line. He'd pretty much crossed it already.

Price's face was completely inflamed, his head dripping with sweat. "Excuse me, Detective, but was that a formal accusation against me or just a snide remark?"

Brian tossed his papers to one side. "I just don't know where your interests lie."

Price stood in Brian's way as he tried to get out of the door. "If you leave this room, Brian, understand that you don't walk back in again. You walk out of this room, you walk away from the case, and you take another big fucking step towards anonymity."

Cassy, approaching the door of the interview rooms, stopped herself when she saw Price and Brian standing off. She backed away slightly.

"What's my alternative?"

Price's eyes twitched. "You re-assess. I'm doing this for all of us, Brian. I'm doing it for the police, for the parents, for all of us. Get the boyfriend back in if you want to. Just stay away from BetterLives for the time being. There's no evidence that anything happened there, not yet. Sure—question their staff like you did, give them a few questions—that's fine. But no more of this charging in bullshit. It's reckless."

Brian's body totally deflated. "Then I'm going to walk out of this door, because clearly you don't know what's best for the case." He shoved past Price and towards Cassy, who watched the pair, wide-eyed.

"Remember what I said," Price shouted. "You walk away from this room, you walk away from the case."

Brian let the words buzz around his head as he stormed out of the office's heat and towards the front door. He needed to get out. He just needed to get out.

"No fucking fingerprints," Brian muttered, to himself more than anybody. "Anyone ever heard of a pair of gloves in the middle of winter 'round here?"

Stephen Molfer trundled through the office with his narrow mouth grinning away as it always did. Today was not a day for his jokes. One word, and...

"Been kicked off the case yet, Brian?"

Brian stopped and squared up to Stephen, who struggled to keep the grin on his face. "Stephen, fuck off," he said, before disappearing out of the offices to a chorus of "Oohs!"

Chapter Eighteen.

The phone rang a few times that evening, but Brian couldn't be arsed with it. It'd probably be some do-gooder from work. Somebody trying to interfere or tell him what they thought was good for him, like they always did. He kicked his shoes off and flopped onto his bed. His hair was greasy as a deep fat fryer as he rubbed his fingers through it. He stared at the TV set, moving images flickering across the screen and the slight hum of white noise cutting through the room.

He picked up the phone. He had to ring Vanessa. He just had to talk to her. To see her.

Maybe if he could just get it through to her that he was sorry for everything. Sorry for all the bullshit and the outbursts. Sorry for what he'd put them through. Maybe things could be okay.

He dropped the phone back to the floor and squeezed the bridge of his nose. It was no use. She'd just kick off—start going on about Davey and her rights as mother, *blah blah, all that bullshit.* Brian held the photograph between his fingers. The BetterLives car. There had to be some other link, something he was missing. But even if he found it, Price wouldn't let him go anywhere near them.

Walters' face as he left the station, slithering away. That soft handshake. Those shifty eyes.

Brian looked over at the bathroom door. His arm tingled. He needed to do it. He needed a release. He couldn't think straight if he didn't.

He walked to the bathroom and sighed at the fresh razor blade sitting beside his toothbrush. He just needed a release. One little release...

He rolled his sleeve up and reached for the razor blade. His arm begged the metal to make contact. *Kiss me, razor blade. Free me. Release me.*

Somebody banged at the door. At first, Brian thought it was one of the doors farther down the block. He didn't really get visitors. But then, another three knocks. He held the razor blade in his hand and waited for someone to speak or go away.

"Brian, it's Cassy." Brian felt like a kid who was just about to be caught wanking by his parents. *Cock in sock. Cock in sock, quickly.*

She'd go away soon. She couldn't see him like this.

"Brian, I know you're in, and I'm not coming to get on your nerves or anything. But I've got your stuff. From work. Price told me he was gonna bin it so I figured I'd bring it 'round. In case, y'know, he changed his mind. Oh—hi, sorry, no, I'm just..." She calmed her voice down as somebody quizzed her in the hallway. "'Just... speaking to an empty door. I—I'll leave these here."

Footsteps pattered away down the corridor, then another door shut as he imagined a weird neighbour no doubt heckled Cassy before disappearing into their own little pit of misery and booze.

So Price had ditched his stuff. It was the same as last time. Probably a few more weeks off work to mope around and sulk. Maybe he had gone back to work too soon. He thought he could deal with it. Vanessa said he'd benefit from the focus.

Showed how much she knew him.

Brian grabbed the small bottle of whisky he kept by his toothbrush and took a swig as the television static hummed through the air.

Then he pressed the blade against his arm, and relief poured out of his body and he was free to think again...

#

Another rattling at the door woke him. He wasn't sure how long he'd been asleep, but the whisky had trickled down onto his cream vest, and saliva dribbled down the sides of his unshaven face. *Fuck.* He really did look like a stereotypical drunk now. He'd make a perfect method actor.

The door rattled again. It seemed to be moving on its hinges. Cassy. Just Cassy, leaving some stuff.

"All right, all right," Brian called, as he wobbled out of bed and made his way towards the door. "I'm not as pretty a sight as I usually am, so close your—oh, I..."

Danny Stocks stood at the door, rubbing his arms. He wore a dark hoodie underneath his leather jacket. He looked up and down at Brian, the whisky stain catching his eye. "I'm not... interrupting, am I?"

"Danny—Mr. Stocks, I..."

"Look, I know this sounds fucked, but I had to find you, 'cause I know you wanted to know more from me. And the police. I saw them again, outside my house, and I heard about—"

"Just slow down, kid. Come in." He ushered Danny through the door, kicking the empty whisky bottle out of the way. He brushed a tiny portion of weed into his drawer. Danny's gaze attached to it like a tracking beacon.

"Could get you into trouble for that," Danny said, a half-grin on his face.

Brian flushed. At least he hadn't noticed the cut on his arm. Nobody noticed the cut. "It's not mine, it... Anyway, I could get *you* into trouble for being here. A lot of trouble. Interfering with the case... doesn't look good for you at all." He pulled a blue shirt over his shoulders and did it up, speaking with a voice of authority despite only having his pants on.

"I know you're not on the case anymore." Danny stared Brian right in the eye. "Which is why I wanted to talk to you. 'Cause... Look, I know you think I'm just a skunk who smokes and wastes his life. And sure, you probably think I'm a jealous little bastard who shagged someone to get back at his girlfriend. But I know you don't think I'm a killer."

Brian slipped some creased trousers on, almost tripping as he dragged them up his chubby legs. "Usually people who don't have anything to hide wouldn't come around to an officer's house to try and convince him otherwise."

"Right. Which is why I'm here. I remembered something."

Brian held his hand up. "Wait, you should probably tell this to the police. If it's official, then you should go to them." He reached around his messy bed for a pen. "I can give you the number of my partner, and she can—"

"No, I need to tell you, because I think you're the only one who has any idea of what's really going on." He tilted his head towards the picture of Robert Luther, stepping out of the BetterLives car, pinned up to Brian's wall.

Brian scratched the back of his neck. "Look, mate, I appreciate your concern and all that do-goodery you're trying, but the BetterLives lead is tired. There's nothing more to it. We're going back to the basics. Colleagues. Friends. Lovers." He emphasised the last word.

Danny smiled. "Right. Which is why I needed to speak to you about what I remembered."

Brian twitched his eyebrows. This wasn't right. He could get into trouble for this. *Ah, fuck it.* "Go on," he said, collapsing onto the edge of his bed.

Danny took a deep breath and straightened his posture. "Well, in the later days, before we, y'know, grew tired of each other... She seemed weird. Like, at first I thought it was just because she'd been with me for a few months, just general shit like that. But I'm not a paranoid guy. I didn't think there was another guy involved, not really."

Brian frowned. "Is there a point to this?"

Danny gulped and squinted. "Well, I never really thought about it before, but just the way she acted and some of the things she said, they came to me. She was obsessed with work. One day, she came in and she just started crying and locked herself in the bathroom. And I just thought—women. Messed up, from Venus, all that. And then I started to suspect there was someone else, and that's when it all just merged together..."

Brian shook his head. "Kid, I hate to be the bearer of bad news, but she was falling out of love with you. She found someone else. Maybe that someone else wanted to kill her. They certainly don't seem too keen on coming forward. But those things, those little signs of deterioration... I've seen them. Shit—I'm going through it at the mo. That's just what happens."

Danny's eyes clouded over. "Sorry to hear about that. But there was something else. Something she was becoming obsessed with. I..." He leaned back against Brian's desk. "I remember one night, we were in the hospital. We were blazing, but she was real high. But her eyes were gone before we'd even smoked, right? And... and I just remember her sitting there and looking at me when I asked her if things were all right, and just saying, 'Dan, they will be soon, but I honestly don't know what's going to happen when everyone finds out.' And alarm bells rang then. I thought she was on about another guy. But I dunno. The more I think about it now, it seemed... different."

Brian frowned as Danny, choking up, said the words. "And what do you make of it now?"

Danny fidgeted with his collar. "I think she might have known something. Maybe it was to do with work. But I think she might have known something, and she might have been killed for it." He looked firmly at Brian when he said it.

"But the girl—Nicola. She was strangled and taken to a brothel. It's a sexually motivated murder. That's what these people do."

"Maybe that's what they want you to believe."

Brian didn't register many words after that. He spoke of normal, everyday things with Danny for a few minutes, but it all kind of buzzed by. He couldn't get that idea out of his head. A *cover-up*. Something more at play.

Something hidden.

He opened the door for Danny. "I hope you find what you're looking for," he said. "I hope you get them, whoever did this."

Brian nodded and waved Danny off.

The little fragments of paper between Nicola Watson's dead fingernails. Was she hiding something?

He sank back onto his bed and yanked the magazine cutting of Robert Luther, smiling as he stepped out of a BetterLives car, from his wall.

"What are you hiding?"

Chapter Nineteen.

Brian took a deep breath as he arrived at the visitation centre, well on time for a change. He hadn't seen Davey for a while—not properly, anyway. Sure, he'd caught a glimpse of him through a car window or something like that, but it wasn't really the same as truly *seeing* somebody. Hearing their voice. Interacting with them. It was weird, how much you could forget about a person when you hadn't seen them for some time.

He swigged back a final painful mouthful of cold coffee and hopped out of the car into the fresh

January air. Even though he'd had his release, his head had been spinning all night.

Danny's visit. The paper between Nicola's fingernails. Was she trying to reach for something? Or trying to hold on to something?

He'd spoken to Vanessa and told her he was off the case. That things were back to normal.

"Are you sure you're in a fit state?" she'd asked. "It's just... just remember the way you were when you last properly saw your boy. He wants his old dad back to the way he was. Are you sure?"

As much as the images of the case and the victim clawed at his consciousness, he said yes. What normal father wouldn't?

"I'll see you at eleven," she'd said.

"I'll be there at half ten."

And now he was walking up to some sort of visitation centre. He'd kicked off a bit when she mentioned that. He'd have just gone round to the house, or spent a little time out and about with Davey on his own. He didn't want to be one of those dads who spent an hour under surveillance asking about fucking grades and new toys. He wanted to be a dad.

The interior of the place was just as dull and sterile as the outside. Fake pictures of painted animals and smiley faces spread across the walls. That sour, sweaty smell of kids running around for too long was ripe in the air.

He signed himself in at reception, where a woman with big glasses gave him a bit of a snarl as he dropped a pen on the floor. He spotted Davey with Vanessa in the far corner of the main room, past the rest of the families and the wannabe dads waving candy in front of their kids' faces to try and appeal to them. Brian raised a hand as Vanessa spotted him and whispered into Davey's ear. Davey scanned the room. His little face lit up when he saw his dad pacing towards him.

"Hello, you!" Brian reached down to hug Davey. His little arms clung around his neck, and Brian remembered what it was like to tuck him into bed. To tell him a bedtime story.

"Are you okay? I was gonna bring you a present, but I got... I had to start the car up, and—"

"It's okay, isn't it, Davey?" Vanessa asked, cross-legged and wearing yet another smart blazer. When had she bought all these fucking blazers? Had she always worn them? Or was it part of her new look?

Davey grinned, revealing a missing tooth.

"And what's that we have missing, eh?" Brian pointed at the gap in Davey's mouth.

"I lost a tooth! The tooth fairy came and leave me a pound! See, Daddy, it's here!" He held a grubby pound coin in Brian's face.

"Well, did she now? You'd better not lose any more teeth too soon, or the tooth fairy might be asking for a loan, eh?" He glanced at Vanessa, who chewed her lip and smirked a little. Davey screwed his eyebrows together.

"Anyway." Brian patted his hands against his thighs and plonked down on a seat. He pulled himself up to the table. "How's things? How's school?"

Vanessa looked at Davey to prompt him to speak. Davey stared at his hands and stood at the edge of the table. "Well, school's okay," he said. "I got a gold star 'cause I worked really, really hard, the teacher said. And Dan got his name on the board, but I didn't get my name on the board because I worked really well."

"Ah," Brian said. "That's my boy, then! And, erm, I hope you're looking after your mum?"

Davey smiled. "Mummy's okay. But Daddy, when will you be home? Because... because Mummy's bedtime stories are good, but you play better than her, and—and you watch the good telly with the 'splosions and the big scary things." He stomped his feet like Godzilla. "But Mummy... Mummy doesn't."

A lump formed in his throat. His little boy. Davey didn't need to go through any more of this crap. He didn't have to suffer because of his dad's job. Brian could be there for him. They both could.

"Well, listen." Brian leaned in towards Davey. "Daddy just needs to spend a bit of time away, but he'll be back soon."

"Has Daddy been naughty?" Davey's brown eyes scanned Brian's face inquisitively.

Brian laughed and looked down at his shaking legs. At least Davey didn't seem to remember the day it had happened. "Well, I dunno, son." He held Davey's hands. "But I guess you'll just have to ask your mummy when Daddy can come home, won't you?" He looked at Vanessa for security.

Vanessa stared into space.

Brian's pocket buzzed. The instant urge to check engulfed him. His hands flinched, then he patted his legs to conceal his intentions, but he couldn't cover it up. Since the Nicola Watson case, answering the phone had become an impulse reaction again, like the need to cough when something was stuck in his throat.

"Aren't you going to check that?" Vanessa looked down at Brian's trouser pocket.

Brian took a deep breath and smiled at Davey. "It'll be nothing. I... I'll just be..." He pulled the phone to his ear. "Hello?"

"Brian, you need to get down here now." It was Cassy. She sounded flustered, nervous excitement in her shaky voice.

Vanessa watched Brian closely, while Davey mumbled something to her, a confused expression on his face. "Now's not a great time, Cassy. And my time on the case is done." He felt like he was in an audition room, saying the right things to prove himself to Vanessa and Davey. *The Good Father Factor.*

"Well, now you're back on it," Cassy said. "Brian, we've got him."

Brian's feigned smile of reassurance turned into a frown. He stood up from the chair and pulled the phone closer to his ear. "What do you mean you've got him?"

"The semen samples, man. We found Danny's there, and maybe that's normal, but there's another, too. Just one more. Brian—it's Luther."

Brian's knees were as weak as jelly. The rest of the room's chattering faded away into the background. "What do you mean, it's..."

"You were right. About BetterLives. It's him, Brian. Get the hell down here now. He's in for questioning. The media are going crazy."

He looked up at the news on the TV screen in the corner. Robert Luther was being escorted through the crowds of media and into the police station. "Watson Murder: Robert Luther Returns for Questioning."

He slipped the phone back into his pocket. The voices in the room became clear again.

"Brian, is everything all right?" Vanessa had her arm on Davey's back.

"I..." Brian, still in a trance, eyes glazed, smiled at Davey again. He squeezed his son tightly. "Daddy's got to go do something very important," he whispered. He rose to his feet and sprinted towards the doorway.

"Brian, what the hell?" Vanessa shouted as Brian raced out of the visitation centre and towards his car.

Chapter Twenty.

The media already swarmed around the entrance to the station. Lights flashed in his face as a group of journalists turned their attention to him, jostling and climbing over each other for a closer view of this crazy show.

"Sir, what can you tell us about Mr. Luther's arrest? Is he the man?"

Brian kept his head down.

Another journalist, wearing a blue anorak, appeared in front of him. His goatee flicked out at the ends as he waved a microphone in Brian's face. "Detective Sergeant, is Robert Luther Nicola Watson's killer? What does this mean for BetterLives? What does this mean for our city?"

Brian shook his head. What did it mean for "our" city? Was that all he was concerned with right now? What mattered was Nicola Watson and finding her killer, not BetterLives. They might have been the city's "great hope", but this was real life. And real life was depressing.

Price was waiting by the door of the interview room as Brian walked down the corridor. His arms were folded, and he chewed at his lip, a frown etched into his forehead. "Wondered when you might turn up to gloat," he said.

Brian tried to smile at him. He peeked in between the half-open metallic blinds at Luther's silhouette. "I'll go in there and have a word. Then, I'll—"

"No, you won't."

The spotlight had spun to him, blinding his eyes. "But I... Look, I know what happened between us, and I apologise for it, but I'm the best officer to handle this—"

"Your ex-wife's just been on the phone. Sounds like you aren't very good at handling *anything* at the moment. I hate to have to do this right now, but I'm temporarily demoting your status as Detective Sergeant. This is my investigation, Brian. Mine."

Brian lowered his head as Price continued to glare at him. *Typical.* He did all the hard work then along came a couch potato to hijack the investigation and claim all the credit. Absolutely typical.

"Ah, Cassy." Price grinned from cheek to cheek and waved for her to join them. Cassy approached, bug-eyed and caught in the moment.

"I figured one of you had to be doing something right, and for a bit of continuity, I've had a word with DS Emerson. She and I are going to speak to Luther. I figured this would be some good experience for her, right?"

Cassy nodded and smiled at Brian.

Two-faced bitch. "So what do you propose I do?" Brian asked, dejected and flushed in the cheeks.

Price looked down at his watch. "Well, DS Emerson and I are going to speak to Luther. Maybe... I dunno, really. Maybe you could head down to Nicola's parents' house and ask them if they knew anything about her dating older men?"

Brian gritted his teeth.

"What's that look?"

He shrugged.

"No, you tell me what the fuck that look was, right now."

"Okay," Brian said, scornfully. "It's just I've spoken to the parents before. They know nothing at all. We've got someone in here with semen samples all over Nicola Watson, and you're asking me to keep myself busy? It just doesn't seem right."

"Keep yourself busy?" Price said, widening his eyes. "It could be important. You're keeping the case under control whilst we move things forward here. Isn't that right, Cas? Go on, cheer the man up."

Cassy shrugged. Her cheeks glowed pink.

"Well, whatever. Good luck." He took a final glance at Luther in the interview room. Upright. Shadowed body. No real signs of emotion. "We didn't take a DNA swab when we interviewed Mr. Luther last time. How did you match the samples?"

Price rubbed his hands. "Turns out our friend Robert isn't as innocent as he'd like us to believe. Was suspected of fraud a few years back. Got away with it, but don't they always? At least he left us a nice gift in the form of his DNA."

"Did he kick up a fuss?"

"Not a flinch," Price said. "Barely seen a man look so defeated."

"And Walters?"

"I imagine he'll be down to sing his man's praises in no time. Now come on—we only have him for thirty-six hours before we have to make a decision whether to charge him. Don't want to have to start worrying about applying for the ninety-six, not with somebody as slippery as him. He's so smooth he's practically oily."

Brian remembered what Danny had said about cover-ups. "Right. I won't be long. Cassy, you get this sorted for us."

She winked at Brian. "I give the orders now, 'Detective Constable'."

\#

Shenice Watson's face grew greyer and more vacant every time Brian saw her. Like a stroke victim seeing a relative and having no idea who they were, she didn't seem to recognise him at first. Then a spark of recognition returned to her eyes, and she gestured him inside without saying a word.

The small pile of sympathy cards that Trevor had collected from the doorstep when Brian last visited were unopened and gathering dust. The Christmas tree shed spikes all over the floor near the entrance. A dustpan and brush lay by its side, Shenice's cleaning attempts clearly half-hearted and disinterested.

Shenice flicked the kettle on as Brian sat down at the table.

"What's the latest?" she asked, cutting straight to the point.

Brian cleared his throat and edged forward in the creaky kitchen chair. He wasn't sure whether or not to mention Luther yet. But then the press...

"No doubt you've seen about Mr. Luther. The man from BetterLi—"

"Was it him?" she asked. Flecks of spit shot towards Brian's face.

Brian loosened his collar. "We're investigating BetterLives as a lead because your daughter spent a lot of time volunteering there. Right now, it's too early to say."

Shenice's jaw trembled. The kettle screamed as the water boiled, but she didn't seem to notice it.

"Mrs. Watson... the reason I'm here might seem a little strange, but I was wondering if there were any little clues that Nicola might have been dating somebody other than Danny Stocks."

Shenice gasped. "Do you think we'd be having this conversation if I knew? Do you think—" She stopped and covered her face with her hands for a moment. "Do you think we'd be arranging her funeral if we had any idea?"

"Sorry. I... I didn't mean to offend you. It's just really important. If there's anything you might have been suspicious about, or maybe didn't think much of at the time, now's the time to tell us."

Shenice paused and squinted. "No. I don't. I don't believe there was 'owt wrong with her, really. She was just our girl. My girl. My Nicola."

Brian heard movement behind him. Footsteps. Scott Watson—Nicola's brother—lumbered towards them in baggy black jeans, hair gelled forward onto his acne-covered forehead.

"Scott," Brian said, nodding at him as he entered.

Scott rubbed at his arm and nervously nodded back.

Shenice clicked on the kettle again even though it had just boiled. She sniffed back tears and sprinkled another spoonful of sugar into her teacup.

"I was just asking your mum here if—"

"There was a ring," Scott said, his lips quivering.

Shenice stopped tinkling her teaspoon against the side of the cup.

"What do you mean?"

Scott reached into the front pocket of his checkered blue and red hoodie and pulled out a little golden ring with a diamond on top of it. He dropped it into Brian's open hand. The ring was shiny and regal. Hell, it would probably have cost more than he'd ever been able to afford.

"Scotty, what is that you have there?" Shenice asked, staring at the ring. Brian looked up at Scott as he continued to rub his arm.

"I didn't think 'owt of it at first or when all this kicked off, but when I heard you saying about the other bloke, I remembered it."

Brian twirled the ring around in his fingers. "How did you get hold of this?"

Shenice marched towards Brian and snatched the ring from his fingers, getting a closer look at it herself.

"Someone delivered it a couple of weeks back. To Nicola. In an Amazon box. And I'd ordered a pen drive through her Amazon account, so I opened her package instead by mistake. I never wanted to tell Mum or Dad about it, 'cause—"

"Why didn't you tell us, Scott?" Shenice gazed directly at her son, venom in her eyes. "Don't you realise 'ow fuckin' important this could be?"

Scott shook and stared at his feet, mumbling something under his breath.

"Just calm down, Mrs. Watson. What did you say, Scott?"

"Because Nicola didn't want me to tell anyone, all right? She didn't want that." The words blasted out of him louder than anything else he'd said. His cheeks flushed at the vocal explosion. Shenice turned back to the kettle before crying out with frustration and throwing the ring to the kitchen floor.

Brian picked it up from a dirty crevice by the corner of the fridge. He moved it between his fingertips again.

"What did Nicola say about this ring?"

Scott blinked fast. "Well, I just thought it was from Danny and that's why she didn't want Mum and Dad to find it first." He turned his stare towards his mother. "But then Nicola just kind of went along with that. She seemed happy. Shocked but happy. She just went along with things. I guess you never look into stuff when it's family, but I did find it a bit weird."

Brian slipped the ring into his pocket. He patted Shenice on the back before walking up to Scott and shaking his bony, spidery hand. "We'll be in touch. Look after your mum."

Scott nodded but avoided eye contact with Brian.

\#

Shenice scooped another spoonful of sugar into her teacup.

Chapter Twenty-One.

Brian thumbed the ring around his palm. Shiny, golden, a little diamond reflecting against the light. Too expensive for Danny to give her, surely.

Could Luther have something to do with it? He clenched the ring in his fist before slipping it back into his pocket and driving through town towards the police station.

Traffic was a nightmare, and Price wasn't answering his phone. Probably interrogating Luther, gobbling up whatever bullshit he and his expensive solicitor were feeding him. Brian bit his nails as rain pounded against the windscreen, engine fuel from the car in front coughing up through the air vent and into his face. He flicked the radio on, some Scottish rock band that used to be pretty decent with another pop song. He switched the channel over. Voices on Radio Four debating some shit or another. He yawned as he looked through the city centre at people scurrying to escape the wind, hiding underneath reversed umbrellas. A fat kid chewed away at a Big Mac whilst his tight-assed mum bit her lip and giggled on the phone.

When the shop caught his eye, he didn't think much of it at first. It had always been there after all.

But when it caught his eye again, he couldn't quite comprehend it.

H.M. Luther.

The honking of the car behind him seemed directed at somebody else at first. On the third honk Brian realised he was holding up the traffic as the green light pierced its way through his window.

He stuck his middle finger up at the driver behind anyway, even though it was his fault.

After getting out of the town's windy roads, crawling with absentminded shoppers and slow moving taxi drivers, Brian pulled in near the bus station and grabbed his phone, his hand shaking. He opened up Safari and closed down the last tab he'd looked at, something about Top 10 Unsolved

Mysteries. He pushed his chubby thumb into the search bar, missed it at first, and pressed it again. He cursed but was luckier third time round. He typed into Google with his sausage fingers. *Fucking not-so-smartphones.* Like hell were they designed for him. FatPhones—they'd be all right.

The search results interrupted his train of thought. He hit the home button and dialled Price again. One buzz. Two buzzes.

"Brian, I was just about to—"

"Price. Before you start—H.M. Luther. It's his father. Y'know, the rich, pompous jeweller?"

Price grunted at the other end of the line. Voices were audible in the background.

"There... There was a ring." Brian struggled to string a sentence together. "Nicola Watson received a ring. Anonymous. The family didn't think much of it, but... I think there might have been something more going on with Robert Luther and Nicola Watson than we first thought."

Price was silent again for another few moments. Other voices muttered somewhere near him.

"Are you getting this? I think Nicola and Luther were lovers. I think there could be more to this than—"

"Brian," Price snapped. "Listen, for God's sake— I'm trying to fucking tell you something here."

Brian was immediately brought back to earth. "Right, right... Sorry. Go on."

Price sighed and mumbled something. It didn't sound all that polite. "You need to get back here, Brian. Well done on your little bit of Sherlock Holmes work—you can have your DS powers back for that. But the lovers thing? We've figured that out, anyway."

"What... what do you mean?"

Price muttered something to someone else before returning his attention to the phone. "Luther's just confessed to an intimate encounter with Nicola Watson. You need to get down here." He cancelled the call.

Brian held the phone to his ear, unable to move it. His head spun with thoughts, but none of them seemed comprehensible right now. Jealous lover? Or coincidence? He needed time. He needed air.

He turned the car around into the private parking area, almost clipping the side of an already bruised silver Rover, before parking and grabbing a ticket. The rain was more violent now, the sky a charcoal grey. He slipped £3.30 into the machine—three hours of parking—perched the ticket behind his police car windscreen wipers, and zipped up his black jacket as he walked through the milder, albeit windy, air, towards the police station.

He needed time to cool off. It was only a five-minute walk. Enough time to compose himself. Enough time to think.

He fumbled around with the ring in his pocket as he walked through the urine stench of the bus station and towards his workplace.

Chapter Twenty-Two.

Price tapped the bottom of his pen against the table. He kept his eyes on Luther, clearly scrutinising every small movement and facial expression as if it was primary evidence.

Luther sat upright, his hands laid out in front of him. The bitten-down skin at the side of his fingernails was beginning to crust and scab. Every now and then, he looked up at Price and Brian to check if they were still watching him, then diverted his gaze when he realised they were. Luther's solicitor, Kayleigh Wallbridge, accompanied him. Her cheeks wrinkled as if she were sucking a lemon.

She blinked frequently as her overgrown bobbed fringe dangled into her eyes.

"Why did you keep it from us, Luther?" Brian asked.

Luther didn't react. He remained focused, gazing at his hands as they rested on the table. Kayleigh made a note and whispered something to him.

Brian sighed. "Luther, you're in a bad position right now. Really, really bad. You're going to want to think about being a little more cooperative." He twiddled the ring around in his pocket.

Luther and Brian held a stare for a few moments. Enough time to make him trust him. Enough time to make him think he had a way out.

He turned away again and gazed out of the blinds. Little streaks of light peeked through into the room, and silhouettes paced down the corridor. Kayleigh leaned back to Luther and whispered something else. He nodded and took a deep breath as if he was preparing for a speech.

"It was just a fling." He tried to raise a trademark confident smile again, but it quivered and twitched at the sides.

"Just a fling?" Brian replied. "I don't believe you."

"Detective Sergeant," Kayleigh said with a soft tone. "Unless you're going to keep on acting on those hunches of yours—which I hear you're becoming quite adept at doing so, may I add—you have no evidence to suggest that Mr. Luther's relationship with the girl was anything more than casual. Two adults leading a healthy, normal lifestyle."

Brian smiled at Kayleigh. He loved it when he had people right where he wanted them. She was clueless about the ring, and so was Luther. His ace in the pack. He was going to milk this for all it was worth. "These hunches of mine. Sometimes they're right. Sometimes they aren't. That's just life. But, Mr. Luther, and I'm addressing *you* directly, can you please confirm that your relationship with Nicola Watson was nothing more than 'casual'? And, come on—be completely honest with us."

Luther glanced at Kayleigh, who rolled her pen between her fingers. Then he faced the detectives. "Yes, I... It was just once. I didn't want it to come out. And then—then her death. I couldn't let that happen. I couldn't let our encounter come out. I was scared. I knew it would come to this, but I was scared."

Brian slipped the ring across his knee. "It's a reasonable enough reaction. In fact, if I were in your shoes—apart from probably being a little out of pocket after buying those shoes—I'd probably have reacted in a similar way."

Luther's eyes widened. It was great when they thought they had a way out. Luther rubbed his eyes. Kayleigh didn't reveal a flicker of emotion.

Just you wait...

Brian slammed the ring onto the table and rolled it over to Luther.

The rest of the room watched as Luther blinked rapidly, a glimmer of recognition in his eyes, just for a moment. Then, a return to the earlier cold, steely grey stare.

"It's—I don't know what it is."

"Yes you do, Luther. You gave it to Nicola Watson."

"What? I did no such thing. It was just a brief fling. Why would I give her a ring like that?"

Brian shrugged. "I don't know, Luther. I don't know. But this is what I think. I think you were in a relationship with Nicola Watson. Maybe it *was* just a short-term thing. Maybe longer. And I think she rejected you when you gave her the ring, or decided she didn't want you anymore. Hurt you badly. So you lashed out."

Luther looked at Kayleigh for support, disbelief in his eyes. "I—Why would I? Why would I do that?"

"Detective Sergeant," Kayleigh interrupted, "are you going to elaborate on these ridiculous claims? What does a ring have to do with my client?"

"I think you killed her, Robert. I think you tried to cover it up."

Luther shook his head. "Because of a ring? Why would you think that?"

Brian nudged Price as Luther and Kayleigh looked on. Price slipped a piece of A4 paper out of the brown envelope and placed it onto table.

"Is this not your father's jewellers?" Brian asked. The picture had been taken some time ago and was in black and white, but the unmistakable "H.M. Luther" sign still peered down onto the Preston city streets.

Luther's nostrils twitched. "Yes."

"And if we paid your father a visit, he'd be able to tell us about this ring and who bought it, wouldn't he?"

"I... I guess so. I guess so, yeah."

"Right," Brian said. "DS Emerson, get on the phone. Ring the jewellers. Ask him about the sales. And if his son bought the ring." He peered into Luther's eyes.

Cassy left the room and keyed in the number. She paced from back to front, waiting.

Kayleigh took some notes in her bumper-sized Pukka Pad. Her lips trembled.

"Did anybody else know about your relationship with Nicola Watson?" Brian asked.

"It wasn't a relationship, okay? And no. No, I don't think so. There was no reason to tell. It's just... It's private. It was irrelevant, in the wider scheme of things."

"Right. Was Nicola Watson irrelevant when you killed her? Is that why you did it?"

Kayleigh coughed to get the attention of the room. "My client does not have to answer to any of these barbaric claims. He knows his rights."

"Mrs. Wallbridge," Price said, breaking his silence. "You're sounding very much like a solicitor with no real defence. If your client knows his rights, he'd better bloody start taking advantage of them, because the way this is going, he's going to have all of those rights stripped away very soon."

Kayleigh backed down and returned to her notepad, muttering under her breath.

"Your assistant, Michael Walters. You wouldn't happen to know why he was removing a CCTV DVD from CityWatch, would you?"

Luther squinted. "I... I don't know. Why?"

"You wouldn't happen to know about his... Let's call them 'relationships', would you?"

"I know he's a single man who just went through a rough end to a relationship. And I know he wouldn't do anything to hurt anyone."

"Oh no, we weren't accusing him. He has an alibi. Just trying to work out how far he'd go to protect his precious boss, that's all."

Luther rubbed the backs of his shaking hands and reached for his cup of water. The plastic cup was clearly empty, but he pulled it to his mouth, sending the final drip of water towards his chapped lips. He squeezed the plastic cup in his palm, his gaze shifting over to Cassy, who continued to move outside. "Okay. I had a relationship with her."

Kayleigh's glare shot up at Luther, who stared at the table. Brian swung 'round in his chair and held his arm up towards Cassy. Cassy entered the room, looking like she'd nodded off for five minutes of a movie and wanted updating.

"Was that a formal confession?" Brian asked, his pulse racing.

Luther's crusty, tired eyes peered at him. "I'm confessing that I was in love with Nicola Watson. And that's all I have to confess. That's all I'm guilty of."

"Detectives, if you'd allow me a moment to talk to my client, please?" Kayleigh's voice was shaky.

Her pen rested against her notepad, completely static.

"Brian," Cassy whispered in his ear, "I just spoke to the jewellers. His dad says there was a ring stolen."

Luther had started sobbing.

"Did you steal the ring?"

Luther clenched his eyes shut, tears dripping down his cheeks. "What do you think?"

Brian turned to Cassy, who turned to Price in return. Nobody could speak.

"I'm... I'm just trying to do the right thing. Just the wrong place and the wrong person. Always the wrong person..." Luther mumbled hysterically. "Just trying to do what's right..."

"Mr. Luther, if you could—"

The sound of the door swinging open tore through the limbo-esque room. Two officers stood at the door. Luther's face reddened in confusion.

"Take him, boys," Price said. "Mr. Luther, we're taking you into custody on suspicion of murdering Nicola Watson. You do not have to say anything, but anything you do say may be used against you in court. Sleep well, Robert."

Price thumped a hard, heavy hand on Brian's shoulder. "Well done, Brian. Redeemed yourself, good lad. Your work's done here."

The guards slipped handcuffs around Luther's wrists. At first, it appeared he was going to protest and kick up a fuss, but he sank his head to his chest and slouched behind them like a prisoner being led to death row. Even Kayleigh Wallbridge was lost for words as she shuffled out behind her client, buzzing around him like a fly.

The guards edged Luther, who struggled, out the door. He twisted back towards Brian and Cassy. "I'm only guilty of loving her," he said before being pulled away down the corridor.

Brian and Cassy sat in complete silence.

Chapter Twenty-Three.

The buzz of people in the background hissed in Brian's ears as he watched the bubbles reach the top of his drink. A group of lads laughed at the corner table, playfully punching one another. Behind the bar, an old greying man wiped the surfaces and looked at his watch. He flipped over some glasses in preparation for the nighttime crowd's arrival. It was always like this in every pub, didn't matter which. The bridge between the afternoon drinkers and the nighttime louts. Brian liked this limbo. Gave him time to think. He was too young to arrive for an early morning pint and too old to mingle with the kids at night. He was just a novelty to them, a "fair play for coming out, old man!" symbol of eternal youth.

Cassy sipped on her Coke, to which she'd added a spot of vodka. "How's things at home?" she asked, half-heartedly. She didn't look at Brian. Her tired gaze wandered 'round the table. It was always hard when something major came to a close. That niggling sense of the unsolved. The unresolved.

"Not quite like the crime shows, is it?" Brian asked.

"No, well... I guess. It's just strange. I mean, why? Why would he?"

Brian took a sip of his pint. "Some things you just can't explain. You *want* there to be more to all these cases and more going on. But these people, I dunno. Sometimes they just snap. Maybe he got jealous. But evidence is evidence. We've just got to get on with that. You'll get used to it."

Cassy watched Brian with her big brown eyes. She rubbed her hands up and down her black tights.

"What?" Brian asked.

She flinched. "Nothing. It's just—"

"No, go on. Say it."

Cassy exhaled theatrically. "I just get the feeling that you aren't done with this case yet, for whatever reason. You should be happy. You can go back to your family now. Instead, you're sat in here supping on a beer. What you doing, mate?"

For a moment, as he slumped in his chair, Brian saw himself from the perspective of a fly on a nearby wall. Fat as fuck, with a waistline growing at the same rate as his discontent. Greying hair greasy from the lack of exposure to shampoo. He'd meant to buy some, but he had to keep up the alcoholic facade. He had to keep on smelling of whiskey, or they might just suspect his reasons for absence after all.

"It's nothing. Just the way it is when a case finishes. You're right—I don't get why he killed her either. But it's done, and soon we'll have more questioning, then the court shit. And the papers... They'll be on to this tomorrow. And we'll have a rough few days, but it'll be on to the next case before we know it." He swigged down a few gulps in quick succession. Cassy bit her lip. She hadn't touched her drink in a while.

"You ignored my question," she said.

"And what was that?" Brian asked, dabbing the corners of his mouth with a napkin.

"Your wife. And your kid. Last I heard, you were off to see 'em, before, y'know—"

"Why do you have to interfere?" Brian asked, sternly. The old man wiping glasses behind the bar shifted his gaze to their table. Brian mumbled and coughed, trying to disguise his anger.

Cassy stayed focused on him. "I care about you. Like, you're my partner, you know? So I give a shit about whether you're turning up on time or whether you're getting drunk to the point you're blacking out every night."

Brian smiled as he took another gulp of his beer. At least she still believed him. "You don't seem too fussed about stopping me." He swilled another large mouthful around his cheeks.

"Oh yeah, how is the beer?" Cassy asked, folding her arms.

"Beautiful." He placed the empty pint glass down on the table. He feigned a groggy throat and made his eyes twirl, slightly vacant and glassy.

"Good." Cassy knocked back her vodka Coke and stood up to walk to the bar. "Another Becks Blue for you, then?"

Brian's skin crawled. "Becks what?"

"Alcohol-free." Cassy smiled. "Hope you're not too much of a lightweight. I hear it still has like, 0.04% alcohol in it or something, so you'd better watch yourself." She winked, then walked towards the bar and ordered him another pint of fake beer.

#

Brian drove Cassy home that night. He'd not drunk an ounce of alcohol, technically, so it seemed like the gentlemanly thing to do. Why did she order him a non-alcoholic beer? Was she trying to catch him out? Get him pretend drunk? Or was she just looking out for her alchie friend?

Brian pulled up outside Cassy's flat. The flats looked more like semi-detached houses, four residents in each little block. Nice area of Fulwood. Plenty of trees. Not a lot of scrotes, apart from the pub at the corner of the street. But that was closed now. A lot of places were closed. Businesses seemed to fall by the minute these days.

"Well, thanks for the lift," Cassy said as they sat in the dim glow of the Victorian style street lamps. "Do you want to come in for a coffee?" She fluttered her eyelashes. "I'm just messing with you, you big romantic. Come in and have a look around."

Brian's cheeks were on fire. Who could turn down a look around a pretty younger woman's home? As long as his wife hadn't moved in next door, he didn't see a problem with that. "Sure. Be nice to see a house that isn't a shithole for a change."

Cassy frowned as she reached for the car door handle. "I didn't say it's not a shithole." She climbed out of the car and slammed the door.

"Don't slam," Brian muttered under his breath. Vanessa always slammed the door. It didn't matter how many times he asked her, she just kept on slamming.

Vanessa. He'd have to see her again sometime. Apologise for the other day. It was over now. He could sort things. They could be happy again.

"The only thing I'm guilty of is being in love with her," Luther had said, his eyes drooping and world-weary as he was dragged away.

Brian stepped out of the car and then walked up the little concrete steps and towards Cassy's front door.

The place was warm inside. A few boxes were piled at the top of a flight of stairs at the entrance. The lounge was spacious, with dark leather sofas covered in old newspapers. Cassy reached for the lamp in the corner and flicked it on. She brushed some papers off the sofa.

"Well, here you are," she said. She didn't quite meet his eye as he looked around the room. Photographs of her and friends on holiday. Her and a girl at the top of Machu Picchu. Independent foreign cinema and classic literature.

In the corner of the room, on an old vinyl player, the new Biffy Clyro album sat on the deck.

"I've worked with you for all this time, and I didn't realise you were a Biffy fan." Brian spun the vinyl around. "What d'you think of the new stuff?"

Cassy cleared her throat. "Well, I know I'm not in the majority, but I like it. They've matured. All bands mature. Side one is good. Not so keen on side two. But Eve and I used to go see bands a lot back in the day. Kind of reminds me of her. Not sure what she'd think of the new stuff." She laughed. "What do you make of it?"

Brian smiled as he turned around to thumb through the rest of Cassy's vinyl collection. "I think it's fucking abysmal."

An awkward silence followed. The humour didn't quite slip off his tongue in the witty manner he had intended.

"So... Eve. She sounds like a clever girl. She your mate on the pictures?" Brian gestured towards the shot of the pair of trekkers up Machu Picchu, the dark haired and olive-skinned girl unmistakably Cassy, and a blonde girl with a toothy grin next to her.

Cassy walked up to a photograph and held it in her hands. "Yeah, me and her back in the day. Had a blast. Tried our first joint together. Travelled the world together. Probably popped our cherries in the same bloody room."

Brian sniggered. "It'd be good to have someone to share all that stuff with. You're lucky."

Cassy sighed as she dusted the table with her sleeve and placed the photograph back into position. "I *was* lucky. She... she passed away last year. Cancer. Brain."

Brian's knees turned to jelly. "I'm so sorry," he said. "Don't mean to bring... Yeah, I'm... Are you okay?"

"It's okay," Cassy cut in. "Really. It's fine. I'm sure you'd have got on with her though, in a weird way."

Brian scrunched his nose. "What's so weird about two people getting on?"

Cassy giggled and looked down at the floor. "You're practically old enough to be my... our dad. Bit of a creeper."

Brian brushed it off with a wave of the hand and a smile. "Only as old as you act."

"In which case, you're older," she said, winking.

Brian slipped his hands into his pocket. The pair were silent for a few moments. "Well, I should, erm..." He pointed towards the door.

"You can always stay." Cassy lurched forward a bit as she asked, her voice rising in tone and excitement. She wiped her hair out of her face, trying to look less eager. "I mean... I can clear up the sofa. You wouldn't have to be late for work that way."

A bit of company. That would make a change.

"Thanks, Cassy. I just... I don't think it'd be a good idea. And I... It's my day off tomorrow. Annual leave. Gonna try and talk to 'Ness. See if I can sort all that crap out. Besides, you wouldn't want a smelly old man on your sofa, would you?"

Cassy's eyes watered, but she smiled and shook her head. "Yeah. Yeah, you're probably right. Have a good day off, you lucky bugger."

"Have a lovely day yourself."

He took one last glance at the picture of Cassy and Eve. He hadn't noticed the bottle of pills by its side until now.

"It's just passion flower," Cassy said. She must have spotted him looking. "Just helps me sleep and chill. Won't be enough to get high off."

"Any more of that and I'll have to report you to Price," Brian said.

Cassy laughed. "That wanker's probably getting stoned off his sour old face every night." They held a stare for another few seconds before turning to the floor. "Anyway..."

"Yeah, I'll... I'll see myself out. Night."

"'Night, Brian."

He stepped over the piled boxes and trotted down the stairs towards the outdoors, towards his car beneath the moth-crowded glow of the street lamp. When he got in, he heard a voice somewhere above him.

"Always welcome to stay."

Cassy leaned out of the living room window. Her brown hair rustled in the breeze.

Brian waved at her. "Gonna get back and have an early night. But thanks. I'll see you..."

She winked and shut the window.

Brian turned the key and started up the engine, nothing but that stupid David Beckham air freshener for company. He flicked on the radio as he turned onto the main road.

Biffy Clyro playing a live gig at Maida Vale. He thought of Eve. Of Cassy, and her loss. The bottle of pills.

The 24-Hour shop caught Brian's eyes as the vocals bashed their way around his skull. He sharply swung the car into the parking space and turned the radio off.

Biffy Clyro's new stuff was still shit.

And he needed a Becks. Not a Becks-fucking-Blue.

Chapter Twenty-Four.

The headaches and the aching forearm were just a part of Brian's morning routine now.

He shuffled around. His bed felt hard. His neck was stiffer than usual. He opened his eyes and realised he wasn't on the bed but the floor. A strand of saliva formed on the side of his mouth.

What time had he got in?

He'd been to Cassy's. Yes, Cassy's... Then he'd just had a few beers...

He looked around the room. An empty bottle of vodka lay on its side, the smell of stale alcohol torturing his nostrils as dust and damp spread across the floor.

Vodka. He didn't remember buying any vodka.

Oh! He'd been out again. He must have got it later on. Before he rang...

Shit. He'd rung Vanessa.

Turning onto his back, he scrunched his eyes together. *Vanessa*. Why did he always have to turn to her when he was at his worst? He let his arms drop to the floor and spotted his phone, the screen face down. He reached over for it with his aching arm, a bandage drunkenly wrapped around it, and pulled it up above his face. The screen swam out of focus.

A couple of texts, one of them unreadable.

Another: "See you at 11 x"

Shit. He jumped to his feet. Why had he been drinking so heavily? It was just a facade. He didn't need it. He'd never been a big drinker, so he couldn't allow himself to drink. He slipped on a pair of creased trousers and sprayed some deodorant underneath his armpits. Nothing but air squeezed out from the pressurised container. It'd have to do.

As he pushed the door open and looked at his phone again—10:51 a.m.—he remembered their conversation. They'd meet for a walk at... the docklands. Talk things through. The case was over now. Luther was being charged. That was it.

BetterLives was down at the docks. Maybe he could pop in and see to some things...

No. Today was about Vanessa and him. Today was about getting things back on track. He threw himself into the driver's seat of his car, probably still a little over the limit, and swerved out of the tiny car park. He left a plume of exhaust fumes in tow.

#

Vanessa stood by the railings, her blonde hair dancing in the wind as Brian's car pulled up. As he jumped out, he smiled and half-waved at her. She nodded back in acknowledgement, barely smiling.

"I... Sorry I'm a bit late."

She shook her head. "I get it. At least you're not as late as you have been in the past."

Brian could only grit his teeth.

They walked down the promenade. It was a grey, windy day, and the water in the docklands crashed against the sides of the walls as seagulls swooped down at scraps of food and disposed materials.

"How's things?" Vanessa didn't look at Brian. She sounded mechanical. Robotic. Strange, how one could go from talking to someone every day of their life to struggling to find the words to make conversation. Even small talk became a struggle.

"I'm all right," Brian said. "The case is closed. We've got the—"

"Yeah. All over the papers." Vanessa gestured towards the BetterLives office blocks in the distance. "Weird, isn't it?"

"What's weird?"

She let out a high-pitched sigh and slowed down as the wind plummeted against her, her hair flying from her head like a cape. "Just, well... That someone you think is a good person can be so... wrong."

"I guess that depends on what your idea of right and wrong is."

"Killing a girl is wrong, Brian. Don't let your warped sense of morality get in the way of that."

Brian began to boil over. "Hang on," he said, before realising he was shouting. He couldn't lose it in front of her. He knew what he'd look like—the psycho suicidal self-harming husband with a twisted idea of right and wrong. He cleared his throat, took a deep breath, and smiled. "I'm not saying it's not wrong. Of course not. Just that maybe to Luther, what he was doing didn't *seem* wrong. Killers, they work differently to you and me, but they don't see themselves as the bad guys. They justify their actions. We'll find a lot more out soon, anyway."

"Do you think it's him?" Vanessa stopped to lean on the railing. She seemed way too concerned about the case. Surely that wasn't what they were here to discuss? He wanted to build bridges with her, put all of what had happened behind them. But she wasn't letting it go.

"Well, it doesn't matter what I *think*. The evidence points to it being him. He had a relationship with her. He bought her gifts. He kept all of that a secret."

"Any DNA of his at the scene?"

"Yes, he... Look, why are you so concerned?"

Vanessa's eyes narrowed and scanned Brian's face pitifully. "Because I've seen what you're like when you can't let something drop, Brian." She looked down at her feet.

Brian's throat swelled up as he struggled to speak. "This isn't like that," he said. "I'm okay now. That's finished. It's—"

"Then why do you turn up late reeking of booze?"

Brian trained his stare on the ground. He wanted to tell her the truth. He wanted to spit it out to somebody. "I... How... How's Davey?"

Vanessa raised her eyes to the sky as they resumed walking. They approached the steps guarded by a black metal railing, leading down to the water. "He's good. Misses his dad. It's hard trying to explain things to a boy that young. I know you think you have it rough but it's almost harder being the one who *is* there sometimes."

Was she screwing with him? He bit his lip and tried not to say anything. Harder being there for her son? She had no idea. Try telling him it was harder being there when she saw the state of his flat. Try living in that shithole and telling him it's "harder being there".

As they carried on, a flock of seagulls kicked up a fuss by the water's edge as they battled for a piece of food. They swooped and flapped around before snapping at one another.

"You should come 'round sometime," Vanessa said. "Just to see Davey. We can go from there. Can't we?"

Warmth grew in Brian's stomach. "Yeah, that'd..." He stopped walking. "Is that...? Oh. Oh shit."

Vanessa squinted and looked over at where Brian was staring. The seagulls were poking at something green. Squawking. Making a fuss.

"Yeah, I'm not..." Vanessa said, but Brian didn't hear her. He'd already thrown himself over the metal railings and started running down the narrow, slippery concrete steps.

"Brian!" she shouted. "What the hell are you doing?"

Brian's heart pounded as he fanned the seagulls away. They departed almost as soon as his shoes splashed against the waterlogged final step. He reached down into the water, sticking his hand into the jelly-like green substance, and then brought his hand up to his face to examine it.

Adrenaline rushed through Brian's body. "Cyanobacteria..." he mumbled.

BetterLives offices stared over them.

"What?" Vanessa shouted. "Brian, come back, you're—"

"Nicola Watson's underwear." Brian turned to look at his wife as the water engulfed his ankles and soaked the bottom of his trousers. "There were cyanobacteria in her clothes. Her underwear, it was..." The substance dribbled down his arm. He remembered Jeeves' close-up photograph. The photograph with no explanation. "Blue-green algae."

"You aren't making any sense, Brian."

"I think... I need to go to the station and have a word with someone."

Chapter Twenty-Five.

Price sighed as he and Brian stood in the corridor outside the holding cells. His nose was even redder than usual, which was hard, considering it was practically purple every day. Little growls emerged from his throat.

"And you say you found it in the docks?" Price asked, holding the little bag of algae up into the light.

"Right by BetterLives HQ. I was with my wife, and... yeah. I saw some commotion and I—"

"What sort of commotion?" Price interrupted.

Brian cleared his throat. "Seagulls, Inspector. I saw some seagulls causing a bit of, um, commotion—"

"Do you always go chasing seagulls when you're meeting the missus, Brian?" A normal man would have smiled. Winked. Given some sort of indication that he was joking. Price wasn't one of those men. He waited, serious-faced, for an answer as Brian's ears began to heat up.

"No. No, I don't."

Price grunted. "It'd explain a lot."

"Look, I found this blue-green algae in the docks, and Jeeves found traces of blue-green algae in Nicola Watson's underwear. Signs that she'd been in water. If I could just speak to Luther, this could all make so much more sense."

Price raised his eyebrows. "I don't see what else there is to say. We've got semen samples. We've got a confession that he was dating the girl. And now this, from right outside BetterLives HQ. It's just an extra. Maybe they had a fight or something. Who knows?"

"It just doesn't add up."

"What doesn't?"

"I just think it's strange. Why would a man try to drown a girl and then take her to a brothel?"

Price shrugged. "We've got people at Luther's at the moment—people inspecting his home and people inspecting his office. It's not looking good for him. You should chill out. Go for a beer. You've done all right."

"Did anything show up in his office? Wet clothes, anything like that?"

Price shook his head. "His office seems relatively clean, as is his house. The only wet clothes were inside the washing machine."

"Wait—there were wet clothes in his washing machine?"

Price smiled. "Of course there bloody well were!"

"And did you have them checked? Did you—"

"There's no need right now," Price snapped. "We've got our man, Brian. We've got him. If we need to check some bloody wet clothes, we will, but right now, you need to let go. Go home, Detective. You've done great."

Brian sighed, defeated. He'd be willing to wager a bet that those clothes had a trace of blue-green algae on them. The question was, why? He had the pieces of the jigsaw in front of him. If he could just speak to Luther, he could slot it all together...

"Granted, you've pissed off the press and made the police look like fucking party poopers again, but it's in the name of what's right, eh?"

Brian couldn't tell quite how much Price was joking and how much was deadly seriousness. "I need to speak to Luther, just for a few minutes. I know it's not ideal, but anything I can learn about this, it's for the better."

Price sighed. He had nowhere to hide now. He needed to give Brian a straight answer.

"No," Price said. "We formally charge Luther tomorrow. There's no way I'm risking you meddling with the case on some hunch. We've made too many mistakes here, Detective Sergeant. Luther's thirty-six hours of holding are almost up, and I am *not* applying to the Chief Superintendent for an extension, not with the bad rep we've been getting lately. We charge Luther tomorrow. Go home, Brian. Go home."

Brian stood helpless as Price walked back inside his office. He turned around to the holding cells, where DC Carlton guarded the entrance. He had to speak to Luther. The blue-green algae wasn't a coincidence. It couldn't be. Maybe it just further implicated Luther, but Brian couldn't shake the niggling feeling that there was more to it than first seemed.

What was Luther hiding? Brian looked down the corridor. A few officers walked by, engaged with their own work. Price's office door was shut. If Brian knew the Detective Inspector as well as he thought he did, he wouldn't come out of that office for anybody at this time of day. Mealtime.

"Fuck it," he muttered under his breath as he headed towards the holding cells.

DC Carlton smiled at Brian as he approached. "DS McDone. How's the case coming along?"

Brian stopped beside him and leaned against the door to the holding cells. Luther's was on the far right. "Not bad, not bad. How's things with you these days?"

Carlton chuckled. "All's good in the hood, as they say!"

Brian laughed in return. Carlton was a wet lettuce of an officer, an absolute suck-up to anybody and everybody. He was friendly, but just too friendly for this game. If Brian couldn't fool DC Carlton into leaving his post for a few minutes, then he couldn't fool anybody.

"Glad to hear it. Say, you don't mind grabbing me a pasty from the shop, do you? I've just realised I've got some reports to log. Don't want to risk the wrath of the powers above, huh?"

DC Carlton shuffled his feet and looked around. "Well, I'm not supposed to leave, but—"

"Don't worry. I'll keep my spare eye on the cells. Leave the keys with me just in case, if you want?"

"Well, I... Okay, okay. Meat and potato?"

Brian paused for a moment as Carlton handed him the keys. He was gullible, but *this*? "Ask for gluten-free meat and potato, please. Failing that, a chicken tikka wrap. Failing that... well, just leave it for now, okay?" He smiled at him. He'd bought himself as much time as he possibly could. Was there even such thing as gluten-free meat and potato? What even *was* gluten, anyway?

DC Carlton nodded and then scooted off from his post, whistling away as he walked.

When Carlton turned the corner, Brian did a final scan over his shoulder then sneaked through the door to the holding cells.

#

He kept his head down as he walked towards Luther's cell. He couldn't actually believe how easily he'd managed to get in here. Poor DC Carlton, at the food counter pleading for gluten-free meat and potato just to put a smile on Brian's face.

Brian turned back 'round as he slipped the key for Cell 241 into the door. If Price found out, he'd eat him alive. But they didn't have much time, and there were things he needed to understand, things that could aid the case. He held his breath and turned the key.

Luther was slumped on the bed wearing his blue pyjamas. He barely reacted to Brian's entrance. His typically well-groomed face had turned a shade of grey, like a dead fish. His hair, usually so slick and parted in the centre, drooped from his head in a grimy, tangled mess.

"Mr. Luther." Brian edged towards the middle of the room.

"Detective." Robert tilted his head up and puffed out his chest as if to cling to some sort of dignity. He was emasculated, totally ruined, as he sat on the edge of that bed. He wasn't even trying to fight.

"Sleep well last night?"

Luther's disdainful eyes narrowed. Stupid question. Did anybody ever sleep well in here? Brian certainly didn't. He'd done his fair share of time in holding cells when he was younger—drunk and disorderly, and the like. No matter how tough he might have appeared to his friends, it terrified him every single time.

"Look, I can't stay for long, but there's something I found that I was wondering if you could tell us anything about." Brian crouched beside Luther.

"Is it going to prove my innocence?"

"It will help advance the case." Brian pulled the blue-green algae sample out of his top pocket and slipped it into Luther's hand.

Luther moved his thumb over it, his eyes focused on the sample, paying attention to every little crevice.

"Cyanobacteria, also known as blue-green algae. We found it in the docklands opposite BetterLives HQ. It was also in Nicola Watson's underwear. Why would it be there?"

Luther slowed down his investigating of the algae sample and smirked. "Of course. More evidence from your guys. That's all you want from me, to use me and destroy me."

"It is pretty conclusive," Brian cut in. "Traces of you inside her. A clear motive. And now this. Bacterial evidence that Nicola Watson was in the water right beside your little HQ. Yet you still claim you're innocent."

"I don't argue because you've already done all the damage you possibly can. Say it turns out I didn't kill her. Say you find something else out, and you release me, and if I am innocent—then what? What do I have to go back to? BetterLives is ruined. My friends won't be able to look me straight in the eye again. I'm finished..."

Brian smiled. "You say *if* you're innocent. Doesn't sound like a man with a lot of faith in himself."

Luther wiped his eyes and shook his head. "You police officers and your way with words..."

Brian stood up and circled Luther. "Look, Robert. I don't have long here. Either you tell us what's going on concerning the water, or you don't. You were in a relationship with her. She turned down your proposal. And who knows what happened next? But Nicola Watson was in the water that night. And you know something about that, don't you?"

Luther's gaze danced around the cold, hard floor. He sighed and scratched at his arms.

"Did you push her in? Is that it? Tried to drown her but couldn't quite bring yourself to finish the job? Did you dump her in your nice company car and have her ditched at the brothel? Is that it?" Brian leaned in and studied Luther's evasive face. "Did you just want to see what it might feel like to kill her? A test run? Hmm? See what that power felt like? See if you had it—"

"I saved her life, okay?" Robert shouted. Saliva dribbled down his mouth, his eyes bloodshot. Somewhere behind Brian, the door swung open and a guard barged into the cell.

"Come on," he said to Brian. "You shouldn't be in here."

Brian held his arm up to block the guard's grasp. "Wait. What did you say?"

Luther rested his head in his hand. "I... I saved her life."

Brian frowned. "What do you mean, Robert? Come on, I don't have all day."

Robert stood up. He took deep breaths and tried to calm himself, but his hands and chin still shook with nerves. "That night. The night it happened. She came to me after I'd had a few drinks at the staff gathering. It was late—no later than she usually saw me—but something didn't seem right. She was distant, and... and she was trying to tell me something, I think."

Brian scurried around in his pocket for his diary. He shoved the guard away from him. "What was she trying to tell you?"

"I don't know." Luther looked Brian in the eye. "She was kind of ranting. Going on about something she'd found out and something the world needed to know, and how she wasn't sure if I could find out yet. I told her to stop being stupid. I was cold. I was cold because I was worried someone would see her there in my office and get suspicious."

"Come on now, McDone," the guard said. "I won't tell you aga—"

"Shut up," Brian said, turning to the guard. "Can't you see? This is fucking important, all right?"

The guard backed down, cowering. Showed him for what he really was.

"What does this have to do with the water?"

Luther slipped his fingers through his hair again. "She left. And then I saw her on the edge of the docklands. She was going to jump. And then... she jumped."

Butterflies tickled Brian's stomach. "She tried to kill herself?"

"I don't know," Luther said. "I don't know. But if I hadn't gone down there... If I hadn't jumped in and got her out, she'd have frozen. Or died."

"Why didn't you tell us about this earlier?"

"Because I knew this would happen. I knew it would all point back to me and ruin the charity anyway, so I just couldn't risk that. Our charity and the implications of our relationship... I was scared. I was just scared."

"Okay, okay." Brian's head spun with theories. "Where did she go after you got her out of the water?"

Luther looked cooler now, and his hands no longer shook. "She came back to the offices. We sat and had a drink to warm up. Didn't talk, just sat."

"And this was at what time?"

"Around twelve. Around then. I'm not sure. It was a blur. I was tired. Bit shocked."

Twelve. So close to the murder. So, so close to the time of death.

"She was worried about someone. She said someone was after her. Then that was it. She went."

"What do you mean she 'went'?"

"I was going to order her a cab, but it was late and the rates were expensive, so I had one of our drivers take her home. That's the last I saw of her."

"Wait," Brian interrupted, goose pimples spreading across his skin. "A driver?"

Luther shrugged. "Yeah. It seemed like the sensible thing to do. Get her home and get her warm. If only I'd known."

Brian's stomach rattled with adrenaline. "Did you see the driver?"

Luther scanned the room. "No... I assumed it was all right. Besides, you've checked the drivers—"

"We didn't check the drivers. We..." Brian remembered Price's words when he'd asked Luther to show him the rota. "*Final straw, Brian.*" Then, nothing more said of it. Nothing more investigated.

"You don't think..." Luther started.

"Where can I see that rota?"

"It should be on my desk, like it always is."

The room swirled as the realisation started to dawn on Brian. He tried to process stimuli as he shook Luther's hand and left the cell. Luther said things to him, asked him questions, but it was pointless.

"Come on, you," the guard said as he pulled Brian into the corridor.

The world buzzed around him.

They were so wrong about all of this. All this time, and they'd been looking in the wrong place.

#

The guard slammed the cell door shut, sour after the disrespect Brian had shown him. He held Brian's arms and pushed him along the corridor like a criminal. Brian thought about apologising for the exchange, but that was no use. If the guard wanted to, he could go away, throw darts at pictures of Brian's face—whatever guards did to let off steam.

Price was waiting for him at the other end of the corridor, shaking his head. Cassy was by his side. "Detective Sergeant, do I need to remind you what I told you five minutes ago?"

"Price, I was right. There's more to it. There's—"

"You've gone against policy, Brian. You've committed a very serious offence, not just against this police department, but against my trust." He snatched the keys from the guard's hands and stuffed them in his pocket. "Is there anything you have to say for yourself?"

"I want some officers down at the Watson household. Right this second."

Price frowned. "What d'you mean?"

Brian yanked free of the guard's grip. "First, I want you to check that rota of Luther's. Y'know, the one you made me dismiss? Is there anyone at BetterLives right now?"

"Well, we can—" Price started.

"Call them. Now."

Price's cheeks flushed. Typically, he would've reminded Brian of their ranks, but he lifted the phone to his ears nonchalantly. "Pete. Yeah, yeah. We have an officer asking about Luther's driver rota here. Got any eyes on it? Yeah, he..." Price shrugged, uncertain of what he was looking for.

"Ask him who's on the rota from twelve to one."

"Who's—Oh, you heard that? Good. Wh... Oh. Yeah, I... Thanks." Price moved the phone from his head. "A driver-for-hire. Sometimes, BetterLives bring outside drivers in. They're a voluntary company, so they don't have much funding for cars."

"Get the cars ready and get a team down to the Watsons' house right now. We need to speak to Scott again," Brian said.

Price's stare followed Brian as he zipped up his coat.

"And in the meantime, I want some more officers down at BetterLives investigating every one of their vehicles. You coming with me, Cassy?"

She waited for Price's approval.

"Wait a second," Price said. "What's going on here?"

"McDone!" DC Carlton bounced down the corridor with a proud smile, holding a pasty in the air. "McDone! I found a gluten-free!"

Price eyed DC Carlton up and pulled a disgusted face. "Get into my office right this second, Carlton, you dumb piece of shit."

DC Carlton's eyes welled up as he looked at the officers with confusion. He slumped and walked towards Price's office, the prize pasty still in his hand.

"Are you going to explain yourself, McDone?" Price said. "Because if you don't, then I have very good reason to—"

"The driver, Price. The driver. Scott Watson was working the town the night his sister died. He was off his face on drugs. Price, Scott Watson is a *driver*. I have reason to believe the last person Nicola Watson saw was a driver." He bit his lip as adrenaline poured through his fingertips. "Price, I think Scott killed his sister."

Chapter Twenty-Six.

Brian pressed his foot against the accelerator and shot down the road, the rest of the traffic wary not to get caught by the speed cameras. They placed the cameras so tactically these days, giving drivers a nice, empty stretch of road to speed down, only to catch them. It was all a trap. But security had to make their money somehow.

"Can I confirm your position?" Brian shouted into the walkie-talkie.

"We're outside the house," DC Thompson said. He rarely got off his arse, but he was a decent enough officer when he had to be.

"Wait for my signal. We want to be smooth about this. Don't want to go in there doing anything rash."

"Yeah, yeah," Thompson said. The radio fizzled out. Cassy scratched her knees in the passenger seat as Brian stepped harder on the accelerator.

"You don't have to worry about how fast I'm going." Brian noticed her gaze wander towards the steering wheel. She winced as he jolted around corners. "Been doing this for years."

"Right." She inched back in the seat. "Hardly reassuring, but whatever."

Two police cars waited as he spun the tires onto the pavement and crept towards the Watsons' driveway. He stopped the car, the engine still running, and raised his hand in greeting at the car on the opposite side of the drive. A hand rose, and a woman dressed in full uniform stepped out of the car.

Brian took a deep breath and reached for his box of paracetamol. He tilted it into his hand, but nothing fell out. "Could've sworn I had a few left."

Cassy rolled her eyes and reached for the door handle.

"Ah-ah, not so fast. DC Thompson and DC Forbes go to the door first. Then we follow." He glanced at the cars in front. Thompson and Forbes moved towards the door, Forbes' blonde hair dangling from underneath her police hat, Thompson as sour-faced as ever.

"Since when did you start settling for backup?" Cassy asked.

"Just gotta do what you're told sometimes." Brian gritted his teeth as Thompson and Forbes approached the front door. Thompson stuck a thumb up at Brian and raised his hand towards the door, knocking three times against the frosted glass.

"Didn't know you were a man to do what he was tol—"

"Right, come on." Brian pulled himself out of the car and slammed the door, then raced towards the house. Cassy barely had time to register his movements as she scrambled in her seat and stepped out of the car, struggling to hit the lock button on the keys.

"What's up?" she shouted.

DC Forbes was messing around with her phone outside the Watson household, DC Thompson nowhere in sight.

"Has he done a runner?" Brian asked.

DC Forbes nodded as she continued to shout things down the phone. "Yes. Yeah..." She looked at Brian. "Follow DC Thompson. See if you can flank him out. He must've just now jumped over the fields. Can't be far. Quick!"

Brian's heart raced before he'd even had the chance to run. "Come on, Cas," he said as he broke into a jog.

They ran around the side of the house and towards the partly open gate in the back garden, still swinging from recent use. The little shit must've seen them coming. He threw one leg in front of the other, trying to build up speed as he waddled out of the gate and onto the field area. In the distance, he saw Thompson, and then another figure, slightly further ahead. They were too far to bother catching up with.

Brian, panting at the edge of the garden, rested his hands on his knees. Cassy almost stumbled over him when she saw him there, gasping for air.

"Aren't we gonna carry on?" she shouted. "We can't just let him—"

"Get back to the car," Brian shouted, struggling for breath. "We'll... we'll try and—and get 'round the back. Only... only place he can end up is the old water works. Nowhere to go." Sweat dripped from his forehead.

"You really need to get some proper exercise, mate." Cassy patted him on the back and jogged to the car.

The specks of DC Thompson and Scott Watson grew ever smaller in the distance.

#

Brian waddled back to the front of the house. He fumbled around for the door handle and shook his head in disbelief as he dropped into the passenger seat.

"Why aren't you driving?" he snapped.

"Because I was waiting for—"

"No time for waiting around, Cas. Get your foot on that pedal and get down to the water works."

Cassy slammed her foot on the accelerator. Brian jolted backwards, wincing as his teeth pierced his tongue.

"I don't mind waiting around for a moment," Cassy said. "I'm a better driver than you, anyway."

Brian, forgetting he'd accidentally bitten it just moments earlier, bit his tongue in anger and yelped in pain. His cheeks flushed. *Fuck*. Totally shown up. He wiped his head and held his breath as Cassy swung the car onto the main road and tore towards the old water works.

"Thompson, any updates?" Brian shouted into the walkie-talkie. The feedback buzzed at him momentarily before Thompson responded.

"—Gone into the water works. Just—can't get far now—can—"

Something exploded in the microphone. Everything went silent.

"Thompson?"

"What was that?" Cassy asked.

"Thompson? Are you there?"

The speaker continued to rattle and whine. Brian was totally silent as Cassy slowed the car down,
approaching the water works.

"Brian? What is it?"

Brian, wide-eyed and in a haze, plucked at his
seat. Memories flooded back into his head. *"Brian,
are you there, Brian? Stay with me, Brian."*

Then the long lie-ins. Vanessa and Davey leaving. The razor blades and the fake alcoholism.

Nicola Watson.

"Brian?"

Brian snapped out of his trance and looked over
at Cassy, who leaned against the steering wheel.
"What is it? Are you coming?"

Brian attempted to crack a smile. "Sure. Sure.
Let's go get him."

#

The water works weren't so much water works
anymore, more a collection of unused pipes under
which the homeless and the junkies hid. Plenty of
spots for a criminal to flee to.

Rain lashed down on Thompson, his hood tightly wrapped around his head. He rushed over to the car as Brian and Cassy arrived. "Sorry about before," he said, biting at his nails. "Dropped my blooming radio, didn't I?"

Brian sighed. *He was okay. He'd just dropped his radio, that's all.* "It's okay. Any sign of him?"

Thompson puffed his cheeks and glanced around the derelict wasteland of rusty pipes and mounds of concrete. "One second I was on to him, the next, nada. But he can't have got too far, you wouldn't think. Skinny lad like that. He'll be round here somewhere. Probably hiding in one of the pipes or something."

Brian moved around the pipes as more rain poured down from the concrete-grey sky. Stacks of empty beer bottles and broken glass filled the interior of the pipes—an absolute haven for drug addicts. The pipes provided shelter and security, at least for a short while, anyway. He walked forward, Cassy and Thompson following, the waterlogged gravel drenching his shoes.

Clatter.

He swung around to face the abandoned pipe up ahead.

Clatter.

Somebody was inside.

He gestured over to the other side of the pipe. Thompson nodded and flanked left, while Brian crept towards the right-hand side. He rested his hand on the side of the pipe. All he could hear was the rain hitting the ground and his pulse racing in his head. He looked over at Thompson, who leaned against the opposite side of the pipe, and held three fingers up.

Three, two, one...

The pair of them swung round and turned into the pipe.

"Oh, for fuck's sake," Thompson said.

Three crows feasted on a dead rat, their sharp beaks scraping against the interior of the pipe. *Clatter. Clatter.*

"Bloody hell," Brian said. "Sick of these bloody animals."

"Brian! Thompson!"

Brian swung around. Cassy pointed to the other side of the water works. He squinted and tried to see what it was.

"He's there," she whispered.

Brian's eyes adjusted. Cassy wasn't pointing towards the other side of the water works, but in fact was pointing to the pipe entrance just a few feet away.

Scott Watson was completely static. He stood in front of the pipe. His distant gaze wandered around, unfocused. "Please, don't hurt me."

Thompson turned, and his jaw dropped as Scott emerged from the pipe behind him. Scott had his hands above his head. Tears poured down his cheeks as he snivelled in the rain. He had something in his hand. Something small. Something dark.

Brian reached for the cuffs. "Keep your hands where I can see them."

Scott sniffed as Thompson threw himself towards him and tackled him to the ground as if he was in a rugby match, knocking the wind out of Scott's lungs. The black object flew out of Scott's hand and into the mud.

"Scott Watson, I am arresting you on suspicion of—"

"It isn't true," Scott shouted, waving his hands around manically. "It's all because of the ring... One big mistake..."

"—I'm arresting you on the suspicion of the murder of Nicola Watson on January 3rd. You do not have to say anything—"

"Just, please, just check it. Check what she found. I was scared. I thought... I've been smoking.

I've been smoking, and I ran because I thought you... Please."

Thompson smacked Scott's back and twisted his hands behind him. He slipped Brian's cuffs around his wrists and dragged Scott, who continued to rant and rave, towards the van.

"Just... just check it, please. Just check—" His cries were drowned out as Thompson threw him into the back of the car, in which Forbes had just arrived, and locked the door. He nodded at Brian and walked towards the front, tossing the key into the air.

"What d'you think he's on about?" Cassy asked.

Brian crouched down and reached into the mud for the object that Scott Watson had been holding above his head. It was a SanDisk pen drive, no larger than a small key ring. He slipped it into his pocket and smiled at Cassy.

"He's stoned as hell, but it looks like we've got our man."

Chapter Twenty-Seven.

By the time the police car had taken Scott Watson back to the station, it was already too late to begin questioning. The sun had set, which didn't take much, thanks to the glorious British weather. Scott had been granted an eight-hour lie-down due to the high levels of marijuana pumping through his system. When he sobered up, he'd have a rude awakening to deal with.

Brian gritted his teeth as he trailed behind Price. "Is there no way you can rearrange so we can talk to him tonight? Just switch a few things around, and—"

"Brian," Price said firmly, turning to face him. "Go home. Get some sleep. We've got him. Officers we sent down to BetterLives have done some digging and confirmed that Scott drove for them at various times, including that night at the time of his sister's murder. And some very interesting reports got back to me that you'll be pleased to hear. Scott Watson's fingerprints are all over a BetterLives vehicle that was out between twelve and one. And to boot, that weed running through the little stoner's system? It looks like it's the stuff Molfer's investigating. Which means that hopefully, we'll get a nice little word on where he got it. Two birds with one stone, Brian. We've got him." He planted his heavy hand on Brian's shoulder and attempted a friendly smile. It didn't suit his face. "Good job." Then he turned around and scooted down the corridor.

Brian looked towards the holding area where Robert Luther was kept. All going to plan, Robert Luther would be back out in the open again tomorrow, free of charge. A formal apology, then off he went. Another day of not knowing. Another day of the press following another lead.

"You okay?" Cassy stepped to Brian as he stood helplessly in the corridor.

"Just want to get it all sorted now. Had it up to here with this fucking case." He pointed towards the top of his neck. "You?"

Cassy sighed and diverted her gaze to the floor. The black edges of her mascara trickled onto her cheeks. "It just... it just all seems so... anti-climactic, you know? Like... I just don't understand why. If it was Scott Watson, I don't understand why."

A lump grew in Brian's throat. A lump of inevitable dissatisfaction that came at the conclusion of any big case. He set his hand on Cassy's shoulder. "Let me drive you home. I know the feeling, I promise."

Cassy pursed her lips. Maybe they'd have a few drinks. Get warm on the sofa. He could do with some company.

"It's all right," she said, avoiding his gaze.

"No, really," Brian said softly. "Let me take you back. We'll have that game of cards we spoke about. If you're in the frame of mind for losing, that is."

Cassy laughed and, shaking her head, looked towards her feet. "It's um... it's all right. I've—I'm seeing someone tonight."

"Who... What do you mean seeing someone?"

Cassy rolled her eyes. "I mean seeing someone," she said. "Meeting a bloke. Having a drink. Maybe see where it goes. Remember what that felt like, Granddad?"

Brian tried to grin as Cassy smiled back at him. *Some bloke. Some lucky fucking bloke.* "Well, he—this bloke, he's... he's all right, isn't he? What's his—his name?"

Cassy raised her eyebrows. "Why you so interested?"

"No, no, I'm just... It's natural for a 'granddad' to show concern, right?"

Cassy nodded slowly. "Right. Truth be told, I'm knackered, but I'm hardly gonna stand the poor lad up."

Stand him up. Stand the bastard up.

"Anyway, you should get some kip."

"Yeah. I might head back and meet a friend. Or something."

"Oh, yeah! Meet a friend. That's a good idea, yeah."

The pair of them walked in silence. *Meet a friend.* Who was he kidding? Was his friend called Jack Daniels?

"Well, enjoy your date," Brian said, waving Cassy off.

"Yeah. Yeah, I will." She disappeared down the corridor.

Brian exhaled and wiped the sweat off his cheeks. Why had he even reacted that way? An old bloke like him would never have a shot with a pretty young girl like her. And still, he had Ness. He had his life to get back to. He and Ness could give it another go. They had to. That was his life.

"By the way," Cassy called.

Brian jumped as Cassy popped her head back 'round into the corridor.

"He's called Ryan." She winked at Brian and vanished down the staircase.

Ryan. Of course. The better fucking name. It was always the Ryans who defeated the Brians. At least she might accidentally whisper Brian's name when Ryan was fucking her.

Bloody Ryan.

#

Brian scrunched the carrier bag in his hands as he hopped up the stairs and entered his room. The corridor reeked of urine. Probably the homeless scrote again. He seemed to be pissing closer and closer to his door the more time progressed. He'd have to get them seen to, have a stern word with them. Now the Nicola Watson case was all but over, he needed something a little lighter to con-centrate on.

A copy of the *Lancashire News* from earlier that day was wedged underneath Brian's door. He picked it up and glanced at the headline: "Local Charity in Jeopardy as Murder Saga Spirals On". A picture of Robert Luther shaking the hand of a passer-by. Smiles all round.

No doubt, tomorrow it'd be news of Scott Wat-son: "Brother Involved in Murder Shocker". It was all just one big soap opera story to them. That's what it was like when they weren't directly in-volved in the reality of it all; they always sought the dramatic conclusion. Sure, the *Lancashire News* might have been the biggest celebrators of the hard work and ethics of BetterLives, but the moment a tiny piece of information about a potential link to something dirty, they were the first to crucify them. Business was business.

And Scott Watson. At first, Brian thought the lad had just smoked a little too much weed. Tomor-row would reveal what led to his sister's death, but it was all starting to click into place. *"I'm a driver,"* he'd told Brian and Cassy back at the first interview in the Watson house. A bloody driver. How'd he let that information slip? And his parents—they never said anything about him working. Never elaborated. Did they suspect some sort of involvement, too?

Brian tossed the newspaper to one side and undid his tie. Takeaway menus and dirty shirts were scattered around the floor. The creased curtains were half-open, the faint smell of body odour in the air. It was only eight p.m. Too early for bed. Too early for a release? His arm ached, begging him for an intervention...

As he took his coat off, something dropped against the floor. He reached down, expecting it to be a loose pound coin, but a red and black SanDisk pen drive stared up at him. The one Scott Watson had been holding, the one he'd apparently ordered from Amazon and mixed up with Nicola's ring. Damn it—he'd forgotten to check it in to property. He scooped it up in his hand and placed it next to his computer.

He picked his phone out of his pocket and began to key in Price's direct number. If he were lucky, he'd get hold of Price before he left for home.

As he typed in the final four numbers, he thought about Danny Stocks' visit the other day. *"Maybe they don't want you to find out."* The urgency to arrest Scott Watson. The timing. Was he being paranoid? 'Course he was. Price had arrested Luther. He was willing to let Luther go down.

Wasn't he?

Brian cringed and swiped the number out of his phone before tossing it to one side and jamming the pen drive into his computer.

He booted up his computer and waited for it to load. Some McAfee thing that expired weeks ago. A woman that he'd accidentally picked up from a porno site creeping across his screen. The little "new devices detected" bubble in the bottom right. He clicked on it, and the contents of the pen drive opened up.

Three folders: *Work. School. Charity.*

As Brian clicked into the *Charity* folder, it became clear who had been using Scott's missing pen drive.

"'Nicola Watson, 22," her rÉsumÉ read. That was the only file in the *Charity* area. Nothing suspicious. He should just ring up and report it in to property. But why would Nicola Watson use her brother's pen drive?

He exited and double clicked on the *School* icon. Perhaps it was just some old work she'd forgotten to delete. He exhaled as the *School timetable* folder spread across the screen. He double clicked it out of curiosity.

Inside, he found another three folders. Inside one of those, another seven.

He clicked more frantically, disappearing into an abyss as the little blue icons tripled in number. Abstract titles.

School.

Healey Way.

Reports.

Brian's heart was in his throat when he saw the title of the final folder.

Proof.

He inhaled deeply and double clicked.

Nothing in there. Empty.

He slammed his fist against the desk, shaking the cursor of the mouse in frustration. All of that effort leading to a dead end. He'd felt so close to something, too. He'd have to call in to property and let them have a look through.

He glanced up at the screen again. His mouse cursor had moved. He noticed a folder hidden away in the bottom corner of the window. He double-clicked it.

Something banged outside his room. Voices and commotion. He looked over at his door to check it was locked then double-clicked on the first document inside the folder.

It was a photograph titled *P.G. 1*. He couldn't initially make out what it showed, other than metal fencing in front of some sort of lock-up, taken from a distance.

But as he flicked through the pictures, all taken at the same location, a figure emerged.

The figure had his back to the camera, so he was hard to make out, but Brian could tell from his wiry hair and hunched demeanour who it was. He walked towards the door of the lockup, and then looked over his shoulder. Then he disappeared inside.

Brian scanned the rest of the contents of the folders, his hand shaking against his mouse. He yanked the pen drive out of the computer, but the photograph didn't leave the screen and stayed imprinted on his retina.

The undeniable photograph of Michael Walters entering the lock-up from distance, taken by Nicola Watson.

Brian might not have known what exactly it meant yet, but one thing was for certain: Nicola Watson was watching Michael Walters for some reason, and she'd died shortly after.

It might have been late, but there was only one place for him to go to get to the bottom of this right now.

Chapter Twenty-Eight.

Moths danced around the light outside Michael Walters' house as Brian's car crept onto the pavement. Rain flickered in the glow of the Victorian street lamp. Michael Walters' front door was large, with a circular brass handle. Hanging baskets of red flowers dangled beside the entrance, dim light glowing from the leaded windows.

The shot of Michael Walters entering the lock-up, looking over his shoulder, taken by Nicola Watson. She knew something. And all of the photos labelled *P.G. 1. P.G. 2.* What did it mean?

One thing was for certain; she knew something about Michael Walters. She knew something about that lockup. And she'd been killed for it.

Brian checked his phone. Two missed calls. Whoever it was could wait. He didn't want to get anyone else involved with what he was doing. At least, not yet. He switched the phone to "silent" and stuffed it into his pocket before stepping out of the car.

Brian hopped across Michael Walters' freshly resurfaced driveway and past his shiny blue Honda. He knocked firmly at the door three times.

A movement in the light, a shuffling around inside. Then the rattling of keys against the door.

What was he going to say? How was he going to handle this?

Michael Walters pulled the door open. His eyes widened when he saw Brian staring at him. He was dressed in a red jumper, wiping a plate in his hand.

"I... Sorry, I wasn't expecting you, Officer. Is there anything I can help you with?" He took a glance over Brian's shoulder.

Brian nodded. "There's just a few things I need to talk to you about. About the case. Luther... your boss. He might be innocent." He bit his tongue and waited for Walters to take the bait.

Play it cool. Give him what he wants.

Walters raised his eyebrows. "Well of course he is. Would you... It's awfully rainy out there. Would you like to come inside for a moment, Officer?"

Brian held his breath and walked through the doorway, his wet black shoes marking the cream carpet, rain dripping down the sides of his face. What was he thinking?

Walters grabbed Brian's coat and eyed up the damp patch Brian's shoes had made on the carpet. "I'll take them off." Brian gestured towards his shoes. Michael nodded and moved through to the kitchen.

Brian followed him in, past the wooden cabinet in the hallway. Photographs of Michael and a woman. Ex-wife. Still obsessed, no doubt. He looked around for signs of keys. Something that would lead him to this lockup from the photographs. He needed to see what was in there. He needed to know what was so important.

Brian walked into the open kitchen/dining room area. The tiles were checkered black and white, the surfaces sparkling clean in the vibrant spotlights. "A drink?" Michael asked, pouring a spot of gin into a glass.

Could he perhaps have one glass? Put across an atmosphere of normality? Brian raised his hand. "No thanks. Just here to check a few things."

Michael shrugged and twisted the top off the bottle. "Well, suit yourself." He knocked back his drink. "You know, I'm not proud of what I did, Officer."

"What you did?"

"The prostitutes," Michael whispered as if people were listening in. "No man is proud of doing that sort of thing. But I was at a loose end. I just want that to be clear. I don't want us to have any misunderstanding about that."

Brian leaned back against the black marble kitchen worktop. "Right. It's... I'm not here about that, anyway. I was just wondering about the night Nicola Watson was murdered. We've arrested her brother on suspicion. He's a driver. Probably the last person to see her."

Michael stared at Brian, gently shaking his glass below his chin. "Is that so? Well, what does that mean for Robert? And for BetterLives?"

How far could he go with this? If Price knew he was here... No. That didn't warrant even thinking about. "There are still a few loose ends. Don't take this the wrong way, Michael, but I just find it hard to believe that you wouldn't have known about Robert and Nicola's relationship if you two were as close as you make out."

Michael's face dropped as he moved to the sink. Cutlery had drained onto the marble surface, bone-dry. "I wondered when I was going to slip up about that."

Brian edged towards the other side of the room as Michael rested his hands against the sink. "So you knew?"

"Yes. Yes, I knew. I... Officer, do you have a warrant to be here?"

Brian gulped. "It's just a personal visit. Just a few questions I had. But they could greatly benefit your boss."

Michael stared at Brian with his squinty grey eyes before sighing again. "Right. The DVD footage I took from CityWatch. I said... I told you I was trying to remove the CCTV from the nights I'd met the escorts. I lied. And Officer, I'm so sorry for this, but it was a DVD of Robert meeting with Nicola. A video of her in the office. I... When I heard the news about the girl's death, I panicked. I didn't think anything of it before then. But I guess I was just looking out for the charity. Just trying to do the right thing."

Michael raised himself from the sink and took a sharp sniff. "I'm truly sorry, Officer." He moved closer to Brian. "Sorry for lying. I thought it was the right thing to do. Evidently not."

"It's okay. Do you have the DVD in your possession?"

Michael stared right through Brian in the room's perfect silence. Was he on to him? He smiled. "I believe I do. It's upstairs. You'll give me a moment, won't you? I'll go get it for you."

Michael scooted out of the kitchen. The sound of his feet clattering up the steps echoed through the ceiling, the floorboards creaking above Brian's head.

Brian glanced around as the floor above continued to creak. A dining area at the other side of the kitchen worktop, and a conservatory style extension with wooden floorboards and a large, cream leather sofa. Brian peeked through the kitchen door to check he was still alone.

As he reached the conservatory area, with various potted plants resting against the windows, he spotted a few books on the coffee table. Aristotle, the latest Clive Barker book, and a little grey notepad with a bookmark sticking out of the top.

The creaking continued above Brian's head. He looked over his shoulder again. He had time just to have a look inside the pad, didn't he? Just a glance?

He scooped the pad into his hand and flipped it open to the bookmark.

Inside the yellowing pages was a list of dates, organised meetings with various charities and individuals. Brian flicked through. The children's hospital. Westholme Psychiatric Clinic. Fair enough. Places in which BetterLives would be interested.

He looked closer between a few of the lines and saw a star and smiley face, with initials below.

*28th Nov - * :)*

P.R.H.

P.R.H. Preston Royal Hospital.

Brian examined the notepad. More lists of dates. More smiley faces and initials.

W.H.B

B.B.F

He needed something. Surely, there must be something.

More creaking above his head.

Pembrokeshire Garage.

He stopped, his heart racing.

Pembrokeshire Garage.

P.G.

The garage from the photographs. He'd seen it before, of course he had. Disused nowadays. Old family business that closed down years ago. But why did Michael Walters need to visit there? And what were the smiley faces all about? Why did BetterLives need the garage?

He shut the book and placed it on the table. He turned around and almost fell back as he looked at the kitchen door.

Michael Walters stood in front of him, holding a DVD in his hand.

They stared at each other for a moment, Brian's whole body shaking and his mind frozen. *Think, Brian. Think.*

"Just... Clive Barker. Not a fan. Never been a fan—"

"I'm of the rare camp that actually thinks his work has improved in recent years." Walters looked down at the books.

He knew.

Brian could only smile and nod. "Right, right."

The creaking. Definitely still creaking upstairs.

"I don't believe you've met Rex, my Rottweiler, have you?" Michael asked.

Brian's hands shook. *Rex.* How many other secrets was Michael Walters hiding?

"He gets awfully active when he smells new people in the house. Very protective. Anyway..." Michael reached for his notepad and aligned it with the edge of the table. "The DVD. It's here, if you want to watch it. Nothing you don't already know, though."

Brian grabbed the DVD and stuffed it in his jacket pocket.

"Again, I am truly sorry for my lapse in judgement, Officer." Michael's eyes narrowed as they scanned Brian's face.

"Not a problem." Brian walked towards the door. "Not a problem. I'll be in touch. It'll all be sorted soon. Thanks for your honesty."

Michael fluttered his eyelashes as Brian stepped out of the kitchen towards the front door. The walls of the hallway swallowed him up. The pictures of Michael Walters and his wife glared back at him. He slipped his shoes back on his feet and fumbled around with the front door. It wouldn't open. The creaking. Rex. *Fuck. Open. Open.*

"You know, it's a real shame, about Nicola." Michael reached over Brian's shoulder and slid the lock open. He could feel Michael's breath on his neck. "Such a life-affirming young girl. Life-affirming, yes. I do hope you get to the bottom of this, Officer." He smiled at Brian and moved back from the door as Brian turned the handle with his shaking hand.

"I thought you never spoke to Nicola Watson." Brian stepped out into the rain and wind, the faulty streetlight flickering above his head.

Michael stood in his doorway and stared at Brian. "I... What I meant to say, was that I got the impression that she was a bubbly girl. Goodnight, Officer." He shut the door, and his silhouette disappeared out of sight.

Brian rushed to his car and threw himself inside. He took a moment to find his breath, rubbing his cold hands against his tingling, hot neck.

He switched the engine on and looked at the digital clock—21.48. It would take him ten minutes to get to where he needed to go. He pulled his phone out of his pocket. Another two missed calls, this time from Vanessa. He'd ring her later. He'd call the police as soon as he found what was in there. But Walters suspected him. He knew he suspected him. That look of knowing. Catching Brian sneaking around in his books.

Brian revved up the engine and pushed his foot against the accelerator, turning out onto the main road. There was only one place on his mind right now.

Pembrokeshire Garage.

What was BetterLives hiding that was worth Nicola Watson's life?

Chapter Twenty-Nine.

Pembrokeshire Garage looked just like it did in Nicola Watson's photographs.

Rain lashed down as Brian rushed over to the metal gating surrounding the garage. A rusty No Entry sign dangled on the fencing outside. His boots splashed in the murky puddles as he ignored the sign and jogged closer to the garage, its blue paintwork giving way to an onslaught of damp and moss.

"Pembrokeshire Garage: First For All You're Motoring Needs". To those who noticed it, the grammatical error of "You're" had become a part of the garage's urban allure back in the day. The owners weren't the sort of people you'd want to point that sort of thing out to. Fat Steve—links with some of the major North West gangs. "Posh toff bastards," he'd say. "We'll say 'your' 'owever we bloody want." Fat Steve was right about one thing; he probably could spell "your" however he wanted, seeing as he was locked in prison these days. After his arrest, the business had collapsed. Fat Steve's kids closed the place up, having decided running a small business was more effort than it was worth in this economic climate. Another place lost to the new world.

Until Nicola Watson's photographs. *P.G.* Michael Walters, sneaking inside. What did it all mean?

When he reached the entrance to the garage, Brian pushed against the door, padlocked shut. *Damn it.* But the padlock was interesting. It shone in the rain, not a scratch on its surface. Newly installed.

Somebody didn't want anyone to see what was inside.

Brian let go of the lock, sighing as he turned back towards the road. His phone vibrated against his leg. Unknown number. Someone selling something. They always called at this time. Ten-fucking-p.m. He hit the red button and tucked it back into his pocket before arching his neck to look over the top of the building, scanning for some sort of entrance.

Down the side of the garage, he saw stacks of old tires, various tools, and a window. Small, but... could he fit through it? He wasn't *that* big, was he?

He rushed to the frosted glass window and looked over his shoulder as a car passed by, splashing rain up onto the pavement. Was he insane? He crouched down to pick up a rock, covered in woodlice, on the floor. He dropped it to the ground before tutting and picking it up again. Seriously, was he going to break in? What if somebody saw him? How would he explain that?

He bit his lip and shut his eyes.

Glass cracked in front of him.

When he opened his eyes again, he couldn't help but smile, like a child enjoying great success at a game of 'Knock a door, run'. He'd made a pretty clean job of the window. He scanned the surrounding area again; no movement other than the rain in the yellow glow of the street lamps. When he saw he was clear, he clawed at the shards of glass spiking upwards from the window ledge, covering his hand with the bottom of his sleeve as he cracked them out of place.

When the ledge seemed clear, he rubbed the back of his hand against the window one final time to check for any loose pieces before propping his head through the glass. The room was pitch black, with a smell of damp, old cardboard.

Was he actually going to do this?

Fuck it. Might as well finish the job.

He groaned as he stuffed his upper body through the gap. In a moment of sheer terror, he thought he wouldn't be able to pull his stomach through. What a sight that would be. It'd be on one of those video-sharing websites. *Robbery Gone Wrong.* A cop's fat arse sticking out of a window, legs waving all over the place. Desperate not to let that happen, he thrust his body in through the gap and held his breath as he tumbled into the garage, landing shoulder-first on the dusty concrete floor below. He winced and clutched at his shoulder but breathed a sigh of relief as he saw the glow of light and rain outside.

He was in.

Finally dragging himself to his feet, Brian grabbed his phone, but the dim screen light didn't reveal much. Cabinets with untouched folders stacked on top of one another. Dusty surfaces and cobweb-covered tyres. Movements, just out of sight. No. Nothing there. Just him. He held his hand out as he edged through the room, searching the walls for a light switch.

When he finally found one, he pressed it, ready to be bathed in light.

Nothing.

Fuck. The electric—probably switched off years ago. Fat load of use he was. He had a torch in the car, too. Idiot. Absolute idiot.

Then he remembered the app Cassy had installed for him. He thumbed the screen of the phone. *You better not have bloody deleted it.*

"God, thank you." He grinned in victory as the Flashlight app beamed to life on his phone.

Maybe apps were all right after all.

He squinted around the room. Nothing visible. More dust. More tyres. Folders and tools scattered around on the floor. Scrunched up papers. He stepped into the centre of the room, every footstep kicking up a cloud of dust.

Something caught his eye near his feet. It glowed in the flashlight; it was small, hard, and unlike anything else around. He grabbed it and turned it over. An Action Man figure. The one with the spacesuit. *Weird.* Not the sort of thing you'd expect Michael Walters to be into.

He gulped as he walked over to the desk and reached into the box of videotapes. *Recess. Hey Arnold.* Cartoon after cartoon.

Then, handcuffs.

And a camera.

Brian's body tensed up as he picked up the camera. The walls felt like they were closing in around him. His hands shook as he flicked the "on" switch.

The camera booted up immediately.

Brian threw it to the ground and collapsed to his knees, heaving.

#

He wasn't sure how long he had been on his knees. All he could think of was the pictures. The images.

It could have been Davey...

No. It wasn't Davey. Don't think of things that way.

He reached for the camera again with his shaking hand and threw it back into the box of videos as if it was coated in venom. His head throbbed. Nicola Watson knew. She knew what Michael Walters was doing—what he was doing in the name of BetterLives—and he killed her for it.

He needed to get out of here. He needed to call Cassy, call the police. Someone. Anyone. He needed to stop Walters, right now.

Brian sprinted over towards the window, stumbling over the Action Man figure, and threw the video box out of the window before pulling himself up. Pain shot through his shoulder as adrenaline pumped through his arms. He winced as a shard of glass nipped at his hand. He tumbled right through the window, into the hard stones and puddles below. A group of nearby youths in hoodies laughed.

"Top lad," one shouted. "Fucking top lad!"

Dicks.

He had to ring Cassy. He had to warn her. He went into his contacts list and hit Cassy's name.

One ring.

Come on. Answer. Answer.

Two rings.

This was serious. It was—

"Hello?"

"Cassy, I... You need to... Cas, just listen—"

"Woah. Slow down, Brian. What's going on with you?"

Brian rubbed his eyes, the taste of metal in his mouth. His left palm streamed with blood. *Shit.* Vanessa would suspect him. The hospital would ask to see his arm, and they'd know what he'd been doing.

No. Focus. Deal with that later. He needed to get this sorted. He needed to get the case solved.

"Cas, it's the case... Michael Walters. You need to get a team down there right now, because I'll be there waiting—"

"Wait," she said. Brian heard voices and the clinking of glasses on the other end of the line. "I'm out at the moment, remember?"

Brian pushed the metal gate to one side and jogged towards his car, his entire body drenched in rain and mud. Her date with Ryan. Of course. "Cassy—it's him. He killed Nicola Watson. The pen drive that Scott dropped—it's the information Nicola was trying to hide. She knew about him, Cas. She knew what Michael was doing, and he killed her because he couldn't risk it coming out. He couldn't be found out."

"You still aren't making sense. Do you want me to put you through to Price?"

Brian sat back in his car and rubbed a hand through his wet hair. "Michael Walters was exploiting BetterLives to access various organisations. Children's hospitals. Orphanages. He was doing nasty things, Cassy. Things no one should ever have to see. Cassy... I have the camera here. I have the evidence. He's sick. Nicola knew. She knew all along. Just get someone down to Michael's place right now."

The line was silent for a few moments. The sound of the rain pattering against the car's windscreen rattled in Brian's head.

"Okay. I'll have a word with Price right away." She apologized to somebody close by. "Brian, you shouldn't have done this on your own. You could have—"

"Thanks, Cassy. I'll see you there in ten minutes." He cancelled the call. His brain pulsated in his head. The camera sat just a few feet away from him. He wanted to smash it up. Stamp on it and smash it up. But he couldn't. He had to stay with it, just for now. He had to stay with it until this was over.

It could have been Davey...

Brian's phone vibrated. "Cassy, I told you I'll—"

"Brian." It was Vanessa. "Where have you been? I've been trying to get hold of you for the last hour."

Brian's stomach sank. "What? Vanessa? It's... Everything's all right, isn't it?"

She sniffed.

"Vanessa, tell me everything's okay. Vanessa, what is it? Is it Davey?"

"He's been hit by a car. He's—he's hurt. We're in the hospital. Brian, he wants his dad here with him."

Brian didn't register the rest of the conversation. His cheeks were cold as he placed the phone onto his lap. His entire body shook. The whole world seemed to crumble around him.

He stepped on the accelerator and followed the road. Michael Walters' house or the hospital?

He could only be at one place at one time, and there was only one place he wanted to be right now.

Chapter Thirty.

Brian paced down the corridor. What did she mean, "hit by a car"? Faces buzzed past him, hazy and out of focus. Hospital equipment bleeped, and the smell of disinfectant was ripe in the air.

"Sir?"

A short, dark-haired nurse watched him as he bombed towards the reception area.

"My son," Brian said, struggling to stay on his feet. "He's... Where is he?"

The woman shook her head and accompanied Brian to a chair. He couldn't sit down. Couldn't focus. He jolted back to his feet again.

"Just, please—tell me he's okay."

The nurse tapped a pen against a pad she was holding. "Okay. You're going to have to stay calm for me, sir. What's his name? Your son?"

Brian scratched his forehead. "Err—um, Davey. Davey McDone. He's..." He stalled. "He's been in an accident."

The nurse scanned her register. "You just wait here for me for two seconds, okay? I'll go and ask around. But please, sir, stay here." She scooted off towards the reception area, taking a sympathetic glance over her shoulder.

Brian rubbed his hands against his legs and winced as his sore hand caught against solid mud caked on his trousers.

The images. Michael Walters, and...

It all seemed so distant. So long ago.

"Mr. McDone?"

Brian looked up to see a nurse staring over him, smiling.

"Sorry about the wait. It's just we—"

"Is he okay?" Brian shot up from his chair.

The nurse examined Brian's muddy clothing and cleared her throat. "Davey's been hit by a car, but he'll be okay."

Brian exhaled a huge breath of relief and threw his hands onto his knees. Tears dripped from his cheeks. *He's okay. He's okay.*

"Nothing more than a broken arm," the nurse continued. "He'll be a bit sore for a few weeks, but he's a tough lad. Took quite a hit."

Brian's eyes clouded with tears as relief washed over him. "Thank you. Thank you."

"Would you like to see him?"

Brian looked down the corridor in the direction of the wards. "Is... Who's with him?"

"His mother and her dad. They've been here since—"

"It's okay. As long... I wouldn't want... We're not together. I wouldn't want to make anything awkward."

The nurse sighed and shook her head. Brian could tell she wanted to protest, for his sake. "Right. Should I tell the mother you were here?"

Brian's head buzzed with the adrenaline of it all. He needed a release. Needed to cool off. Something to make the pain surface then disappear...

"Yeah, I—"

"Brian!"

Vanessa was power walking towards him. He tensed up and readied himself for the barrage of insults. She always said his name in that high-pitched tone when he was in trouble.

"Where have you been? I've... I've been trying to..." She rushed towards him, black coat drooping at either side, eyes red and streaming.

"I'm sorry. I thought... It doesn't matter. I'm here now. I'm here." He opened up his arms as she stopped in front of him awkwardly, an invisible barrier between them.

"I... Thank you. Thanks for coming. You're so... muddy."

Brian looked down at his trousers and shoes. "It's a long story. But it'll be worth it in the end. Can I see Davey?"

Vanessa and Brian's gaze held for a moment. Her watery eyes shimmered in the light. "Sure. Sure. He's just this way." She held her hand out.

Brian smiled back at her as his phone vibrated in his pocket. He reached for it and cancelled the call before grabbing Vanessa's hand.

They walked down the corridor towards Davey's room as his phone started to vibrate again.

\#

Davey sat upright against his pillow as Brian rushed into the room. A brace elevated his arm, and a clear drip poked out of his purple wrist. He was wearing his blue-striped pyjamas that Brian had bought him at Christmas.

Brian grinned at him, his eyes stinging with tears. "Hello, soldier."

Davey waved his free hand as Brian crouched beside his bed. "Where have you been, Daddy?"

Brian laughed. "I've been fighting monsters and aliens so I could find my way to visit you!"

Davey's gaze spun around in delight, his tongue poking through the gap in his teeth where two milk teeth had fallen out. A little red bruise above his left eye and a few scratches on his neck, but otherwise he looked in fit shape. "Were they really scary monsters, Daddy?"

Brian sighed as the images clawed through his mind. "They... they were really bad monsters, Davey. But they are nothing to worry about now. Daddy's sorted them." He kissed Davey's hand and leaned his head against the pillow beside him.

"Granddad says he's going to get you a copy of the Highway Code next Christmas, doesn't he?" Vanessa held her elbows as she stood above Davey and Brian.

"It was like... There was me and then, BOOF!" Davey held his hand in the air and moved it around in front of him, using his fingers for legs. "But it only hurt my arm, and it was like it didn't happen, but it happened in a dream."

Brian brushed his fingers through Davey's wispy blonde hair. "You don't worry yourself about it too much, son. You just focus on getting back to strength. Get those bones strong again, right?"

"And then will I be able to fight the monsters with you, too?"

"I hope not," Brian muttered. He approached Vanessa. Her arms were wrapped around her body. Brian put his arm around her shoulders. It felt awkward, like a first date in the back row of a grubby cinema. She seemed out of place. She didn't slot into his chest like a missing piece of a jigsaw anymore, not like she used to.

But right now, they needed to stick together.

"Where is your dad?" Brian asked.

Vanessa grunted. "Don't you worry about him. He left just before you got here. Otherwise we'd have to get another hospital bed set up for one of you."

Brian scratched his cheek. His hand tingled.

"Jesus, Brian, what's happened to your hand? You... It isn't, is it? You should get that seen to whilst you're here."

His hand—of course. Blood dripped from the deep, muddy cut right through the middle of his palm. The clot was having a hard time forming. How had he let himself forget about his hand? "It's not what it looks like, okay? I swear it's not what it looks like. I'll... Yeah. I'll go get it seen to quickly before I leave."

"Is everything... all right?" Vanessa eyed up the dirty patches on Brian's trousers.

Brian wiped his eyes and tried to keep a straight face. "Not really, Vanessa, no. I found... It's the Watson case. I found..." He glanced over at Davey, who was pretending his fingers were little legs running away from a roaring monster. "I don't really want to go into it right now."

"Then don't." Vanessa's leg rubbed against his. They were so close.

Brian's phone vibrated.

His cheeks grew hot, and his throat swelled up. *Bloody phone.* If only they could leave him alone for five minutes. They were perfectly competent officers. They had their orders. What was the problem?

"I'll leave it," Brian said.

"No." Vanessa smacked him on the back. "You get back to your job, Detective Sergeant. We're not going anywhere."

"Are... Really? Are you sure?"

Vanessa smiled. "We're really glad you came, aren't we, Davey?"

Davey stopped his game and grinned. "Glad you beat the monsters!"

"Well, what are you waiting for?" Vanessa asked as Brian's phone continued to vibrate.

Brian kissed her on the cheek then scooted out of the room. He pressed the phone to his ear and waved at Davey as he left.

"What is it?" he asked in the corridor.

"Brian, where have you been?" *Cassy.*

"Long story. Have you got him?"

Cassy paused. Other voices accompanied her. "We're at his house now. You'll want to come down here as soon as possible."

"Right." Brian marched down the corridor and smiled as he walked past the nurse from earlier. "I'll be there. Make sure you don't let him go anywhere. I've—"

"Brian, you—"

"I'll see you down there." He ended the call and slipped the phone back into his pocket.

After a voluntary nurse quickly bandaged his hand, he emerged from the hospital and back out into the rain. A feeling of purpose ran through his body. A feeling of reunion. The worst possible circumstances had made him feel better than he had in months. He didn't need a release anymore.

He sat in his car and turned the engine on. Biffy Clyro were playing again. Same song as the other day, the same new mainstream crap. But he didn't mind. It was music to his ears. *Ha!* Even that sounded funny in his head.

He looked down at his passenger seat, and the camera stared back at him. His stomach knotted. It would be over soon. He could be there in five minutes, and it would be over.

He turned out of the hospital car park and headed back down the main road. Michael Walters couldn't hide any longer.

This was going to end, right here.

Chapter Thirty-One.

A sea of flashing blue lights engulfed the street outside Michael Walters' house. It was impossible to believe that this was the same location, robbed of its peace and serenity, that Brian had been earlier. The rain had given up its assault, but water still fell from the trees lining the road. Price was there, wearing a suit as usual despite the torrid conditions. Cassy stood beside him as other officers in white coats scattered around. One of them struggled to attach black and yellow tape to either side of the driveway.

Brian got out of his car and rushed over towards Price. Price gave him a double take as he chatted to a shorter, fatter DC and gestured back at Michael Walters' house. His face wasn't as red as usual.

"Brian," he said. "Where the bloody hell have you been for the past—"

"At the hospital. My son's been in an accident. What's the latest?"

Price's eyes widened. "Um, well... First off, good work. I don't agree with your methods but... yeah. It looks like you were on to something."

Brian pointed back to his car. "The camera in the passenger seat. It's all on there. Pembrokeshire Garage, Price. Michael Walters was using his position and status in BetterLives to abuse kids. Making little dates with children's hospitals. Orphanages. He was exploiting the weak and voiceless. The sick, sick bastard."

Price nodded. His eyes were distant. Empty.

"What's going on?" Brian asked. "You're scanning the house. Have you found something? Where is he?"

Price held his hand out to Brian and shook his head as Cassy emerged. "I think you'd better show DS McDone inside, Emerson."

Cassy tilted her head and half-smiled at Brian. "Come on," she said.

The lights were all off, but makeshift fluorescent lighting spread around the hallway and staircase cast a soft glow around the house. White sheets covered some of the surfaces. An officer in a blue jacket inspected the desk by the door. He picked up the photograph of Michael Walters and his ex-wife and sighed before placing it back down again.

There was a large plastic mat along the hallway leading towards the kitchen and dining area, where Brian had stood just an hour or so earlier. It was strange, seeing so many people in the house, like a morbid party. A police fancy-dress orgy, but without the fun.

Cassy stopped Brian at the kitchen doorway. "You're okay, aren't you?" She looked down at his muddy trousers and the bandage on his hand.

A sickly feeling grew in Brian's stomach. He'd seen houses like this before. He'd been in the job for enough years to know what he was walking into. That same sense of anti-climax. Nobody had to say anything; everybody knew. He nodded and entered the kitchen.

The first thing he saw was Michael Walters' shiny brown shoes hovering above the kitchen worktop.

Brian scratched his forehead as he walked over to him. Walters' eyes were still open. One of them had popped out of his head and dangled against his cheek as a thin white cord hugged his neck. His hands were purple, and his glasses lay on the floor beneath his feet, one of the lenses cracked. His body swung lightly, like a car air freshener.

"When did you find him like this?" Brian asked the dark-haired younger DC. He jotted things in a notepad, his jaw shaking and hands twitchy.

"Um... I—We got here about, about um, ten minutes ago?"

Ten minutes. Michael must have done it right after Brian had left. He looked up at Michael's one good eye, staring out with fear. Inevitability. He'd known. He'd seen the suspicion in Brian's eyes earlier when he'd read his diary, and he'd known. Suicide was the only way to escape without being punished.

"A man can't live with the guilt of something like that."

Brian turned round to see Price approaching him.

"Have you seen the camera?"

"Yes, yes." He waved at Brian. "You did well. Not method, but good work. I do need a word, though. In private. Lance, would you mind?"

The nervous younger DC hopped up from the worktop and scooted into the conservatory.

"Could've picked a nicer venue for our chat," Brian said. Michael Walters' body still swung from the wire a few feet away.

"Brian, I'm quitting my role of Detective Inspector for a while as of tomorrow."

Brian tried to speak but his mouth hung open. *Price... quitting?* "What... Why would you do that? You... The police. It's your life. Isn't it?"

"The press. They're going to crucify us tomorrow. They say we've shown negligence towards BetterLives. They say we've let this shit go on right under our noses."

Brian gritted his teeth. "And have we?"

Price couldn't quite meet Brian's eyes.

"Oh, Price. Price, you... What the hell?"

"It was just an anonymous claim or two, Brian. For fuck's sake, an anonymous claim. How many anonymous claims do we get a day? It was nothing serious. Nothing to link BetterLives or Michael Walters to Nicola Watson—"

"Nothing serious?" Brian shouted. "Price, this man has been exploiting his fucking charity to abuse innocent children over God knows how long a period. It's been pretty fucking clear for a few days now that Nicola Watson knew something important. And you think that somehow it's not serious?"

Price rubbed his hands against his face. "Y'know, back when I was a Detective Sergeant, I used to be all moral, like you. But the further you climb up the detective ladder... Brian, there's bigger things at play. But you did good. You did the right thing. I can't fault your work or commitment."

Brian barged past Price towards the door.

"Where are you going?"

"Home. I'm going home, and I'm going to go to sleep early, and I'll be up tomorrow for the briefing so we can put the nail in the coffin of this fucking thing."

Price scratched the back of his neck. "I didn't know, Brian. If I'd have known, I would've done the right thing, I swear."

Brian shook his head at Price, like a parent to a misbehaving child. "How much did BetterLives pay you to keep quiet about this, hmm? Hundreds? Thousands?"

Cassy emerged from the hallway. She looked between the two of them, confusion in her eyes.

"It's not like that," Price said, calmly. "It was two anonymous reports, Brian. Two anonymous reports."

Brian tensed his fists and started to walk towards Price.

Cassy grabbed his arm. "Come on." She eased him back outside the kitchen. "Let's go get a drink."

"I'll be there for the briefing in the morning," Brian said. "I hope you stick to your word, Price."

Price's eyes watered, and his shoulders slumped. "I'll be gone in the afternoon." Michael Walters' swinging body cast a shadow over him.

#

"It's so unsatisfying, isn't it?"

Brian and Cassy leaned against the bar. Students, downing drinks and shouting nonsensical chants, surrounded them. *Student nights.* A reminder of a long-lost youth that didn't look quite as appealing as it seemed at the time.

"What is?" Brian asked.

Cassy's chin slumped into her hands. "Well, when you told me it'd be a disappointment when we got him, I didn't quite believe it. But... he got away with it. He got away with all those horrible, evil things in his life, and he'll never have to pay for it. And Nicola Watson—her family, the charity, the children... They are the ones who've had to pay."

Brian sipped his rum and Coke as a wobbly eyed, drunken student staggered up to him. "All right, Officer? Sick fancy dress! Where's your truncheon?"

Brian narrowed his eyes and clenched his jaw as the student stumbled back towards his giggling mates.

"You learn to get used to it," Brian said.

"Hmm." Cassy sipped her drink. "What was all that about between you and Price?"

Two anonymous reports. He could sympathise with Price, to an extent. They received a whole bunch of unfounded reports and conspiracy theories every day. It couldn't have been easy doing the job he did, especially when the media and major institutions were pressuring you and pushing you in certain directions.

"The press aren't going to be happy with us tomorrow. Negligence, they'll call it. Price is acting the martyr."

"But I don't get *why*. We were pursuing every lead we could. It was an accident that the pen drive turned up. I just... Why do they have to punish us?"

"Because that's what the vultures do. They can't punish Michael Walters because he's dead. They won't punish BetterLives because they're Preston's fucking saviours. So they poke the finger at us. If you can't get used to that now, you probably never will. How was your date? I hope I didn't ruin it too much."

The last question seemed to catch Cassy off guard. She messed with her hair. "Oh, *that*. Yeah, thanks for saving me. I don't think Ryan or I will be seeing each other again. He's too... well, creative."

Brian raised his glass towards Cassy. "To independent life."

Cassy smiled at him. "Fuck you, Granddad."

Brian finished the last drop of his drink as nightclub lights pulsated around him. The warmth of the drink seeped down his neck. He looked at his watch. 12:07 a.m. now. "Time for another drink?"

Cassy shrugged. "Whatever you're having, I'll have a double." She winked at him and downed the remainder of her vodka lemonade.

Chapter Thirty-Two.

Brian's head pulsated as he squeezed his eyes together, desperate not to let the light in. The back of his neck was splitting, and his stomach was heavy and rumbly. His arm didn't ache today, though. Something was different. Where was he?

His sweaty body was naked from the waist down, his shirt clinging on by one button at the collar. *Shit.* He hadn't... had he?

He turned to the opposite side of the room. Cassy's record player. *Of course.* He'd come back with her. Kipped on the sofa. But his trousers...

Where were they? The kitchen door opened, and the smell of fried sausage cut through the room.

"Morning, stranger." Cassy glanced down at Brian's floppy penis with a grin on her face.

Brian's cheeks warmed as he grabbed a cushion and threw it in front of his bare crotch. He shuffled around on the sofa, careful not to reveal his arse in the process. Cassy looked on, fully dressed in work gear, sausage sandwich in hand.

The smell made Brian's stomach turn, the distant taste of musty alcohol still coated across his tongue. How many drinks had he had? Probably too many. But it wasn't like usual. It wasn't like the nights alone, the whisky showers and the razors. It was a celebration. It felt strangely good. Normal.

"I'm all right." Brian cringed as Cassy poked the sausage sandwich into his face.

She shrugged and stuffed half of the sandwich into her mouth. "More for me, then."

Brian turned his attention back to his uncovered lower half. Was Cassy ever going to give him a moment to dress?

"Oh, your trousers are in the hallway." She pointed towards the door. "You seemed to think it was a good idea to leave them in there last night. I tried to stop you, but you were fairly adamant..."

Brian clenched his jaw, his cheeks on fire. He realised Cassy was looking at the scars on his forearm and trying not to say anything. "Well, could you, um?"

"Oh, go get them yourself, Brian," Cassy said, one hand on her sausage sandwich, another on her hip. "You've been lying on that sofa with your own bloody sausage on display all night. No point getting all shy about it now."

Brian grumbled as Cassy walked back into the kitchen.

Three, two, one...

He made a lunge into the hallway, his naked arse visible, and quickly pulled his creased trousers on. His head seared with pain as he stretched to fasten his buttons. At least he'd headed back to his flat before he'd gone out last night and changed from his dirty clothes.

"I'll just finish this and meet you in the car if you want," Cassy said with a mouthful of sausage. She tossed the keys at Brian, who dropped them, his coordination still lagging.

"Sure. I'll um... I'll see you in there." He rushed down the stairs and out into the open air, where he retched into the drainpipe beside Cassy's flat.

Fucking sausage.

#

Cassy joined him a few minutes later as he wrapped his hands around himself in the passenger seat. He didn't like being a passenger at the best of times, but after a rough night on the town, it was even more painful. An awkward silence permeated the car as Cassy approached the station.

"So... did you sleep all right?" Cassy glanced at Brian then looked back down at the steering wheel, a grin on her face.

He wasn't sure what was more awkward—the fact that Cassy had seen his "sausage", or his cuts. "Look, Cas. It was just a cock, all right? I had my cock out. Big deal. If you're gonna giggle about it like a schoolgirl all morning, I'll walk to work."

Cassy spluttered as she tried to hold her laughter back. "*That* was a cock? I didn't see anything. You sure about that?"

Brian imitated a childish "ha ha" before looking out of the window. A small crowd of six or seven journalists with cameras and notepads gathered around the entrance to the police station. *Bloody media...* "Anyway, you'd better pull yourself together. Looks like we've got some company."

Cassy stopped the car before the crowd noticed them. She sat rigidly in her seat.

"What're you doing?"

"The scars, Brian," Cassy said, staring out of her window. "You were telling me about what happened last night. And then I saw the scars. I know you're not a real drinker, Brian. You're too much of a lightweight to be a real drinker. Maybe it's time to bury the hatchet. The case is over, so why don't you offload your burden, too? Why don't you tell me what drove you to cutting yourself?"

Brian folded his arms, his cheeks heating up. He looked around the car, everywhere but Cassy's face. "You got me drunk and still didn't manage to get an answer out of me. Poor effort, DS Emerson."

"Okay, okay. You don't have to speak right now. But just tell me, what chance do I have of, like, ever finding out?"

Brian opened the car door and waved at the press. One of the men with a camera patted his friend on the shoulder and sent a flock in their direction, like seagulls around dropped ice cream. "Maybe if we survive this lot, I'll consider it."

#

"Officer, what do you have to say about the repeated arrests of Michael Walters? Why were adequate searches not carried out?"

"Officer, if the police had figured out what Michael Walters was up to sooner, could Nicola Watson's life have been spared?"

The press assassination. He bit his cheeks and focused on the approaching entrance to the station as the media continued to shuffle around him.

"Officer, what do you have to say about the arrest of Robert Luther and the arrest of Nicola Watson's *own brother*? Is there any way you can repay BetterLives and the poor girl's family for almost bringing them to the ground?"

"You go inside," Brian whispered to Cassy. He faced the crowd as they gathered around the steps. His head still ached, and he felt a little wobbly from the height. Maybe he was still drunk. "I know it's a very confusing time for all of us right now—"

"Too damn right it is!" a bald-headed man shouted.

More heckles echoed through the crowd, gaining momentum.

"I know it's a confusing time," Brian continued, "but we've just started to put the pieces together of a very complex jigsaw, and we're still trying to get to the bottom of the true extent of things."

"Officer, what do you have to say of the *Telegraph*'s report that there was a cover up of Michael Watson's activities within BetterLives and the police department?"

Brian thought back to Price's words as the microphones dangled into his face. *Two anonymous reports.* He cleared his throat and half-smiled. "We'll know more as the day goes on. Right now, you need to allow the police to do their job. No guilty parties will get away with this, I promise you." He turned away from the crowd and entered the police station as the mob of voices roared on behind him.

A quietness ran through the offices and corridors of the station as Brian walked through. It always did after a big case. Phones rang on, not answered quite as immediately as during the case. The chatter of keyboards was less frantic. Brian took a seat at his desk.

"Good job on the Watson case, Brian," DS Stephen Molfer said, not quite making eye contact with Brian.

"What was that, Stephen? I didn't hear you—say that again?"

Stephen shook his head and rolled his eyes. "Good job."

"Cheers," Brian said, smiling smugly. There was something bittersweet about the happiness, though. A man had hanged himself. Children had been involved. An innocent girl had been killed because she was on the verge of leaking that information. Nothing to be happy about. It was only the beginning of a bigger investigation. BetterLives.

Police negligence. How deep did it all go? He got the feeling they had only scratched the surface.

"Brian."

His ears pricked up. The voice was shakier than usual. Price stood by the door, his tie loose around his neck. He waited for Brian to speak. Brian held out.

"I was..." He rubbed his hands against one another as the rest of the office looked up at him, curious. "Could I have a word?"

Brian stayed in his seat, but some of the other officers were starting to whisper. He stood up. "Sure."

Price led the way back to his office.

#

"We've just been clearing the loose ends up and getting everything back in order," Price said. "Scott Watson's still in custody, but we're playing it cool with him. We're very, very curious about how his prints just so happened to be all over the murder vehicle. Looks to me like Walters might've had a driver do his dirty work for him, but we've nothing to prove it yet. Robert Luther's back at BetterLives, but we're keeping an eye on him." Price, his hand shaking, stuffed his whisky flask into his rucksack.

"What did Luther have to say?"

"Obviously he's gutted. His best friend just turned out to be a nonce, then topped himself. In a bit of a haze. Went straight back to work."

"And there's no sign of any foul play on Better-Lives' part? No sign of any sort of cover-up of what Walters was up to?"

Price shrugged. "We've spoken to a few members of staff this morning, and they're all as stunned as the rest of us. They've given us records, documents, all sorts. Looks like one bad egg using his privileges to his sick personal advantage. But we keep on investigating BetterLives. It all starts here, Brian."

"Right."

Price regarded him with narrowed eyes. "Look, I know what you think about me. I know you can't forgive me for my misjudgement. But Brian, it's just how it works. I made an error, and I'm paying for it. I can't do anything more than apologise." Price scratched his stubbly cheeks.

"What happens now?"

Price walked back to his chair and spun it around with one finger. "I finish my day's work, and I go home to my family. I've done this for too many years. No doubt you'll be in my shoes some-day."

Brian took a deep breath. "Actually, I came to hand in my notice. I'm... I'm leaving."

Price's jaw dropped. "You don't have... But Brian, you're a great detective. Why?"

"I need time to get my life back on track. My family—they are what matters. This whole thing has made me realise what I really value. The stuff with Walters and the kids, and y'know, what happened to Davey. It's just made me realise how much I'd hate for him to have nobody to look out for him."

"You're a good man, Brian. The department will miss you." He reached out his hand. "Thank you."

Brian reluctantly placed his palm in Price's, and they stared at each other for a moment. It was strange, being so intimate with Price. In his many years of working with the police, Brian had never seen Price's defences broken down for such a prolonged period.

"I'm sorry it had to end this way for you, Detective Inspector," Brian said.

Price grinned and tightened up his shoulders again, the redness returning to his nose. The doctored photographs had been taken down, meaning Price must have noticed. Good job he wasn't in the office when that went down. "Don't you fucking 'Detective Inspector' me," he said. "It's Dale."

Brian smiled as he turned out of Dale Price's office space. *Dale.* He didn't look like a Dale, not one bit.

Brian grabbed his coat and slung it over his shoulders. He slipped the packed lunch Cassy had rustled up for him under his arm.

"Where d'you think you're going?" Cassy asked as Brian strode towards the exit.

Brian grinned. "I'm going home to see my wife and my kid."

He walked out of the office and into the open air.

Chapter Thirty-Three.

Brian shook his dusty curtains and wiped the condensation from the window. He always let it get so murky in here, to the point where it seemed beyond saving. But not today. Today, he had to get things right. He had the chance to make a good impression on Vanessa and Davey. The case was over, so he could focus on rebuilding things.

For a moment, the room almost looked nice. Almost.

He picked up the three used razor blades and empty whisky bottle from the floor and tossed them into an overflowing black bin bag, which was stretching at the sides with the weight of the litter. The thought of cutting himself sickened him. He'd spent the last hour or two cleaning, but now he was free. He'd enjoy his time off for a few weeks then get some easy job down at the shop, or maybe he'd go back to the police but something administrative. No more of this Detective Sergeant bull-crap.

On the floor by his black workbag, Brian found a bunch of newspaper clippings. Scott Watson, Robert Luther, BetterLives, an assortment of things related to the case. He shoved them into a cardboard box. He wouldn't need them again.

He looked at his watch. Two p.m. He still had two hours to kill. What did unemployed men do? Sit around? He'd just about got away with sitting around on his extended leave, but most of those months were spent under a cloud of moping and feeling sorry for himself. Being happy and sitting around all day seemed mutually exclusive concepts.

He jumped back onto his bed and winced as something pointy stuck into his side from underneath his coat pocket. He reached in to see what the culprit was. The DVD recording that Michael Walters had handed him. *Damn.* He'd been so focused on getting things sorted that he'd pretty much forgotten about it. In the end, the DVD had become nothing more than a decoy. The fact that Walters had been hiding the DVD probably showed that he'd left the private party earlier than he'd originally claimed, or something like that. Must have known what his fate was going to be when the police watched it. That'd be why he killed himself. *Good job, Walters—solved the case for us.*

Out of curiosity, Brian pulled the DVD out of the white card holder and slipped it into the DVD slot in the bottom of his portable telly. He hit play, and blurry images moved across the screen, not quite in black and white but devoid of colour.

It started at three p.m. Nothing much happening: a recording of Luther's office. Michael Walters coming in and out with papers. Luther writing something. Luther walking around the room. Brian yawned and slipped his hands behind his neck.

When it got to eight p.m., his attention picked up.

Walters, Luther, and a couple of other charity workers in the room, laughing and joking over a drink. *The BetterLives party.* If the facts added up, the guests would leave, Luther would rendezvous with Nicola Watson, she'd come back into his office soaking wet, and she'd leave. Michael Walters would probably follow her.

Nine p.m. A glimpse of someone in the corner of the room, slightly out of focus. Luther stepped up from his chair and disappeared. Brian fumbled around with the remote to rewind it, cursing as he accidentally changed the channel. He flicked back and rewound.

Sure enough, at nine p.m., Nicola Watson's recognisable figure arrived at Luther's office. Luther shot to his feet, hands against his face, as the other men looked on. Then, Nicola and Luther disappeared out of the room. Walters hung his head in the corner of the room and attempted to make conversation with the other men.

At 9:06, Robert Luther returned to the room, shaking his head and apologising to the other men. The party went on. Nicola would be heading to meet Danny. They'd smoke a few joints, and then Nicola would leave and return to BetterLives. She'd jump into the docklands and return to the office, only to be met with her death some time later.

Nothing much of interest happened in the following hour, so Brian hit fast-forward. At ten thirty, the first man left. Another one left shortly after him. Before he knew it, it was just Robert and Michael. Michael would leave the room soon. Luther would get a call from Nicola and bring her in, soaking wet. They'd spend some time there for a while.

But Michael and Luther stayed in the room. Ten minutes became fifteen. Fifteen became twenty. Luther rubbed his head in his hands. Michael slumped against the wall. Something didn't seem right. They didn't seem like lifelong friends or two men who had just enjoyed a company New Year gathering.

At last, Luther pulled his phone to his ear. This was it. This was where he left to save Nicola. This was where Michael left the room and waited, eavesdropping or knowing what she was about to say. Luther stood up, and Michael blocked his exit.

Something caught Brian's eye.

He had to rewind the DVD to catch it properly, but it was definitely there. Luther, squaring up to Michael before he left the room and looking him directly in the eye, just for a few seconds.

Then he was gone.

Brian dropped the remote to the floor and fumbled for his phone. He keyed in Luther's office number without even taking time to think.

One ring. Another ring.

"Hello, Robert Luther speaking, how may I help?"

Brian rubbed his eyes. "Luther... Robert, it's Detective Sergeant McDone. How are you doing?"

"McDone. Not great, not great. Trying to get my head around things. Is everything okay?"

"Yeah, just I found the DVD that was removed from CityWatch. Michael Walters gave it to me before he... passed. There's just a couple of things I need to clear up with you."

The crackle of mobile static cut through the conversation.

"Of course. Such as?"

Brian closed his eyes. "Before you went down to save Nicola from the water, you and Michael exchanged words about something. Can you remember what they were?"

Luther let out a puff of air. "Maybe he'd cocked something up again? He could be a bugger with his spelling sometimes."

Brian watched the images flicker behind the shaking static of the television, Luther squaring up to Michael. "No, no. I don't think it was, Robert."

"Is there something you'd like to talk about? I've got a free hour or so if you want to come down to BetterLives HQ and get things sorted?"

Brian looked at his watch again. An hour and forty-five minutes before he was due to meet Vanessa and Davey. He could make it there and back in that time, couldn't he? "Sure. I'm sorry about this. It's just a technicality or two."

"It's fine, Detective. I understand how it is."

They said their farewells, and Brian put the phone down. He took another glance at the pause screen in front of him. Michael Walters had hidden this DVD. He'd claimed it was an accident, and he'd got the wrong DVDs.

He'd tried to hide something, and he'd killed himself because he knew it was about to be discovered.

As Brian slung his coat over his shoulders and grabbed his car keys, he couldn't get a niggling idea out of his head. The look of malice in Luther's eyes as he squared up to Walters.

Had Nicola managed to tell Robert about what Michael was up to after all?

Did Robert Luther know about the atrocities being committed in the name of BetterLives?

Brian's head spun with thoughts as he revved up his car engine, but all of them led to the same final question.

Was Robert Luther willing to be wrongly arrested for the murder of Nicola Watson, rather than allow the truth about Michael Walters and Better-Lives to come out?

Chapter Thirty-Four.

Brian arrived at BetterLives ten minutes later. Luther had a pot of tea ready to greet him as he entered his office. An unusual sobriety inhabited the place. Volunteer workers whispering to one another, holding up newspapers. "Charity at Centre of Child Abuse Scandal", the *Lancashire News* already read. Sensationalist bastards. Always had been. They were quicker to turn on their supposed city saviours than Brian had expected. Perhaps the police weren't the whipping boys for a change.

Robert Luther's eyes were dark underneath, his skin paler than when Brian had last seen him.

Signs of a beard sprouted from his face, and he seemed strangely distant and detached.

"Take a seat, Detective." He gestured towards the leather chair opposite the desk. It was the chair on those DVDs in which Michael Walters had sat. Luther stared at it for a few moments before shuffling some papers on his desk and sidling into his own chair. He rubbed his hands together and stared at his desk with a glassy glare.

"Firstly, I'd like to apologise," Brian said. "I know it must have come as a shock to you to find out about your colleague." *Play the cool card. Test the water.*

"Sixteen years. Sixteen years. That's a long time. A long time to know someone and then to find this out about them. It's just..." He shook his head and scratched his hands aggressively.

"It's just I feel guilty. For not knowing. For all of this happening. If I'd have known, I'd have—" He dropped his head into his hands. "How did I not know? How could I not know?"

Brian cleared his throat. "I know this isn't ideal, but did Michael ever give off any indications that maybe all wasn't as it seemed? That maybe he had... well, let's call them 'alternative interests', for the purposes of this conversation?"

Robert moved his hands away from his face. His hair drooped onto his forehead. "If you'd asked me that an hour ago, I might have said no. You see, that's the thing. The more I think about Michael— the dates he had, the weird times he'd go disappearing away, the little off-hand comments he'd make—the more I think... you know?"

Brian nodded. "Do you... do you have any idea why Michael Walters might have removed the CCTV footage of your office?"

Luther's eyebrows twitched.

"The CCTV footage of this office from the night of Nicola Watson's murder. Why would he hide that?"

Luther shook his head slowly. "I—I don't know. I really don't know anymore."

Fuck. He'd hit a loose end. He shouldn't really be here anyway. Price didn't know, and Cassy didn't know. He looked at his watch—only an hour until Vanessa and Davey paid a visit. He was wasting his time here. The case was over. He had to let it go.

He pulled himself up from his chair and straightened out the bottom of his jacket. "Look, I'd better leave—"

"You don't have to leave. I'm just... I appreciate you're doing your job. Be honest with me if you have to be, Detective."

Brian scratched the back of his neck. "It's just there's something I'm not getting with all of this, Robert. The argument—the exchange—between you and Michael before you left to meet Nicola Watson. I can't help but feel…"

Robert's bottom lip started to shake as his glazed eyes stared at Brian. "What?"

Brian took a deep breath. "I think you knew what was going on, didn't you? I think Nicola Watson told you what Michael Walters was doing in the name of your charity, didn't she?"

Robert Luther slumped his head back into his hands and brushed his fingertips through his hair.

"And I think you suspected it was Michael Walters who killed Nicola all along, didn't you?"

Robert, digging his nails into his forehead, shook his head in defeat.

Brian edged around the desk. "I think you suspected it, and you knew, but rather than see your goody-two-shoes charity crumble, you waited, didn't you? You waited and hoped things sorted themselves out? Waited for the wrong person to be arrested?"

Robert continued to shake his head in his hands, increasing in momentum as Brian approached.

"I think you sat in that prison cell prepared to go down for what Michael Walters had done because you couldn't bear for that information about your charity to come out, could you? I bet when you heard Michael had been charged, you were disappointed. Deep down, all your legacy falling ap—"

"No!" Robert shouted. His eyes were bloodshot, and the corners of his mouth quivered. "No. These claims are completely unfounded. Now if I could politely ask you to leave. Please leave, Detective." He pointed towards the door.

"You knew, didn't you? You knew?" Brian stepped closer to Luther. Luther's faltering arm was still aimed at the door. "You can talk to me about it, Robert. You can talk to me."

Every muscle in Robert Luther's body went slack. He let out a long, deep breath. A tear rolled down his cheek. "Everything I worked for."

Brian's heart began to race. *Holy shit. Ho-ly shit.* "Thanks for your honesty, Robert."

"What will it mean? For me? And for Better-Lives? What will it mean?" He walked backwards and forward on the spot, rubbing his shaking arms, his face twitching. He was like a frantic animal just experimented on.

"We just have to see, Robert. We'll just have to see how things go."

Robert covered his face with his hands, and then pulled them away. He moved up to Brian with wide, tearful eyes. "I have files. I have everything. We can help you. I can help you." He pulled a chain of keys out of his pocket and struggled to unlock his filing shelves. When he finally managed to turn the key, he began to throw books to the floor, tearing folders and files from their place with no real direction.

Brian noticed a bunch of papers on the floor, their pages slightly curled and a few chunks of paper missing from the top corner. Brian reached down and picked them up as Luther continued to hunt at a manic pace for whatever he was hunting.

Brian studied the papers. On the front, a seemingly incomprehensible list of dates:

28-1-09 - CCS.

04-4-09 - BCD.

Brian flicked through the pages. The same seemingly illogical pattern of numbers and letters sprawled down each side.

"This is my private cabinet," Luther said, saliva flying out of his mouth. "Nobody goes in here but me. Not staff, not Michael—nobody. I can help you,

Detective. Something in here will help you. There has to be something..."

And then, *CCH. Corpus Children's Hospital. 06-07-09*. Approved and signed by Robert Luther.

Luther tossed more folders to the floor. The filing shelves were almost completely empty. He looked back down at the slightly crumpled paper in his hand, and his stomach turned as he remembered why he'd noticed the marks on the side of the paper in the first place.

The paper between Nicola Watson's fingernails.

"This is my private cabinet... Nobody goes in here but me."

Brian felt the room closing in around him. "You... you did it."

Luther pulled his head up from the bottom level of the filing shelves and frowned at Brian. "What?"

"This paper. You approved a visit. You approved all these visits. You knew for years and you... This paper. This paper was between Nicola's fingernails. It... it's in your private filing shelves, and it was between Nicola Watson's fingers." Brian stumbled backwards towards the doorway as he searched his pocket for his phone.

Robert Luther advanced towards Brian, sweat dripping from his greasy fringe. "If I can just have a look—"

"I'll have to ask you to step back." Brian, still moving backwards, held his hand at Robert. He thumbed through his phone but hit the wrong button. *Fuck.* Stupid hammy fingers. *Keep cool, keep cool.* He went back into his contacts—Cassy's number was last in his recent call history. He hit her name and pressed the phone to his ear. *Answer. Answer, goddammit.*

Luther retreated from Brian and walked over to his desk. A defeated smile spread across his face.

Brian had to get some backup. Somebody else had to find out about this.

The dialling of the phone gave way to Cassy's voice.

"Hello?"

"Cassy," Brian shouted, his words forced and breathless. "Cassy, if you can just—"

He felt a sharp crack against his head. The next thing he knew, he was on the floor. The room drifted around his eyes. He was floating into the distance and up into the air. Something cold brushed against his eyes.

"Hello? Brian?" Cassy's voice sounded miles away. It disappeared as something reached down for his phone. He saw the figure above him, slightly blurred. It pressed a button on the phone and dropped it back to the floor.

Then everything faded away, and Brian rose up into the clouds...

Chapter Thirty-Five.

At first, he thought something cold slithered down his neck. Was he outside? His vision blurred as he lifted his heavy head up and peeled his eyelids open. Everything in front of him looked fuzzy and distant as the light stung his eyes. He reached to scratch his aching head but realised he couldn't move his arms or his legs. They were locked.

Someone stood in front of him, shaking his head and fidgeting with his hands.

Robert Luther.

Of course. He'd been at Luther's, and there was the file, and the paper, and...

"I'm sorry about your head." Robert hunched in front of Brian. He cast a wide, glassy-eyed stare at the mass of papers covering his office floor. "But I did what I had to do. I didn't know what else to do. It's like with a fly, you know? When a fly keeps on buzzing and buzzing and buzzing, and eventually you've just got to..." He exhaled and shifted his gaze to the other side of the room.

Brian edged his neck forward to look at his hands. Plastic ties, just like the ones digging into the flesh of Nicola Watson's ankles, held them together tightly. A sticky, oily fluid coated his skin and drenched his clothes. His phone was at the other side of the room, the screen cracked and flashing.

Robert Luther stood up with his hands behind his back and leaned against his desk. "At first, I didn't know what to think. I nearly killed myself, you know?" He looked at Brian again. Brian's head pounded, his neck stiff and tender to every twitch of movement, like a hangover from hell.

Luther turned back to his desk and gazed out at the grey clouds through his window. "I didn't know what to do when I found out that Michael was exploiting BetterLives. I thought about going to the police, but then I figured, why should I pay for Michael's sick habits? And Michael said he had a way to implicate me. So I left it, just for a short while. I dunno, maybe I did the wrong thing. But I did it for the right reasons. I would've ended what Michael was doing in BetterLives' name. I swear I would've ended it."

"Why didn't..." Brian winced, trying to squeeze words out of his sandpaper-dry throat.

Luther shifted his head slightly but stayed transfixed on the office window. He barely acknowledged Brian's presence. "And then the girl came along." He laughed. "Ah, such a pretty girl. Lovely, driven, motivated. Girl of my dreams, you know? But she started digging and digging. Like a rat. She started digging and digging, and I just..." He raised his hand in front of him and, shutting his eyes, clenched it into a fist. "I just panicked."

The truth of it all dawned on Brian. His heart started to race. Here he was, in the same room as Nicola Watson's killer who had murdered her to hide a secret. A secret of corruption and sickness that had gone on right under his nose. A secret that was worth a life to save his reputation. To save his empire. His legacy.

"Why did you... Why?" Brian spluttered. It was all he could say.

"Why?" He frowned as if what he'd done was the only logical option. "Because the city *needs* BetterLives. The people need strength right now. The jobs, the hope—it's all gone. No, I did what I had to do. It was the wrong thing to do, but those secrets couldn't come out. No. They couldn't come out, not yet. Not yet."

Brian scanned the room for a way to pull himself to his feet. He tugged at the ties around his arms and legs, but they were too thick and his body was too weak. Luther stood tall above him, wide-shouldered, as if delivering a speech to the public.

"You see, Brian, people at the top—we have to make these big decisions." He crouched down in front of Brian. Brian smelled sweat as it dripped down Luther's forehead. "I'm not saying it's the right decision—no, it was wrong, so wrong, and I'll pay for it. I'll pay for it, I will. But I had to do it, Brian. I couldn't risk it. You see that, don't you? You're a clever man. A great detective. You see that?"

Brian stared back at Luther as he struggled to convince himself of his righteousness. "I think you're a fool for telling me this right now. Michael Walters—your sick friend—you're worse than him."

"No. Michael wasn't my friend, not after everything he'd done. He needed me, though, and I guess I needed him too, after approving all of his...

visits. But Nicola—God, she was so lovely, and I truly am so sorry about what I had to do to her."

Brian's head spun. The back of his head stung from the blow. "The water, and the blue-green algae. Why did you save her if—"

"I didn't save her." Luther's arms shook. "I... She'd found out what Michael was up to, and she'd been to see me about it. Confront me. I told her, 'Not tonight, it's the office party, not tonight.' Didn't want her showing up like that, making a scene. Embarrassing. And then she called and said she was back, but she couldn't accept me letting it go. She sounded drunk or stoned, or whatever it was she did with that awful boyfriend of hers. She told me she wanted us to be together, but we had to 'do the right thing'. About Michael. You know? And she just kept going on and on and on, so I... I pushed her into the docks. But then I realised I was being stupid. Stupid! So I finished her off in the hooker den. I made sure it looked like a prostitute murder, or something like that. Just something to buy us some time to figure things out. But it had to be done, you understand that, don't you? These things—these secrets—we all have them. I had to do it. For the city. You see that, right?"

Michael Walters *had* left to fill his car with petrol, then gone straight home. Or maybe he'd gone back to BetterLives. He'd removed the DVD the following day because he didn't want his friend linked to the death of a missing girl. He'd done all those things, those terrible things, but he hadn't killed Nicola Watson. "What about Scott Watson, her brother? Why were his prints all over the car? Why didn't he have an alibi?"

Luther smiled. "You know, I really, really thought I was in the clear with that one. I really did. Scott Watson does drive for us. I only realised that the night of... Yes. But he does, and that's an awfully good coincidence, isn't it? Yes, poor Scott came rushing to us, late for work, all drugged off his face, eager to please. So I put her in the boot of his car and had him deliver her to Foster Road. Shit—it was a foolish move of mine. Bloody foolish. But I'm not a killer; I'm just a politician. Luckily, fate was on my side that evening. I'd made sure Nicola was... I'd made sure she was sleeping. And he had his music up loud—very loud—so it wouldn't have mattered anyway. So I made sure I was at Foster Road when he arrived and... Well, you know the rest."

Scott, stoned off his face on that new blend of cannabis, driving his sister down to Foster Road, blissfully unaware of what he was doing. *"Lowers inhibitions,"* Stephen had told him. Luther, waiting there to finish her off. Maybe Scott, in his drugged up stupor, had remembered visiting Foster Road at some point that evening. But he knew what it would look like if he admitted it. Everything had fallen right in place for Luther.

"Granted, it was a little more complicated than I'd hoped. I had Michael go down to CityWatch to check for incriminating CCTV that I could kindly deliver to you. I figured we could use his little prostitute-visiting story as a motive for trawling through the footage. When he brought the two DVDs back, though, I'd only gone and revealed myself in the shot of the car arriving at Foster Road, hadn't I? If I hadn't, then that would've been perfect. It would've showed Scott arriving in the BetterLives car at exactly the time I needed him to. But alas, I had to get rid of the DVD. What falls into the docklands rarely surfaces, you know that. But I figured it would work out in the end. And it almost did, I suppose. Almost fell very nicely indeed. Not ideal, but... better than it could've been."

The missing CCTV DVD. Michael must have taken two DVDs all that time, and not just one, the shifty bastard. Walters hadn't killed Nicola, but he must've known. He must've suspected. "You deserve each other." Brian's jaw trembled. "You and your twisted nonce friend deserve each other."

Luther wiped his finger against the damp patch on the floor and raised his finger to his face. "Have you ever seen something burn in petrol?"

Brian's heart thumped.

"It's not like the films, or anything like that. There's something... calming about it. Hell, what am I talking about? I almost sound completely insane." He laughed and brushed his hand through his floppy, sweaty hair.

"You're finished, Robert," Brian spat out as he continued to try breaking his hands and feet free from the ties. "I don't think you see quite what you're doing or how this can possibly help you. You're done. So please, just stay calm, and—"

"Ha," Luther said, laughing into his hands. "Don't you dare take the moral high ground with me. I know where I stand. I know you're off-duty. Oh, I know very well where I stand, thank you very much, and that's an unfortunate turn of events. But there's no way I'm going anywhere, and neither are you."

Brian's stomach sank as Luther pulled a red canister out from underneath his desk. He sprinkled some more oil onto the papers and documents scattered across the carpet and then tipped it over his head, rubbing it through his hair like a shower.

The vein in Brian's neck pulsated as he shuffled his hands and feet as rapidly as he could. "Luther, you don't have to—"

"Don't you tell me what I do or don't have to do, Detective," he shouted, before throwing the empty canister towards the door. "Don't you dare. I loved Nicola. I loved her, and I'm so sorry." Tears streamed down his cheeks as his eyes turned red and bloodshot. He reached into his pocket and pulled out a matchbox.

"Whoa, whoa!" Brian's chest tightened. Luther disregarded his cries and struck a match against the box. "Please. I have a kid. Please. I've done so many bad things, too, and I've not been there for him. I'm supposed to be seeing him soon. Please, Robert. We'll go. We'll walk out of here. You can go. Just, please. Give me another chance. I don't want to die anymore!" Brian squeezed his eyes shut. Thoughts of Davey and Vanessa and Cassy flashed through in front of his eyelids.

Cassy. What a lovely partner. He'd never have the chance to tell her how highly he thought of her. A lump grew in his throat as his entire body tightened.

Robert looked on in pity, tears streaming down his face. "I'm so sorry. I really am sorry for all of this and for the inconvenience it has caused you. I pass on my best to—"

The door smashed open. Everything else happened in slow motion.

Cassy barged through into the room.

Robert swung round as she pelted towards him.

The match slipped to the floor, and Robert went up in flames.

Brian gritted his teeth and stared at a horrified Cassy as he waited for the fire to approach. He saw his leg on fire before he had the chance to process the pain.

When the pain did hit, he screamed like a pig in an abattoir. Then, everything drifted away again, as the searing worked its way up his body and enveloped him like a hot blanket of water.

Chapter Thirty-Six.

Cries around him. Something tugging at his leg.

"Get out of here!"

Then a crack. His hands were free, but a different sort of resistance bound them. His feet—they were still stuck. Cassy leaned over them, battling with the flames to untangle his ankles. No—she should go. He tried to shout, but his throat burned with the smoke and the fumes.

Go... go...

\#

A beeping echoed around his head. A chill in the air as he took a deep breath through his nostrils and out through his mouth. Where was he?

He opened his eyes. The familiar white tiles of the wall, the heart rate monitor next to him. He must've been visiting Davey and got in a hospital bed, or—

No. Luther. The flames. Cassy untying his feet.

The bleeps of the heart rate monitor increased in pace.

The door opened at the other side of the room. The nurse to whom Brian had spoken about Davey stood there, notepad in hand. She stepped over to the side of his bed with a large, sympathetic smile.

"Mr. McDone," she said. "Welcome back to the world. Didn't expect to be seeing you again so soon."

Brian winced as a searing pain shot through his body. White bandages wrapped his left leg, padding spread across his chest.

"How long have I—"

"A few hours," she said, smiling again. "You just focus on relaxing right now, and we'll have someone in to explain everything shortly."

Brian's chest stung with hot pain, as if flames still covered him. "Wait."

The nurse stopped at the door and turned around. She wasn't smiling anymore.

"Please, the least you can do is just tell me... things are okay. My friend—she helped me out. Is she okay?"

The nurse half-smiled and turned back to the door. "Detective Inspector Price is on his way to visit you. We've got someone else to see you now, though."

The nurse whispered to somebody outside. Then Vanessa walked in, hand in hand with Davey, his tongue sticking out.

"Hello you!" Brian tried to sit upright. "Look at you, on your feet again."

Davey ran over to him and wrapped his one good arm around Brian's arm. He winced with the pain, but it didn't matter. Davey was here. He was okay.

Davey pulled back. He had a sling on his arm and a "Brave Boy" sticker on the front of his coat.

"You're okay to be up and about right now, aren't you, lad?" Brian looked up at Vanessa for approval. From the redness in her eyes and the twitching of her eyelids, she had been crying.

"Nurse said I could come see you. Daddy, did the monsters beat you?" His face was curious, his eyes blinking rapidly.

Brian laughed. "No, Davey. I told you, the monsters *never* beat me." He rested his hand on the back of Davey's head again and planted a dry-lipped kiss on his short hair.

Vanessa rubbed her arms. "You... What happened, Brian? What—" She broke eye contact and gritted her teeth, her eyes welling up.

"You two don't have to worry about anything anymore. I've finished fighting the monsters for now."

"You said that last night."

"I mean it today." He smiled at Vanessa.

The nurse appeared at the door again as Davey showed off the multicoloured cast on his arm.

"I think you'd better let your dad have some rest, young man." The nurse brushed her hands through Davey's hair. "Mr. McDone, DI Price is here to see you."

Price. He'd been wrong to force him into stepping down. Now that Brian saw the truth, Price would be able to acknowledge what BetterLives had been covering up as an institution. He had a chance to make things right again. The press could try to spin it whichever way they fancied, but it wouldn't be enough. He and Price, they could handle this together.

Brian gave Davey a final hug. Vanessa patted Brian on his arm. "We'll be outside," she said. "I'll... I hope things go well with Price." She turned away and left the room. Davey stuck out his tongue as they disappeared.

The nurse held the door, and Brian's body seized up as Price walked in. It was unusual to see him dressed in normal clothes. He wore a brown fleece zipped right up to his chin and faded blue jeans. He looked like a regular ageing man. *Dale Price.*

"Brian. I... I'm so sorry this happened to you."

Brian tried to shrug, but his shoulders nipped against the bed sheets. Was there any part of his body that didn't hurt?

Price cleared his throat. "How are you... how are you doing?"

"Price, just tell me something. Cassy—I saw her there, didn't I? She... she untied my hands, and then somebody else came in for me. Price?"

Price's head slumped against his chest as he looked towards the floor. He couldn't make eye contact.

"Price, she's okay, isn't she?"

Price took a deep breath and stuck his hands into his pockets. He returned to his police officer stance, detached from the situation. "Detective Sergeant McDone, I'm sorry to have..."

Brian's head spun as Price recited the words. The room seemed fuzzy, distant, as it buzzed around him. All of the pain and aching in his body receded.

"...to tell you this, but Cassandra Emerson died in hospital two hours ago."

A warm tear slipped down Brian's cheek. His throat was dry. It felt like a bullet had pummelled through his chest and knocked him back against the bed in which he already lay.

"She... Why? How?" He knew the answer. He just couldn't process the words. It couldn't be happening. It couldn't be real.

Price's jaw shook as he wiped his cheek. "She... she took your call. Said your location came up on Location Services or something and found it weird, so she went to check it out. She saved your life, Brian. She sacrificed her life for you."

Location Services. She'd set it up for him before they'd investigated the old hospital. *I always prefer to be cautious...* "No." Brian sniffed. "No—fuck. No, no no. Why the fuck would... She had... Get out."

"Brian, you need to calm down—"

"Don't fucking tell me to calm down," Brian shouted, rattling his arms against the side of the bed. Price's face was grey and filled with grief, too. The lump in Brian's throat took hold of his entire neck.

The pair was silent for a moment, only the bleeping of the heart rate monitor cutting through the air. After what seemed like hours, Price broke the silence again.

"She was a brave officer, Brian. She was like nobody we'd had in years. The best acting DS I can remember. So much promise. I hope you... I think she'd like you to say a few words at her funeral."

Brian dug his teeth into his bottom lip and shook his head. *Her funeral.* This wasn't right. It wasn't real.

Price stood up from the seat at Brian's bedside and walked to the door. "I should go and let you rest. Sorry. I just thought I should be the one to tell you."

"What happens now?"

"What with?"

Adrenaline rushed through Brian's body. "Robert Luther. He killed Nicola Watson because she was threatening to open up about corrupt activities in BetterLives. It wasn't Michael Walters. He was in the wrong, and he was doing horrible things, but he didn't kill her. We need to get back to Better-

Lives. We need to do a thorough investigation. We need to punish Luther—"

"Brian. Robert Luther killed himself and burned down his office. You know that."

"We need to investigate his office. We need to find out if anything else has gone on in the past and for how long. I was only there for a moment, but I saw stuff. I saw stuff, Price."

Price stared at Brian. "I'm not sure what you're talking about, Brian. Robert Luther killed himself because he'd lost everything. His best friend and longtime assistant had been abusing his position for years, then murdered Robert's lover, and the charity looked to have collapsed without any hope of resurgence. You should get some rest."

Brian's mind froze. How could he let Luther get away with this? How could he let Walters take the blame?

"No, it's not right. I was there for a reason, and he tried to kill me. He fucking killed Cassy, Price."

Price halted and turned back to face Brian. Accusation glimmered in his eyes. "Brian, sometimes you've got to make the tough decisions. BetterLives is no more. Luther's documents were incinerated in the fire. Michael Walters will be formally charged with the murder of Nicola Watson. Besides, it's easier for the public to take. It's easier to accept a twisted paedo did this and not the city's symbol of hope. People would go mad, Brian. The city would kill itself."

"I thought I was wrong about you."

Price pulled open the door. "You should have let it go, Brian. You should have let it go." He exited into the corridor.

Grief and misunderstanding ran through Brian's body. Cassy's death was all for nothing. It was all his fault, and it was all for nothing. Price was happy to use Michael Walters as the scapegoat. Luther had killed Nicola Watson, but he wasn't dangerous. He just had his secrets to cover up. It was in the interests of the people.

Tomorrow, the press would portray Robert Luther as a shamed and embarrassed martyr. A victim of circumstance.

And there was absolutely nothing anybody could do about it.

The door clicked open again. It was Vanessa, on her own this time. He tried to keep the frog in his throat at bay. Tried to keep the tension behind his eyelids from letting itself all out.

"Are you okay, Brian?"

Brian's jaw shook as he tried to smile. "Yeah, I'm... No. No I'm not." His body exploded with emotion as he crumbled with tears.

Vanessa cradled his head against her warm chest and cried with him.

Chapter Thirty-Seven.

The sun shone down on the church. The grass was a rich shade of green, and premature daffodils sprouted from the ground. The church was in one of the nicer spots just outside of town in the little village of Woodplumpton. People always said it would be a nice place to be buried. Brian wasn't so sure the buried would be all that fussy.

"Are you not going to go inside?"

Brian sucked on a hard-boiled sweet as he sat in the car park. The hearse had arrived a few minutes ago. He'd made sure to miss the coffin being carried inside.

"I shouldn't. I... I'll wander up to the grave later. Say my piece." He turned 'round to Vanessa and smiled.

She tilted her head in understanding. "You're going to have to stop blaming yourself, Brian. It's just got to stop."

If she knew what Brian knew, maybe she'd understand. It wasn't just the fact that Cassy had untied him, saved his life, and lost hers in the process. It was the repression of the truth, the truth about Robert Luther and BetterLives. Her death was, ultimately, for nothing.

Vanessa turned the page of the newspaper quickly before Brian had the chance to see it, but he knew what it was already. "BetterLives Closes Amidst Crisis". And then the footnote: "Funeral for Police Hero Today". A "horrendous accident" had resulted in her death, apparently. That seemed to work for the press. A horrendous accident where two officers heard news of Robert Luther's attempted suicide, and one of those officers lost their life trying to prevent it. That was the truth to the people of Preston and the people of the country.

The nearby echo of music played through the church hall. Biffy Clyro's first song, "Hope for an Angel". Brian smirked.

"What you laughing at?" Vanessa asked.

Brian shook his head and wiped his nose. "Nothing, it's... She always said she wasn't keen on the old stuff. I wondered if she was telling the truth or not."

Vanessa looked back at the newspaper and read the piece on inflation or deflation, or whatever the economy was doing nowadays.

A few minutes later, people started to emerge from the church. Brian tensed up in his seat, his legs still sore from the rubbing of the bandages.

"It's okay. We don't have to stay if you don't want to."

Brian glanced back at the open church door. Officers he recognised from work, holding their hats against their laps, arms around each other. A shadow grew near to the door, and he knew what it was they were carrying.

He hit the clutch and reversed out of the car park, driving away from the church and leaving the guests behind.

The journey to drop Vanessa back at her dad's was a quiet one. Vanessa coughed when they reached the Guild Merchant roundabout—it was always her way of asserting her presence.

"I know it can't be easy, Brian. She was your partner. But you've tried, and that's the main thing.

People would love to see you, though. They know you were both heroes."

"I'll drop you off at your dad's, yeah?"

Vanessa nodded and returned back to her silent shell. She was wrong about the other officers loving him. Perhaps on the surface, they'd celebrate him and pretend he was heroic, but he knew what they'd be thinking deep down: *It should be you in that coffin and not our daughter. Our sister. Our friend.*

He thought back to his phone conversation with Nicola Watson's parents earlier that day. Something about it sent a chill up his spine. "Is it over?" Shenice Watson had asked. "Michael Walters. He's the man, isn't he?"

And Brian had just gritted his teeth and said yes.

Maybe Price was right about best interests all along.

Brian pulled up outside his father-in-law's semi-detached house. Years of wear and tear stained the grey brick front, the paint flaking. He looked through the smoggy window and saw Davey waving at him. Vanessa's dad placed a hand on Davey's shoulder and moved him away.

"You should come inside," Vanessa said, reluctant to meet Brian's eyes.

"I... I don't know. I mean, your dad..."

"Oh, he's just a silly old man. He'll get over it."

Brian swallowed the lump in his throat. The sun peered through his windscreen, forcing a squint out of him.

"Yeah, I will. But there's something I need to go and get first. Something for Davey. That's okay, isn't it?"

Vanessa shrugged and hopped out of the car. "Don't be long." She walked over to the front door and let herself in. Brian watched the three of them behind the window, smiles on their faces, their lungs filled with conversation. He started the engine and drove back towards the roundabout.

#

The churchyard wasn't as busy when Brian returned. A few visitors dressed in black, but not many people here for Cassy, not anymore. He reached into his CD case and pulled out the album artwork of Radiohead's latest album—Cassy loved it, Brian hated it.

He stepped up to the bed of flowers and makeshift wooden cross. Something seemed abstract about it, something less than human. The gold-plated name plaque on the coffin shone up, reflecting against the sun. *Cassandra Emerson.*

Brian smiled down at the coffin. "I thought I'd bring you something to listen to. I figure you'll get more use out of it than me." He looked over his shoulder. Their own losses, their own visits, occupied the other visitors.

He dropped the artwork onto the coffin and turned away, but he still had something to tell her. Something niggling at him. "Offload the burden," she'd told him. He kneeled down beside the open grave and took a deep breath. "In September, I came in from work, and I felt this loathing in my body. My mum had just died a few weeks earlier, and my dad was as good as dead. And my wife, she was nagging on at me—'You're an incompetent husband. You're a shitty father.' So I got a rope and I hung myself. I wrapped my neck with rope, and I jumped from the bannister. And I remember the last thing I saw." He sniveled and wiped the salty tears from his face. "I saw Davey walking in through the front door, Ness behind him. I saw his face, and I remember just seeing that look in his eyes. That look of, 'Why? Why, Daddy, why?' But I was sick. I was at the end of my tether. I was pressured at work, and I was sick of it all. It wasn't me."

Brian crouched by the grave for a few more seconds, his hands buzzing as the burden lifted from his shoulders. He plucked some grass from the ground. "'Ness knew it wasn't me, too, but I needed to get away. I needed to see a therapist and spend some time away from them, because Vanessa didn't want Davey to remember his dad like that. It was the right thing—for everybody. But I didn't go to the therapist, not much. I controlled it myself. I cut myself, and I drank a little to convince everybody that I was just an alcoholic. Nobody asks questions of an alcoholic. I got worse and worse, and I punished myself. And now I know what I have to do. Now I know what's right and wrong. Now I don't need a release. I feel free. I feel better. Thank you." Brian took one last look down at the coffin, a tear dripping onto the polished wood. "Thank you, Cassy. You saved my life in more ways than you can ever imagine."

He stood up and walked away from the church-yard.

#

Brian stepped into the 24-Hour shop just down the road from his father-in-law's house.

"Can I help you?" the shop assistant asked. Brian wasn't sure whether he'd served him before, or whether it even mattered. His furry top lip was in need of a shave, his red t-shirt begging for a wash.

Brian looked up at the whisky and then back at the shop assistant. "I'll just have a Chocolate Kinder Egg, please. For my kid."

The cashier raised his eyebrows as Brian smiled and paid for the chocolate egg. "You not a Gillette man anymore, sir? Just we have them on special offer. Two for a fiver."

Brian took a deep breath. "I think I'll pass. I prefer electric razors these days. Thanks." He left the shop and drove back round the corner to Vanessa's dad's.

The three of them were still visible through the front window. Brian clutched the chocolate egg in his hand and took a deep breath as he stepped out of his car and walked to the front door of the run-down house.

He knocked on the door. Words he had recited spun around his head. Should he go for a hand-shake? Was a hug too far? Or just a friendly "Hello"? He'd gauge it on the greeting. He'd work it from there.

The flaky white-painted door opened, and Vanessa's dad stood tall and wide, blocking the view to the back of the house.

"Hi again, Fred."

Fred reached out and shook Brian's hand, his wrinkly face attempting something that resembled a smile. "Welcome back."

Brian peered out of the rectangular window at his car. He thought he saw himself still sitting out there, an outsider looking in with a razorblade in his hand.

"They're just outside now." Fred pointed towards the small garden at the back of the house.

Brian smiled and turned away from the window, the phantom of himself outside in his car left behind.

"Thanks, Fred. Thanks."

They stepped out into the garden, side by side. Back to his family. Back to reality.

Thank You For Reading!

Enjoy Brian's journey and dying to know what happens next?

To be notified as soon as Ryan launches a new book in the *DS Brian McDone* series, visit the following link:
http://bit.ly/rcmlist

Your email address and details will never be shared and you are free to unsubscribe at any time.

*

ABOUT THE AUTHOR

Ryan Casey is the author of several novels, novellas and short stories. He writes a wide range of dark thrillers and mysteries, but refuses to be confined by the limitations of genre. Casey lives in the United Kingdom and enjoys American serial television, is a slave to Pitchfork's Best New Music section, and wastes far too much of his life playing Football Manager games. He posts a weekly blog at RyanCaseyBooks.com, discussing writing, publishing, and whatever the hell else he feels like.

Ryan is also the author of:
Killing Freedom
What We Saw
The Painting (The Watching, #1)
Dead Days
Something in the Cellar
Silhouette

Visit Ryan at ryancaseybooks.com

Printed in Great Britain
by Amazon.co.uk, Ltd.,
Marston Gate.